Death
Benefit

Also by this author

Dead on Account

Dead Ringer

Death Duties

Salvation Hall

Death Benefit

A Rose Bennett Mystery

MARIAH KINGDOM

~ Perceda Press ~

First published in digital form 2020 by WL Fowler

This paperback edition Perceda Press 2020

ISBN 978-1-8380834-3-4

Cover design by www.ebooklaunch.com

Annual income twenty pounds, annual expenditure nineteen pounds, nineteen and six, result happiness

Annual income twenty pounds, annual expenditure twenty pounds, ought and six, result misery

Charles Dickens: David Copperfield

.

1

Toby Dugdale took another sip of the whisky that he shouldn't have been drinking. It did nothing to quell his anxiety.

He'd been waiting for Leo Pearson for almost three quarters of an hour now, forty-five excruciating minutes during which Verity Pearson, Leo's wife, had tried to diffuse the situation with meaningless small talk and repeated calls to her husband's mobile phone. He could hear her now, out in the spacious hallway of their mock-Tudor home, the hiss of urgent, admonishing words carrying through to him as she berated her husband for being late for the meeting.

For goodness sake, Leo, where the hell are you? Toby has been here for nearly an hour. We need to get this sorted.

Need to get it sorted? That would be an understatement. He took a final sip of whisky, and then looked up from the glass to see Verity appear in the doorway.

She leaned against the doorframe, her green eyes wide and blinking, her glossed lips pursed into a practiced pout. 'Toby, I'm so sorry. I just can't seem to get through to him.'

She crossed the lounge to the sofa and lowered herself slowly down beside him. 'He was so keen to have this conversation. We know we have to sort this mess out.' She checked herself, casting her eyes upwards with a sigh. 'Not that it's really a mess, is it? I mean, we have a solution that suits everyone now. It's just a case of the timing.'

Toby leaned slightly away from her. 'The timing *is* the solution, Verity.' She was sitting close to him, too close, and the strong aromas of her musky perfume were beginning to envelope him. 'If we don't get this sorted out by Friday, there's a very real possibility that I will lose my job.'

She moved in a little closer and gazed at him through long, dark lashes. 'It's not going to come to that, Toby. We're not going to let that happen.' Her voice was silken now, a persuasive purr. 'Look, I don't know where Leo is. I've been told that he left the shop just after five o'clock. You know that the journey home from Scarborough usually only takes him about three quarters of an hour. I can only think there's been some sort of hold up on the road. Perhaps there's been an accident? The roads around here can be lethal.' She lowered her chin and furrowed her brow. 'I've called his mobile four times in the last twenty minutes, and he just isn't answering.'

'He's almost an hour late.'

'I know. And I can't apologise enough.' She wafted a manicured hand in the direction of a mahogany cabinet against the wall. 'Are you sure that I can't get you another Scotch?'

'No.'

'No, you're not sure? Or no, you don't want one?'

'No, I don't want one. I don't even know why you're asking me. You know that I have to drive home.' He cursed under his breath. 'Look, I can't wait here all evening. And I can't leave without getting the confirmation that I need.' There was a sleek black laptop case propped against the side of the sofa and he reached down into it and pulled out a small neat laptop. He placed it on his lap and lifted the lid, and then clicked at the keyboard to power it up. When he spoke again, he kept his eyes firmly on the screen. 'As you are also a director of the company, Verity, I'm going to have to ask you to answer my questions in Leo's absence.'

She didn't respond, and he dared to cast a glance in her direction. Her brow was still furrowed, her lips moving silently as if she were whispering to herself. Finally she let out a gentle laugh, a ripple of audible astonishment. 'Oh Toby, for heaven's sake. Is there any need for this?'

'Yes, I'm afraid there is.' His tone was formal now. 'Please can you confirm for me that the sale of the business, registered as L & V Pearson Ltd, and trading as Pearson the Bookmaker, is scheduled to complete on Friday, October 16th?'

'We hope so.'

'I need to record your confirmation as the business owner that the sale will go through. I need a "yes", not "we hope so".'

'You know it's going through on Friday, Toby. Leo promised you that it would.'

His fingers clicked briskly at the keyboard, unmoved by her attempt to convince him. 'And you confirm that all the required due diligence has been carried out by the buyer, and the buyer has confirmed that everything is satisfactory from his point of view?'

'Yes.'

'And all the final paperwork is being prepared by your solicitor, and will be signed by the purchaser on Friday?'

'Yes.' A note of mild irritation was beginning to creep into her silky tones. 'I don't know why you're being like this. We've had to bring the sale of the business forward to help you out. We didn't have to lean on the buyer to bring the date forward. We were quite happy for the sale to complete at the end of the month. It's not our fault that your stupid bank has decided to move the goalposts.'

He felt a flush of anger sweep into his cheeks and he sucked in a deep breath to dampen the heat. 'And it's not my fault that Leo chose to structure his finances in such a way that he needed to borrow more money than he could afford to repay.'

His response struck a nerve. Verity stiffened, and then she leaned back and observed him coolly. 'Perhaps not. But my understanding is that until now you've always been happy enough to arrange things the way Leo wants them. So I'm sure there must have been something of benefit to you in the arrangement.' She looked away for a moment, and when she turned back to him the green eyes were uncharacteristically direct. 'To be perfectly honest, Toby, if this situation is beginning to backfire on you, then maybe you should stop and think before laying all the blame at Leo's door. Because from where I'm standing, it looks to me as though Leo wasn't the only one trying to play the system.'

Rose Bennett settled back into the well-worn Lloyd Loom armchair and lifted her feet up onto the footstool. She wriggled a little to find a comfortable position, and then glanced down at the ever-hopeful face of the aging West Highland terrier that was hovering somewhere close to her knees.

She raised a teasing eyebrow in the dog's direction. 'Really? Are you sure? You do realise that Clive is going to call me any minute now?'

The terrier hesitated and blinked his one good eye, and then answered the question by scrambling clumsily up onto the armchair and down into Rose's lap, circling twice for good measure before curling up and settling down for a snooze.

His small body was a warm weight against her legs. 'I think you need more exercise, and less pork scratchings.' She put out a hand and rubbed it into the fur of his neck. 'Maybe we both do.'

She let out a self-deprecating sigh and cast her eyes around the conservatory. Too bright by day, even in the autumn months, it was always cosy in the evening, warmed by the heat from a small log burner, and lit by a single large standard lamp in the corner. It was an ill wind that had blown her to seek refuge in the comfort of her Aunt Lu's cottage. But she knew she couldn't hide away forever.

She stretched out her free hand to a nearby coffee table and picked up her mobile phone. She had barely glanced at the screen before the expected call came through, and she swiped at it with her thumb to answer. 'Clive? Could you be any more punctual?'

It was a good-humoured jibe and Clive Barden took it in good part. 'I am aware, Rose that you have been languishing on this sabbatical, or whatever you like to call it, for too many weeks now. I wouldn't like you to think that the rest of us have become lax in our habits during your absence.'

'Heaven forbid.' She laughed softly into the phone. 'How many weeks is it now? I'm not used to so much leisure time. I've almost lost track of what day it is.'

'It's Monday, and I believe it's been about three weeks since you last graced the East & Northern Bank with your presence. I am beginning to worry that we have lost your services for good.' He coughed to clear his throat. 'I hope that I'm not speaking out of turn. I appreciate that I'm not known for my interpersonal skills. My role as the bank's Head of Risk rarely calls for me to show that I have a human side.' There was an unexpected sensitivity in his voice. 'I do understand that things have not been easy for you of late, and whatever you may think, I do hope that you have found some peace in Market Melbourne.' He coughed again, a splutter of embarrassment. 'I hope that the rest has done you good. And that perhaps you might be ready to return to work, and take on a new assignment?'

Rose smiled to herself. She knew that small talk wasn't Clive's strong point, and she found his attempts almost touching. 'How could I refuse you, Clive? You know my heart beats solely to serve the ENB.'

He drew in a noisy breath. 'I have missed your assistance in the workplace, Rose. I cannot stretch so far as to say I have missed your flippancy. Perhaps if I might be permitted to outline the problem to you, before you make a decision?' He clicked his teeth in censure, the fleeting moment of humanity gone. 'As you know, the ENB has a rather bespoke approach to lending when it comes to our commercial customers. We prefer to look at each request for business funding on its own merits, rather than taking a one-size-fits-all approach. It is an approach which I believe gives us a competitive edge in the market place, and I am sure that we have appropriate processes, training and controls in place to avoid any unnecessary risks.'

'Has something happened to make you think again?'

'I fear so. I know I do not have to tell you that there are times when processes, training and controls are not enough. We also rely heavily on the discretion and trustworthiness of our colleagues. And for that reason, we find it necessary to run random checks from time to time to ensure that our trust is not being abused.' He let out a sigh. 'Regrettably, our latest random checks have shown that we have a commercial customer who has benefitted from what we might call "irresponsible lending". In short, we have loaned far more money to his business than we believe it can comfortably afford to repay.'

'Forgive me, Clive, but that doesn't necessarily mean that something dishonest has been going on. It could just as easily mean that your processes need reviewing and updating. And you already have colleagues who can deal with that. Why would you need an independent investigator?'

'Well, as I see it, there are two possible paths that could have led to this outcome. One is that the customer has in some way influenced his account manager to lend the money outside of normal lending rules, knowing that he couldn't afford to repay. The other is that the account manager has offered to lend the money in order to boost his own commission, without due regard to the risk for the customer.'

'So you would like me to investigate whether this account manager has acted dishonestly?'

'Yes.' He hesitated. 'But there is more. I have repeatedly given my fellow board members my personal assurance that our approach to commercial lending is a safe one. I have assured them on numerous occasions that I do not believe our processes are inadequate, nor that any member of our staff would abuse the privileges given to them to exercise their own judgment in deciding how much to lend to their customers. But in this case ... well, frankly, it looks as though I might be wrong.' An uncharacteristic humility had crept into his voice. 'If I use an internal team to investigate, the results of their investigation will be available for everyone at the ENB to access.'

'Would I be right in thinking that if a dishonest colleague has slipped through the net, you would like to know how and why he did it before everyone else does?'

'Indeed. Then, if and when I am challenged on the subject, I can assure the board that I am aware of the issue, and have the matter in hand.' His voice became a conspiratorial whisper. 'And for that to happen, I need an independent investigator to crawl all over this case for me, and flush out the facts.'

Rose drew in a deep breath and slowly blew it back out again. 'No pressure there, then, Clive.' She tilted her head back against the armchair, and considered an obvious risk. 'What happens if I crawl all over this case for you and *can't* flush out the facts?'

At the other end of the line Clive Barden uttered a long, low groan. 'If you crawl all over this case and can't give me the facts, Rose, then it won't be long before the East & Northern Bank start looking for a new Head of

Risk, and I will be looking for another job.'

The fire was beginning to take hold now.

The heat was beginning to burn his cheeks and he took a step back, almost losing his footing on the rough, uneven ground. But he couldn't take his eyes away from the growing conflagration. The flames were hypnotic, the swirls of smoke mesmerising as they circled the car's interior, casting tiny shooting stars of sparks as they went.

It was a criminal waste, he thought, to see that beautiful piece of craftsmanship begin to disintegrate. It hadn't taken long for the sumptuous leather upholstery to catch alight, for the lovingly-polished paintwork to blister, for the solid, workmanlike rubber of the high-performance tyres begin to melt. Forty thousand pounds' worth of unmitigated luxury wiped out by a gallon or so of carelessly thrown petrol and a thoughtfully placed lighted match. It wouldn't be any great loss for the leasing company. Just another car to write off. Just another desperate dream up in smoke.

He put a hand up to his face and rubbed across his skin, wiping the growing perspiration away with the cuff of a shabby, coarse-spun jumper that had escaped from the sleeve of his coat. The unwelcome aroma of unwashed wool seeped from the fibres, and he screwed up his face at the smell of it, then dug deep into the pocket of his overcoat and pulled out a small leather-bound hip flask.

He pulled at the neck of the flask to release the stopper and then held it to his lips and drank. The whisky burned at the back of this throat, drowning out the smell of dirt and smoke, and he took a second pull for good measure before thrusting the flask back into the pocket. Sometimes, he thought, you have to do the worst of things for the best of reasons. Sometimes, there just isn't any other way.

The fire was building dangerously now, the heat growing in intensity, an orange glow beginning to light up the damp, dark, depressing October sky. Soon he was going to have to back away further, and before long he would need to leave the scene altogether. He cast a glance behind him, in the direction of the main road. There was nothing to see, no traffic, no headlights to cast a glow. It was time to make a move.

He turned and stepped forward to a shape on the ground, and bent down to pick up the small folding bicycle, already open and ready to mount. It would take him about forty minutes, he reckoned, to make his way back to the Barnfield estate. There wouldn't be any traffic to hinder his progress. It was still too late at night, or perhaps too early in the morning, for anyone else to be around.

The ground ahead of him was too rough for the cycle to handle, and he walked purposely towards the main road, pushing the bicycle beside him, his face down, his chin obscured by the cheap acrylic scarf pulled close around his neck, his eyes almost masked by the woolly hat pulled down low over his brow.

Close to the road now, he stopped and glanced over his shoulder for one last look. The moon was still obscured by clouds, but the scrubland was lit by an eerie crimson glow. He sighed, resigned to the horror of his own creation, and as he did so the petrol in the car's tank ignited and the car imploded with a sickening sound of shattering glass and twisting metal.

He took in a sharp intake of breath, stunned by the noise and the heat of the blast, and then turned once more in the direction of the road. There was nothing to do now but make for home.

2

Detective Inspector George Mulligan shivered inside his overcoat. It was cold on the cliff top, the bleak scrubland exposed to a biting wind off the North Sea that carried with it a vague, insidious drizzle, and he was briefly overwhelmed by a nagging and familiar thought.

I'm getting too old for this game.

It wasn't as if the drama unfolding before him was unfamiliar, nor that he lacked the skills to cope. Perhaps he just couldn't help thinking that after the best part of thirty-five years in the force he could be doing better things with his time than investigating a vehicle fire in the middle of nowhere.

There was a salty sting to the breeze pummelling against his cheek, and he put up a hand to shield his eyes, and scanned the scene for sight of his detective sergeant. It only took a moment to locate Ian Scott, standing just beyond the burnt-out car, deep in conversation with a uniformed colleague. Mulligan muttered under his breath. The affable Scottie was looking far too cheerful for a cold, damp, miserable morning.

He stepped away from his car and picked his way across the gorse, waving to catch DS Scott's attention as he went. Scott nodded to him in recognition and set off towards him, and as their paths collided just a few feet from the wreckage Mulligan paused and cast a questioning glance in his direction. 'Joyriders?'

DS Scott grinned at him with his customary good humour. 'Come on, George, I hope you know me better than that.' His gentle Welsh lilt sounded incongruous with the bleak Yorkshire surroundings. 'Would joyriders leave a body in the car when they torched it?'

'A body?' Mulligan's heart sank. 'I suppose I'd better take a look then.' He pluffed out a begrudging sigh and walked the last few paces towards the driver's side of the car. A thin, white plastic sheet had been draped across the door, and he lifted the edge with a tentative finger and peered in through what had once been a window. He winced at the sight within, and swallowed hard to keep down his breakfast. 'Poor sod.' He straightened his back. 'Have we run a check on the car yet?'

'We have. The rear registration plate was still readable.' DS Scott pulled a notebook from the inside pocket of his overcoat and flipped it open. 'You wouldn't know to look at it, but this used to be a dark grey Jaguar XF saloon, seven months old, registered in the name of Leo Pearson. The address is in Kirkby. Kirkby Park to be exact.'

'Any report of it's being stolen?'

'Nothing yet.'

'And our friend in the driving seat?' Mulligan cast a wary glance back in the direction of the charred remains. 'Any report of this Leo Pearson going missing?'

'Nope. Not so far.' DS Scott snapped the notebook shut. 'The fire was reported at about 5am by a passing motorist. He was on his way to an early shift at the fish processing plant when he caught sight of it, and he parked up to call the fire service.' He turned towards the main road behind them and nodded in its direction. 'He reported that the blaze was well alight, and it took the brigade twenty minutes to reach it. It didn't help that the car had been driven off the road and across this rough ground. Anyway, I've been told that it was still burning pretty fiercely when they got here. It wasn't obvious that there was anyone inside until the fire had been damped down.'

Mulligan thrust his hands deep into his coat pockets. 'We're in the middle of bloody nowhere. What the hell was he doing up here?' He frowned and glanced around him. Down to the right, sleepy villages mingled along the coast with almost-deserted caravan parks. Up to the left, the cliff top undulated towards Scarborough, obscuring the view of the town, leaving only the sketchy outline of the distant castle ruins visible through the mist. He twisted his neck to look over his shoulder. 'Why would he drive up here at night? We must be a good quarter of a mile away from the road.'

'Some sort of tryst?'

'Or maybe he was trying to avoid being seen. Maybe he'd been drinking, and was looking for a place to sleep it off.'

'Are we assuming that it was Leo Pearson inside the car?'

The senior officer shrugged. 'I don't think we can assume anything at this stage.' He turned back and peered again into the wreckage of mangled metal. A noxious smell of molten rubber, and worse, hit his nostrils and he pulled a large white handkerchief from his pocket and clamped it across his nose before bending forward to take a closer look. 'The identification isn't going to be easy.' He turned his head, casting his eyes quickly over what might once have been hair, skin, hands, fingers. Something on the ash-strewn floor of the car caught his attention and he took the handkerchief away from his face, and gingerly reached into the wreckage with it to pick up the small metal object. It was still warm. He pulled it up to his face to take a closer look, and then he rubbed it between his thumb and forefinger, cleaning away a sooty residue with the handkerchief. 'It looks like a wedding ring.' He pulled a small plastic bag from his pocket and dropped the ring into it. 'Whoever he is, he's somebody's husband.' He turned back to DS Scott. 'Where's Jimmy Miller?'

'An emergency appointment at the dentist. He'll be at least another hour.'

'An emergency …?' Mulligan rolled his eyes. 'I suppose even pathologists get toothache.' He heaved another sigh. 'Well, I suppose we'd better make a start, and see if we can find out who the poor sod is. Let's take a trip over to Kirkby Park and see if this Leo Pearson has missed his Jaguar yet. I'll drive.'

He turned towards his car and began to stride back across the scrubland, the sergeant following in his wake. It seemed too cruel a way to tempt fate, he thought to himself, as he picked his way through the gorse, to wonder whether Mrs Leo Pearson was missing a husband.

Julia Spencer's office was on the second floor of the ENB's Kirkby headquarters. As Rose Bennett sank into the visitor's chair beside Julia's desk, she felt unexpectedly flustered. 'You'll have to forgive me this morning, Julia. I've just had three weeks out of the office, and I'm still feeling a bit giddy. Still,' she reached down into the briefcase at her feet and pulled out a pen and a soft leather notebook, 'even if that wasn't the case, I'd struggle to work out what Clive expects of me. He hasn't exactly given me a lot to go on.'

Julia, a cheerful-looking woman with shrewd brown eyes, and a voluptuous hourglass figure optimistically squeezed into a navy pinstriped two-piece, peered at Rose over the top of tortoiseshell reading glasses. She held her gaze for a moment, and then her mouth curled with a knowing smile. 'You've come to speak to me about Toby Dugdale.' She leaned back in her seat and folded plump hands into her lap. 'What do you want to know?'

'Well, just about everything, really.' Rose rested her notebook on the edge of the desk, and opened it up to a clean page. 'I understand from Clive that there has been some irregularity around credit advanced to one of Toby's customers. I think that Clive wants to know if it was a deliberate attempt by the customer to defraud the bank in some way, or whether Toby was simply careless when he calculated how much borrowing the customer could afford.' It was almost the truth. She knew that Clive wouldn't thank her for giving Julia the whole story.

Julia's brow folded into a studious frown. Then she said 'Toby Dugdale has only been on my team since January. He has seventeen commercial accounts to handle, and his performance so far has been more than satisfactory. He's had all the prescribed training required for his role, and he hasn't given any cause for concern until now.'

'Is he new to the bank?' Rose jotted in the notebook as she spoke.

'No, he's been here since he left school. He started in the Retail Division, in the Scarborough branch. I believe he was there for about six years. After that he took a transfer to Kirkby, to work in Customer Services. He worked on complaints, as a case handler, for about four years, and moved up into a supervisory role. Six years after that he applied for a move to the Commercial Division. His performance and work record were good, so we took him on as a junior Account Manager.'

'Do you know much about the customer involved?' Rose licked a finger and used it to leaf back through her notebook, searching for the name. 'L&V Pearson Ltd?'

'I know a little. The directors are Leo and Verity Pearson, although I understand that Verity is just a sleeping partner. They trade as Pearson the Bookmaker, from premises on the Kirkby Road in Scarborough.'

'Pearson the Bookmaker? You mean they're a turf accountant?'

'Yes. I know that not every bank likes to deal with the gambling industry, but the ENB have never had an issue with it.' Julia hesitated, and then asked 'it's not a problem for you, surely?'

'No. Actually, I have a friend who is a turf accountant. He could come in handy if I need any of the finer points of the business explaining.' Rose laughed softly under her breath. 'Now there's something I never thought I would hear myself say.' She tapped her pen on the notebook, thinking. 'Has the customer lodged any kind of complaint about the way Toby has handled their accounts?'

'Not that I'm aware of.'

'So to all intents and purposes, there was nothing to give any cause for concern on either side, until a random check threw up a flag that the ENB had advanced them too much credit.' Rose pushed the notebook away from her a little and dropped the pen onto the page. 'I understand from Clive that the firm's accounts were due for their annual review in November. Even if Clive hadn't commissioned a random check, surely these irregularities would have come to light then?'

'They would.' Julia rested her elbows on the arms of her chair, and steepled her fingers under her chin. 'At its last review in November of last year, Leo Pearson's business was just about breaking even. In January, he applied for a second commercial mortgage on his business premises, and the application received a borderline approval based on the value of the property. It just scraped through. But in February, and then again in May, Toby sanctioned significant increases to the company's overdraft limits, and he must have either used a false statement of accounts to achieve that, or at least turned a blind eye to the truth. I don't believe that the business was turning enough of a profit to cover the cost of the borrowing.' She nodded to herself. 'The business was put up for sale in the summer, and I think that Toby was hoping it would be sold before the next scheduled review in November. If the outstanding borrowing was repaid, and the customer's accounts closed, then it's just possible that we would have been none the wiser.'

'The review wouldn't have been conducted if the accounts had been settled and closed?'

'I think you already know the answer to that, Rose. We wouldn't waste time digging into the past if the matter was settled. If the outstanding debts to the ENB were paid in full, we would simply close the accounts and file everything away.'

'And does Toby know that the accounts are under investigation now, and that the date of the annual review has been brought forward to next Thursday?'

'He does, yes.'

'And how has he taken it?'

Julia swivelled around on her chair and glanced out the window at nothing in particular. 'I've heard on the grapevine that Toby has persuaded Leo Pearson to bring the date of the sale forward. So that it will complete by the sixteenth of October.'

'That's this Friday.'

'Correct.'

Rose let out a low whistle. 'So he's taken deliberate steps to bring the sale forward, so that the accounts will be settled and the review won't be necessary? That's a bit damning, isn't it?' She rested her elbows on the edge of the desk. 'What the hell is this all about, Julia? Why would he sanction excessive lending to this customer, knowing he shouldn't do it, and then take steps to try to cover his tracks by ensuring that the sale proceeds come in ahead of any review? I mean, I can see what he's done. What I can't see is why he's done it. If he believes that money raised from the sale of the business will cover all the outstanding debt to the ENB, what has he gained? And what has the customer gained?'

Julia turned back to look at Rose. 'I've been asking myself the same question. Toby didn't make a great deal of commission from the additional lending, so all I can think is that the business had cash flow issues. Perhaps they needed additional funding to tide them over, Toby bent the rules for them, and now those issues are over they are voluntarily selling the business and settling their debts. I asked Toby why they are selling. He said they plan to take early retirement and move abroad to Portugal.'

'And what happens if the sale falls through?'

Julia let out a shrill cackle and slapped a beringed hand on the desk. 'Well then we'll all be up to our knees in the brown smelly stuff, won't we? We all need this sale to go through. Leo Pearson's business debts will be settled by the sale proceeds. Toby's indiscretions won't go unnoticed, but he'll probably get away with a rap on the knuckles. And most importantly of all, the ENB will get its money back.'

'Always assuming, I suppose, that the new buyer is willing to pay a high enough price to cover off all of the outstanding debt.'

Julia's plump cheeks dimpled. 'Well let's hope that he is, eh, Rose? You know that there's no room for sentimentality in banking. For what it's worth, I don't think Leo Pearson's business is worth its stated book price. But if he's managed to find a buyer foolish enough to pay over the odds for it, let's hope that no one tips that buyer the wink before the ENB has managed to recover its money. I'd hate to think the buyer would wriggle off the hook and leave us with a substantial unrecovered debt. And I certainly wouldn't want to be the one to have to break a piece of news like that to Clive Barden.'

DI Mulligan perched awkwardly next to DS Scott on the edge of Verity Pearson's generous lilac sofa. The sofa was at the garden end of a lounge which was both sizeable and comfortable, a room which overflowed with warmth and elegance. He glanced around, taking in the simple Regency-stripe wallpaper, the large gilt mirror hanging above a carved alabaster mantelpiece, the collection of expensive-looking botanical prints in their heavy gilt frames. A scattering of coloured sheepskin rugs littered the floor, and billowing floral drapes framed a south-facing French window out onto an expansive York-stone patio. He gave an unobtrusive sniff, and registered the aroma of affluence. The place had a feeling of luxury, colourful and tactile.

It occurred to him that there was a luxurious, colourful and tactile feel to Verity Pearson, too. Seated opposite Mulligan and Scott on a small damask-covered chaise, her slim frame was sheathed in a teal-coloured velvet dress that stretched down over footless tights to tanned and pedicured bare feet, and her hair fell to her shoulders in a rich mass of vibrant burgundy curls. As his gaze came to rest on her heart-shaped, ageless face, he realised that she was observing him with a cool, almost impassive curiosity.

He cleared his throat with an uneasy cough. 'Can I ask when you last spoke to your husband, Mrs Pearson?'

'Yesterday afternoon. I spoke to him on the telephone at around four o'clock. He was at the shop.' Her voice was calm. 'We have our own business, it's a betting shop on the outskirts of Scarborough. On the Kirkby road.'

'Pearson the Bookmaker? Is that the one?'

'Yes.'

'Were you expecting him home yesterday evening?' Mulligan watched her face closely as he spoke.

'No, I wasn't. He'd arranged to meet up with some friends. It was a little embarrassing, because we had a meeting arranged with a business associate. But he didn't want to attend.' She looked uncomfortable now. 'I'm afraid I lied on his behalf. I made out that he had left for the meeting, but that he must have been held up in traffic.'

'Does he often ask you to lie for him?'

She appeared to consider the suggestion, and then dismissed it with a shake of the burgundy curls. 'It isn't the first time he's asked me to do it, but I don't make a habit of it. And it wasn't a problem. As it happens, I am also a director of the business, so I was able to deal with the meeting on Leo's behalf.'

'You were expecting him to be out all night?'

'Yes. He told me that he was going out for a drink with some friends, and then I think there was meant to be a game of poker afterwards. He told me not to wait up.'

'Did he tell you which friends he would be with, or where he would be spending the night?'

'I'm sorry, he didn't say.' She licked her lips, a nervous flick of the tongue. 'Inspector Mulligan, has something happened that I should know about?'

He kept his voice as level as he could. 'A vehicle has been found just outside Scarborough, parked up on the cliff top near Cayton Bay. Based on a registration check, we believe it's your husband's Jaguar.' He saw the green eyes blink. 'I'm sorry to have to tell you that there was a body in the vehicle, in the driver's seat.'

There was a brief uncomfortable silence, and then her voice became a husky whisper. 'Have you identified the body? Was it my husband?'

The policeman hesitated. He couldn't exactly say that there wasn't much left of the driver to identify. 'We're still waiting for the results of a forensic examination. I'm afraid that the car had been set alight. It will be a complicated procedure to identify the victim. But we did retrieve an item from the vehicle that might help us.' He slipped his hand into the pocket of his overcoat and pulled out a small, clear plastic bag. 'Do you recognise the item in this bag?'

For a few seconds she just stared at his outstretched hand, and then she took the bag from him and opened it to take out the plain gold band. She lifted it up to her face and stared at it with expressionless eyes. 'It looks like Leo's.' She turned it around and squinted at the inner edge. 'Yes, it has my name engraved on the inside. Verity.' She drew in a deep, slow breath through her nose and blew it out again between clenched teeth. 'The stupid, idiotic ...' Her voice trailed away, and she turned her head to stare out of the French windows and into the garden.

'Of course, this is just circumstantial evidence, Mrs Pearson.' DS Scott's gentle lilt broke into the silence. 'It's possible that the car was stolen, that for some reason your husband might have taken off his ring and dropped it in the car before it was taken. But we think you should be prepared for the worst. We're very sorry.'

She turned to look at the sergeant. 'He would have been wearing a gold neck chain under his shirt. Eighteen carat gold, he never took it off, not even in the shower.'

'Thank you. We'll make a note of that.' Scott paused, and then asked 'is there anyone we can call to come and sit with you? A friend or a family member who could stay with you until we have more news?'

'Sit with me? No, that won't be necessary. I wouldn't expect you to understand, but our marriage wasn't exactly a sentimental affair.' She pushed herself up from the chaise and walked slowly over to the window. Eventually, she turned to look over her shoulder at DI Mulligan. 'So what happens now?'

'When the forensic examination of the vehicle is complete, we'll ask you to take a look at any further items we think can be used to identify the driver. And we'll let you know how we believe the fire was started. The site of the accident,' he wasn't sure what else to call it, 'will be cordoned off while we investigate, but we'll let you know when it will be possible to visit. In the meantime, if you hear from your husband, or from anyone who knows where he is, please let us know.'

'Of course.' She lowered her eyes. 'Is that all I'll need to do, to identify that it's Leo in the car? Confirm that anything you find belonged to him?'

Mulligan exchanged a glance with DS Scott, and then began to push himself to his feet. This wasn't the time to talk of dental records, or to ask if Leo Pearson had any physical deformities that might show up in the structure of his bones. There would be plenty of time for that when the news had sunk in, and even then, he thought, only if it were really necessary. Even the most distant of wives was entitled to be spared an unnecessary trauma. 'We'll let you know if we need anything else.'

He turned to look down at Scott and motioned with his hand for the sergeant to stand up and follow him. Scott frowned and then rose to his feet, but instead of following DI Mulligan to the door, he turned to look at Verity Pearson. 'I'll try to pop back this afternoon, and give you an update. Will you be at home?'

'If I know you're coming back, Sergeant Scott, I will make sure I'm here.' Verity looked up at him through the long, dark lashes. 'Why don't I let you have my phone number, and you can let me know what time to expect you?'

For a moment George Mulligan wondered whether he was the only one present who had remembered the gravity of the occasion. But a glance at the sergeant's face, and the glint in Ian Scott's eyes as he gave his senior officer an almost imperceptible wink, only served to reassure him that yet again, Scottie had picked up on something that he himself had missed.

3

Toby Dugdale tilted his head towards the firmly-closed door of Julia Spencer's office, and wondered what was going on behind it. She had been closeted with a stranger for almost an hour now, a cool-looking redhead in a dark grey woollen suit who had greeted his manager like a long-lost friend. It had been his first ever sighting of Rose Bennett, although not the first time he had heard of her. If the rumours were true, and he had no reason to think that they weren't, then the visitor was Clive Barden's personal Rottweiler.

He puffed out a sigh and turned his attention back to a small, neat laptop in front of him. But forcing himself to stare at the screen wasn't going to do anything to alleviate his mood. His desk was at the end of a bank of six, and he turned to look briefly over his shoulder. The office was busy, every desk occupied, and the low-grade chatter of hushed conversations and confidential phone calls hummed interminably in the background. At least no one was paying him any attention.

He put out a hand to the telephone on his desk and began to lift the receiver, and then thought better of it. Instead, he pulled his mobile phone from the inside pocket of his jacket, and jabbed at the keypad to find Leo Pearson's mobile number. The call went straight through to voicemail for the seventh time in an hour, and he cut it off with an angry thumb, and then clattered the phone back down onto the desk.

How could Leo put him through this?

He lifted a hand up to his forehead and rubbed at it, trying to ease a growing tension. He still didn't understand what was going on. He'd always played fair by Leo, and until yesterday he'd believed that Leo would always play fair by him. To discover his mistake was a bitter pill to swallow.

He picked up the phone again and stared at the screen. Verity wasn't returning his calls either, but it had to be worth one more try. He tapped at the phone with his fingers, and tried the number for Kirkby Park. To his utter astonishment, the call was answered almost immediately.

'Hello? This is Verity Pearson.' Her voice sounded odd, hoarse and heavy with sorrow or some undisclosed torment. 'Who is this calling, please?'

'Verity, it's Toby.'

She didn't reply.

'Verity, I really need to speak to Leo.' The words spilled out of him in a hurried and anxious whisper. 'I've been through all the numbers again this morning. Even if the sale of the business goes through on Friday, it won't realise enough capital for Leo to repay everything that Pearson the Bookmaker still owes to the bank. The sale of the premises will cover the outstanding mortgages, but the proceeds from the shop fittings, the goodwill, and so on … they will go some way towards settling the overdraft, but there will still be a shortfall. Leo promised me that if this happened, he had a solution. He said there was nothing to worry about. But I need to know that the shortfall will be covered this Friday when the sale goes through, otherwise there will still be a significant business debt to the ENB.' There was still silence at the end of the line. 'Verity, are you still there?'

'Yes, I'm here.'

'Do you understand what I'm saying? I need to speak to Leo so that I can understand how he's going to cover this shortfall.'

'I'm afraid that isn't going to be possible now, Toby.' She sounded vague, distant at the other end of the line. 'There is no easy way for me to tell you this, but I don't think you're ever going to be able to speak to Leo again.'

The Crown and Anchor had once been a busy coaching inn on the main road from Kirkby into Scarborough, but now it was part of a modern pub chain. It served food, accommodated families, and still had an attractive beer garden at the rear for those who enjoyed the nip of sea air with their alfresco refreshment. But its main appeal for George Mulligan had nothing to do with the hospitality on offer, and everything to do with its location, which was directly across the road from Leo Pearson's business premises.

He edged his bulk into a seat at the window, dropping his coat onto an adjacent chair as he went, and hitched up crumpled shirt-sleeves to better rest his elbows on the edge of the table. Settled in, he tilted his head first to the left, where DS Scott was taking possession of two half pint glasses from the bar, and then to the right, to contemplate an uninterrupted view through the window of a busy main road, and beyond it a small row of shops.

'So that's the place? The double-fronted unit between the newsagents and the bakery?' Mulligan squinted again through the glass as the sergeant dropped into a seat at the other side of the table. 'It doesn't look anything out of the ordinary.' He pushed out his lips in contemplation. 'Does it look prosperous enough to you to fund a fancy house in Kirkby Park, a luxury saloon, and that sporty little number of Verity Pearson's that was parked on the driveway?'

'It's difficult to say, George. You can never tell with these bookmakers. If the place was too swish, it might put the punters off. Just because the premises are basic doesn't mean it isn't taking money.' DS Scott folded his arms onto the table. 'I take it we're going over there after lunch to see what we can find out?'

'It's as good a place to start as any. We have a body which may or may not be Leo Pearson. His wife can't tell us where he was last night, and it's too early in the game to make any assumptions about what happened to the victim. We'll have a better idea when we get the forensic report. Until then, the best we can do is talk to Leo Pearson's staff. One of them might know where he was going yesterday evening. It's possible we might even find out whether there were any enemies. The more we can find out from the staff, the less you will have to tease out of Verity Pearson when you go back this afternoon.'

'Do you think it could have been an accident? What if he'd had one over the eight, and knew he wasn't fit to drive? He might have driven up onto the cliffs to sleep it off. The car might have developed some sort of mechanical fault and caught alight while he was sleeping.'

'Wouldn't the smoke have woken him?'

'Not necessarily. Cars are made from all sorts of nasty man-made substances these days. Burning upholstery can give off toxic fumes. So can burning rubber. What if he was drunk when he parked up, he fell asleep, and then the burning began and the toxic fumes overcame him while he slept? The fire takes hold, the victim is dead to the world, and he doesn't stand a chance.'

Mulligan considered the suggestion. 'I suppose it's possible, given one or two variables. But I still think we should go ahead and question the staff. We don't know anything about him yet, let alone whether he was a heavy drinker.' He turned his head to take another look out of the window.

DS Scott pulled a glass of lemonade towards him, concentration ridged across his brow. 'If this turns out to be murder, it's going to be a bit tricky coming up with a suspect before we've identified the body. We could waste a lot of valuable time searching for a motive, means and opportunity if we make the wrong assumption.'

'And we could be giving a suspect a lot of valuable time to make a getaway if we don't at least make a start on the case.' Mulligan pushed his own glass to one side and leaned forward in his seat. 'Let's begin with the assumption that the body is Leo Pearson's. It's a reasonable assumption, because as far as we know Leo Pearson hasn't been heard of since yesterday afternoon, and the body was found in his car. We believe the victim was wearing his wedding ring, and we have information that he always wore a gold neck chain. If that turns up during the search of the vehicle or the examination of the remains, then that would bolster the case.' An inquisitive smile began to play around his lips. 'What made you think that the old charm offensive might be a good way to play it with Verity Pearson?'

Mischief flickered across DS Scott's face. 'Dolled up to the nines even though it was only mid-way through the morning? Not overly concerned that her old man had been out on the tiles all night? I thought it would be obvious, George, even for you. Verity Pearson is lonely. She's a good-looking woman, and she has all the trappings of a luxury life, but she's married to a man who would rather be out all night playing poker.'

'Good-looking and lonely she might be, but I hope you're going to tread carefully.'

'You know me, George. I'll just be a shoulder to cry on.'

'Well while she's crying, make sure you find out as much as you can. She said that Leo Pearson had a business meeting scheduled that he didn't want to attend. See if you can find out who that meeting was with, what it was about, and why he didn't want to attend it. Maybe there were repercussions. Maybe the person he was due to meet with didn't like being stood up.'

'You don't murder somebody just because they didn't

turn up for a business meeting.'

'That,' Mulligan countered, 'depends on just what sort of business you were planning to discuss, and what sort of person you were meeting to discuss it with.'

Evie Green dialled the number of Pearson the Bookmaker for the third time that day, and waited for someone to answer. The phone still pressed to her ear, she tilted her head to look over her shoulder, a furtive glance through the doorway at the far end of the hall. Liam was still at the kitchen table, his young nose deep in a comic, his fingers clutching a doorstep sandwich. She watched intently as he licked at the edge of the bread, concentration wrinkled into his brow, his attention torn between the entertainment of the story and the gratification of salty Cheshire cheese and spicy pickle squashed between slices of soft, spongy bread. At least it was easy to keep him distracted.

'Pearson the Bookmaker. Can I help you?'

The brisk female voice at the end of the line broke through her maternal musing, and she swung around to face the wall, and cupped the phone's receiver with her hand to muffle her voice. 'I'm sorry to bother you again, it's Evie Green. Could I speak to Neil Redfern, please?'

The voice on the line softened. 'Evie, it's me. It's Beverley. Has Neil still not shown up?'

Evie felt a lump begin to rise in her throat and she swallowed hard. 'No. I'm so sorry to keep calling, but I'm at my wits end. He isn't answering his mobile, or his landline.' She glanced again over her shoulder. 'I'm going to have to miss my shift tonight. I can't leave Liam on his own.' She sighed out her frustration. 'I'm sorry, Beverley. I know there's nothing you can do. I'm just worried sick about him. Neil's a lot of things, but he wouldn't leave me to worry like this. And he wouldn't let me down when he knows I've got to work.'

'When did you last speak to him?'

'Yesterday teatime. I called him to make sure he was going to babysit for me tonight, and to tell him to come early and eat with us before I went to work. He said he would call me this morning to let me know what time he'd be here, but I still haven't heard from him.'

'Have you tried calling any of his other haunts?'

Evie laughed, a low, bitter snuffle. 'He doesn't have any other haunts. Why do you think he spends all his time gambling at Pearson's? No one other than Leo Pearson will give him credit.'

'Well what about the police? Could you ask them to look for him?'

'They'd say I was wasting their time. I'm sure they've got better things to do than hunt around for my brother.' She paused, and then ventured a hesitant question. 'I don't suppose you could ask Leo Pearson for me? Ask him if he knows where Neil is? You know that Neil sometimes does odd jobs for him.'

There was a sound at the end of the line that sounded like a sharp intake of breath, and then the voice behind it took on a curiously elusive note. 'I'm sorry, Evie. Leo hasn't been in to the shop today either.'

'Could you call him?'

This time there was an elongated silence. Eventually, Beverley said 'it's a bit difficult just now, Evie. But I'll ask around in the shop again, there are still one or two of the regulars in. We don't close until eight tonight. If I hear anything, I'll be straight on the phone to let you know.' It was a firm but gentle refusal.

Evie blinked to push back a tear, and then spoke quietly into the phone. 'I'm sorry to have bothered you again, Beverley. Thanks for your help.' She placed the phone's receiver gently down on its cradle, and then rested against the wall, wrapping her arms around her own petite frame in an attempt to hug away the worry. There was nothing else to be done, then. She would have to cancel her shift. But cancelling the shift was the easy bit.

Finding her missing brother? Now that was going to be more problematic.

'I'd like to introduce you to Rose Bennett.' Julia Spencer ushered Toby Dugdale into her office, and pointed to a small meeting table in the corner.

Rose, already seated at the table, turned her head and looked up at him with an amiable smile. He was a good-looking young man with waves of thick blond hair and pale blue eyes, sharply dressed in a grey herringbone suit and a crisp white shirt. But the blue eyes looked troubled, and instead of smiling back he merely blinked and stared at her. 'How are you, Toby?' Rose glanced across at Julia, who responded with an uncomprehending shake of the head as she took her own place at the table. 'Is everything alright?'

Toby hesitated, and then sank onto the chair beside her. 'I didn't mean to be rude. It's ... I've ... had some bad news this morning.'

'I'm sorry to hear that. Would you prefer to meet with us later?'

'No, now is fine.' Despite his words, he sounded uncertain. 'Actually, now is good, if it's Leo Pearson's accounts you want to speak to me about.'

'I see.' Rose glanced down at her notebook, open on the table in front of her, then she pushed the book away and turned in her seat to look directly at him. 'Why don't we talk about this off the record? It sounds to me as though you already know why Julia has asked you to meet with us.'

'You want to talk to me about the state of Leo Pearson's accounts.'

'We'd like to ask for your help, Toby. So that we can understand how you came to sanction so much borrowing for him. We want to understand whether there is a flaw in the process, or in your training. So that it doesn't happen again.'

'It won't happen again.' He spoke so quietly that she could barely hear him. 'I did know what I was doing. I sanctioned more borrowing than he could afford, and I shouldn't have done it.'

The unexpected admission hung in the air, and then Rose raised an eyebrow in Julia's direction. Julia leaned forward across the table and gently put a hand on Toby's arm. 'As your line manager, Toby, I have to advise you that such an admission might leave you open to disciplinary action. Are you sure you want to talk about this now?'

'Yes, I'm quite sure. I think I've sort of backed myself into a corner, and I don't know how to get out of it. But I would like to do the right thing, as far as I can. And I suppose that means telling you what I've done, and why I did it.' He clasped his hands and placed them down on the table in front of him, and focused his attention on some indeterminate point on the polished wood. 'You know that Leo Pearson already had two commercial mortgages on his business premises, along with an overdraft facility. And I suppose you already know that I increased the lending limit on that overdraft facility twice, once in February and then again in May.'

'And you did that,' Rose asked, 'knowing that the company's position wasn't strong enough to support the borrowing?'

'Yes. Leo had drawn up an interim statement of accounts to support the application, but I didn't bother to file a copy.' He turned towards Rose. 'The accounts weren't worth the paper they were written on. Not by the time Leo had finished with them.'

Rose frowned, thrown by the candour of his confession. In her experience it was unusual for a colleague to so willingly confess to their sins. 'Well, I do appreciate your honesty, Toby. Would you be prepared meet with me again this afternoon and talk about this in more detail?'

'Of course.' His handsome face clouded. 'I wonder … in return would either of you be able to advise me on what to do next? It's just that I've realised this morning that when Leo's business premises are sold, the sale proceeds won't be enough to cover the outstanding debt to the bank. The sale is still due to go through on Friday, but there will be a shortfall of around forty thousand pounds, give or take a thousand. How do I handle that from the bank's point of view?'

The usually-affable Julia pursed her lips. 'Assuming that you took the necessary personal guarantees when you sanctioned the lending, the bank will seek to recover that shortfall from Leo Pearson in person.'

He turned towards her. 'And what will happen if Leo can't pay off the shortfall?'

'It depends what you mean by "can't". If you mean that he doesn't have sufficient personal assets to settle the debt, then we would probably seek to set up a repayment plan for the money to be paid back to us over an agreed period. Depending on his circumstances, we may be prepared to advance him a personal loan to cover the outstanding amount.' Julia pouted, and then sucked in a breath of disapproval. 'I do hope, Toby, that you're not going to tell me that Leo Pearson is not in a position to repay the debt on a personal level.'

Toby winced, and turned to look at Rose. The colour had drained from his cheeks, and his pale blue eyes looked suddenly rather young and unexpectedly vulnerable. 'Am I going to lose my job, Rose?'

Rose gave a gentle shake of the head. 'I can't answer that, Toby. It isn't my decision to make. But I can promise you that if there's something you need to talk about, you can talk to me in confidence when we meet this afternoon.' She let him consider the possibility, and then asked 'I take it that you already know Leo Pearson is going to find it difficult to repay what he owes?'

The young man turned his face up to the ceiling. 'I don't know. I mean, it might be possible. But I can't ask him. I can't ask him anything.' He blinked hard, and his voice crackled with an unexpected grief. 'I'm still waiting for it to be confirmed, but I've been told this morning that Leo Pearson might be dead.'

4

The business premises of Pearson the Bookmaker were an unprepossessing affair, shabby and old-fashioned. DI Mulligan paused in the doorway, and then pushed down on the tarnished brass door handle. An old-fashioned bell chimed as he pushed the door open, and a gaunt elderly man in a threadbare Crombie turned and nodded as Mulligan stepped over the threshold, his attention momentarily drawn away from a dog-eared copy of the Racing Post. Mulligan nodded back with a grunt, and turned his head to extend the courtesy to two men over to his right. Factory workers, decked out in faded navy overalls, both turned their faces to the television screen up on the wall without a hint of acknowledgement, assiduously avoiding his gaze.

The policeman grumbled under his breath. Maybe they had recognised him, and maybe they hadn't. Either way, it was no novelty to him to be identified as a police officer. He'd never found any reason to apologise for the fact, and he certainly wasn't going to start forming the habit today.

There was a counter at the back of the shop, a functional affair with three separate stations for taking bets, and beyond he could see two young women chatting, their faces partly obscured by a thick glass screen that ran the full length of the counter. He walked up to the screen and coughed loudly. 'Would it be possible for me to speak to Leo Pearson?'

The women fell silent, and exchanged glances, the flow of their gossip cauterised by his question. Then the taller of the two, a pale, waif-like creature with thin blonde hair and worried eyes, stepped forward. 'Mr Pearson isn't here today. Can I help?'

He peered through the glass at a name badge pinned to the shoulder of her blue nylon blouse. 'Beverley? Can I have a word with you in private? It's about Leo Pearson.' He pulled his warrant card from his pocket and held it up for her to see. 'My name is Detective Inspector Mulligan. Is there somewhere we can talk without being overheard?'

For a moment he thought she would demur, and then she walked to the end of the counter and unlocked a gate for him to pass through. 'We can use Mr Pearson's office. It's just in here.' She held out a hand to usher him into an adjoining room. 'I'm sure he wouldn't mind.'

All things considered, Mulligan was sure too. He followed the girl into the office and waited until she had closed the door, and then offered her a disarming smile. 'Have you heard from Mr Pearson at all today, Beverley?'

She shook her head. 'Mrs Pearson called this morning to tell me that he wouldn't be in today.'

'And that was all she said?'

'Yes.' The girl looked nonplussed. 'Is there something else?'

'I understand that Mr Pearson was in the shop yesterday, but that he left at around five o'clock. Did he happen to mention where he was going?'

'Not to me, no. He just said that he was leaving for the day.'

'He didn't mention that he was meeting up with friends? That he was going out for a drink, or planning to spend the evening playing poker?'

'That's not the sort of thing he would share with me, Inspector.'

'Does he usually leave the shop at around five o'clock?'

'It depends, really. If we're busy or there's a big race

meeting on, he sometimes works on through the evening.'

'Did you see him before he left?'

'Yes, he spoke to me on his way out. Only to say that he was leaving, and to call him on his mobile if I needed anything.'

'Did he seem to have anything on his mind? Anything troubling him?'

'No more than usual.' She relaxed a little. 'Has something happened to Mr Pearson? Is that why he hasn't been in today?'

'We don't know, Beverley. That's what we're trying to find out. We've found his car, up on the cliff top near Cayton Bay. Can you think of any reason he might have driven up there?'

'I can't think why anyone would want to drive up there. Especially at this time of year.'

Mulligan sank uninvited into the plush leather chair behind Leo Pearson's desk. 'When I asked you just now if anything might have been troubling him, you said "no more than usual". What sort of things is he usually troubled about? The business? Are things not going well?' He jerked his head towards the door, and the betting shop beyond. 'It looks pretty quiet out there this afternoon.'

A hint of suspicion settled into Beverley's grey eyes. 'I can't say one way or the other. You'll have to ask Mr Pearson about that, when you find him. Or Mrs Pearson.'

'So Mrs Pearson does get involved with the business, does she?'

'Only when Mr Pearson isn't available.'

'Is he a good boss, Beverley? Do you enjoy working for him?'

She gave a shrug. 'It doesn't really matter now whether he is or he isn't. I won't be working for him for much longer.'

'You're planning to leave?'

'No. It's Mr Pearson who will be leaving. The shop is being sold. The transfer is due to go through at the end of the week.'

The policeman blinked, and tried not to reveal his surprise. 'Will you lose your job?'

'No, we're being kept on. I'm sure it will be fine. It's just … well, you never know, do you?'

'Do you know why Mr Pearson is selling the business?'

'He's retiring. I think they're planning to move to Portugal.' She looked uncomfortable now. 'Have you spoken to Mrs Pearson yet? I'm sure she'll be able to answer any other questions you have.'

Mulligan bit on his tongue. He'd spoken to Mrs Pearson alright, but he obviously hadn't asked her the right questions. 'Do Leo and Verity Pearson get on well, Beverley?'

The directness of his question brought a faint flush to the girl's pale cheeks. She glanced down at her hands. 'I've never heard them argue. But then Mrs Pearson doesn't visit the shop all that often.'

'Does Mrs Pearson have any feelings about the sale of the business? Is she supportive of it?'

Now the flush in the girl's cheeks deepened. 'I think it was Mrs Pearson's idea for her husband to retire early. At least, that's what Mr Pearson said.'

'I see.' Mulligan nodded to himself, and smiled at her again. It wasn't quite a direct answer to the question, of course. But sometimes an indirect answer could be so much more useful, especially if there was a possibility that you'd been asking the wrong question.

'Inspector Mulligan thought I should bring this over to you as soon as possible.' DS Scott stretched out a hand, his eyes fixed firmly on Verity Pearson's face as she stared at the long, gold chain hanging from his index finger. 'We were just finishing our lunch when we heard this had been found in your husband's car. We were already in

Scarborough, so I left DI Mulligan in the town and drove over to Cayton Bay to collect it.'

Verity hesitated, and then placed her fingers underneath the dangling chain, and slowly lifted it up for a closer inspection. 'Yes, this is Leo's.' She turned her green eyes up towards his face. 'May I?' She lifted the chain from his finger and suspended it from a manicured one of her own. 'I gave it to him on our first wedding anniversary.' Her voice was calm. 'Was he wearing it? Did you find it on the body in the car?'

'It was found in the vehicle.'

She dropped the chain into the palm of her other hand and closed her fingers around it. 'May I keep it?'

'Of course.' They were seated in the lounge, Verity herself comfortable on the lilac sofa, DS Scott perched awkwardly on the edge of an adjacent armchair. He was studying her face, and it discomforted him to realise that her expression was more one of resignation than of sorrow. He cleared his throat. 'Is there anything that you would like to ask me?'

'Yes.' She spoke quietly. 'Will I have to make a formal identification of the body now?'

'Given the circumstances of the death, that may not be possible. We will do everything we can to confirm your husband's identity by other means. We already have the jewellery he was wearing, and the body was found in his own vehicle.'

'And isn't that enough?'

'I'm afraid that will depend on the cause of death.'

'The cause of death? But he died in the fire, didn't he? You said that the car had been burnt out?'

'We need to be sure that there were no suspicious circumstances around the death. The car was found about a quarter of a mile away from the main road. It had been driven across scrubland towards the cliff top, well off the beaten track.' He waited for the information to sink in, and then asked 'did your husband have a habit of parking up at that spot, Verity? Did he have connections to the Cayton Bay area? A friend living there, someone he might have been playing poker with?'

Verity blinked, and looked away from him. 'I've already told you, he didn't tell me who he was spending the evening with.' She swallowed hard to hold back the risk of tears. 'I'm sorry, I thought I would be able to handle this, but it's too soon.'

The policeman dug a hand into the pocket of his jacket, and pulled out a crisp, white handkerchief. 'Here, take this.' He held it out towards her. 'I'm sorry if this is difficult for you. But I will still have to ask you a few more questions. It would be helpful if you could confirm your husband's height and weight for me. And if you could let me have a recent photograph of him, preferably a full length shot. Both of those will help with the identification.'

She dabbed randomly at her tears with the handkerchief, and forced a smile. 'He was about five feet eleven inches tall, and around thirteen and a half stone in weight.' She pushed herself up from the sofa and headed for a bookcase against the wall. Her mobile phone was resting on the top, and she picked it up and swiped at it repeatedly, and then turned and handed the phone to the policeman. 'I took that picture last year. We were on holiday in Portugal.'

Scott looked down at the phone. The man in the picture was slim but paunchy, a once-fit specimen who had let himself go to seed. Thinning sandy hair framed the top of his square face, and a single gold tooth glinted at the right-hand side of a crooked grin. He was wearing grey linen trousers and a short-sleeved orange polo shirt that stretched over an unmistakeable beer gut. His arms and face were tanned, and a gold chain glinted against the skin of his neck where the collar of his shirt was open. Leo Pearson looked relaxed in the picture. More than that, Scott thought to himself, he looked smug. Self-satisfied. He glanced up at Verity Pearson and couldn't help thinking that she deserved better. He'd never been able to understand what attracted women – especially women like Verity – to men like Leo Pearson, swaggering, brash, over-confident. He could only guess it was the money.

He handed the phone back to her. 'There's an email address on the business card I gave you earlier. Could you send that picture to me as an email attachment?'

'Of course.' She dabbed again at her eyes. 'What else did you want to ask me?'

'We'll be making enquiries now into sightings of your husband after he left the shop yesterday.' His voice was gentle. 'I don't mean to be rude, but I find it a little strange that you don't know who your husband was planning to meet, or where he might have been going when he left the shop.'

'I'm his wife, Sergeant Scott, not his keeper.' The words came out just a little too harshly. 'I'm sorry.' She gave a contrite shake of the head. 'Leo doesn't really go in much for friends. He's a member of the Kirkby Golf Club. Perhaps he was planning to meet with some of the other members.' She rubbed across her brow with a finger. 'And you could try his business associates. He has an accountant and a solicitor, of course. I suppose it's possible that he may have spoken to one of them yesterday. I can give you the contact details for both.'

'And there's no one else? You really can't think of anywhere else that he might have gone after leaving the shop? To a club? To visit a relative?' He hesitated, and then gently added 'to meet with a girlfriend?'

A fleeting scowl crossed Verity's face, and then her green eyes refilled with tears, and she bit at her lower lip. 'Oh, there have always been girlfriends, Sergeant Scott, but I've never made it my business to ask who they were. What would be the point?' She looked down at her hands. 'I'm Leo's wife, and no one can take that from me.' She gave the handkerchief a petulant shake, and then crumpled it up in her hand to dab with it at her nose.

DS Scott tried his best to look sympathetic. This wasn't the time or place, he thought, for anyone to point out that she was probably no longer Leo Pearson's wife, but his widow.

Rose Bennett picked up a teaspoon and stirred idly at the frothy cappuccino in front of her. 'I'll be honest with you, Toby. I'd much prefer it if we could keep things fairly informal. I know that's not the way things are normally done at the East & Northern Bank. But as I'm not an employee, I'm not really tied to the bank's processes and procedures.' She placed the spoon down on the table. 'Obviously, as we're having this meeting in the staff canteen, we'll need to be discrete. I wouldn't want anyone to overhear us.'

Toby looked around him, surveying the landscape of empty white melamine tables and unoccupied blue plastic chairs. 'I don't think there's any danger of that. It's always quiet this late in the afternoon.' He looked tired, and dark circles had begun to form underneath his pale blue eyes.

Rose leaned back in her seat. 'I have to say, it's quite refreshing for me to work with someone as cooperative as you. People usually make a dash in the opposite direction when they see me coming.'

He attempted a smile. 'I realised that Clive and Julia had already worked out what I had done. What would be the point in delaying the inevitable? Now that Leo's … now that there's no way I can speak to Leo to discuss how the full debt will be repaid, the best thing I can do is help his wife to complete the sale of the business, and take responsibility for the shortfall.' He looked away. 'I guess Julia's pretty mad at me for not making sure that Leo could cover the debt.'

'Julia's only doing her job, Toby. If you screw up, then it reflects badly on her as your manager. And she will feel responsible for that. She'll be blaming herself for not giving you more support when you needed it.'

'It wasn't support that I needed, though, was it?' A guilty flush seeped into his cheeks. 'I knew I was breaking the rules.' He frowned, and then the crease in his brow relaxed. 'I suppose the first thing you want to know is why Leo Pearson needed the additional borrowing?' He didn't wait for an answer. 'In a nutshell, Pearson the Bookmaker was in trouble. For a number of years, the business had been stable, but in the middle of last year a local factory closed down and laid off its workforce. Like most of the businesses in the area, Pearson's lost a lot of custom in the process. But on top of that, gambling habits are changing all the time. Young people don't want to go into a shabby shop to place a bet. They want to gamble on line, in the comfort of their own homes. Leo talked about investing in the shop, but Verity wasn't keen. According to Leo, she wanted him to cut his losses and retire. So he decided to sell the business.'

'But I thought Leo was planning to upgrade the premises? Back in January he made an application to the bank for a second mortgage on the property, and that was approved on the understanding he would spend the money on an upgrade to the building. Didn't I read on the application form that the roof needed repairs? And that he proposed to spend the rest of the money on shop fittings and fixtures, and a new set of betting terminals?'

Toby glanced away. 'He was hoping that the business would be sold, and the mortgages settled, before the bank asked what he had done with the money.'

'I see. And the extensions to his overdraft?'

'He said it was to ease cash flow for the business, so that he could pay the staff's wages and still keep covering his own personal expenses. He was struggling to find a buyer.'

'So basically Leo Pearson was using money borrowed from the ENB to shore up his lifestyle until his business was sold, and then he was going to sail off into the sunset and call it retirement?'

Toby glowered. 'If they had found a buyer straight away it might not have been necessary. But he'd run out of personal credit at the beginning of the year, and he just didn't have enough coming in to cover his mortgage, the cars, their personal debts ... the business was his last resort.'

Rose considered him with an appraising eye. There was no doubt in her mind that he was still hiding something. 'Does Leo hold his personal bank accounts with the ENB?'

'I believe he has a current account with us. And a mortgage. His cars are financed through a leasing company. I'm not sure about his credit cards.'

'And what about Verity Pearson? She's a co-owner of the business. Does she have any income of her own?'

Toby scowled. 'Verity doesn't work, and she relies on Leo for everything.' He drew in a breath. 'Do you think that Clive and Julia will let me continue as the account manager for the business until the sale is complete? Verity's not very good when it comes to money, but she's used to dealing with me.'

It was an oddly personal remark. Rose tried to sound noncommittal. 'I'm afraid that call isn't mine to make.' She studied his face. 'You still haven't told me why you were prepared to break the rules for Leo Pearson. You must have known that you were risking your own job?'

A glimmer of shame passed across Toby's face. 'Leo Pearson is my cousin, Rose.' He let out a doleful sigh. 'His father was my mother's eldest brother. There was fifteen years between them, and I'm the youngest of four children, so there is quite an age difference between us, almost twenty years. But I've idolised Leo for as long as I can remember.'

Rose whistled softly under her breath, and placed her hand on his arm. 'Toby, I'm so sorry.' She squeezed his arm gently. 'Of course I'm sorry for your loss, if something has happened to Leo, but you do realise that you should have reported that? That you should have advised Julia that there is a personal relationship between you, a conflict of interest?'

He scowled into his coffee. 'Yes, of course I know that. But I already knew that Leo was struggling. When I was offered the role in commercial banking, and they told me that Pearson the Bookmaker would be one of my accounts, I just couldn't believe it. I thought it was a chance to help him.' He sounded earnest. 'I wasn't trying to defraud the bank, Rose. I was just trying to help my cousin sort out his financial affairs. I thought I'd be able to help him with the additional lending, and I'd convinced myself that the business would sell and the bank would get their money back before anyone noticed.' He spluttered a self-deprecating laugh. 'Evidently I'm not as clever as I thought I was.' His face contorted. 'Clive and Julia are going to hang me out to dry, aren't they?'

'I don't know what Clive and Julia are going to do, Toby. I think the first thing we have to do is nurse the sale of Pearson the Bookmaker through to completion so that we can get the associated bank accounts closed and off the books, and then look at how to recover the shortfall. I will suggest to Clive that although there is a personal connection between yourself and Verity Pearson, it would be in the ENB's interests to let you stay on as the account manager under my guidance, at least until the business is sold.' She drew back her hand. 'Are we absolutely certain that this sale is going to complete? There's no risk of it falling through?'

'Not that I'm aware of. Leo's solicitor confirmed yesterday that all the paperwork is in place, the buyer is on board, and contracts are due to be exchanged on Friday.'

'And the buyer is reliable?'

Toby nodded. 'He's an existing turf accountant looking to expand his business. I haven't met him myself, but Leo and Verity thought they'd died and gone to heaven when he decided to make an offer. I believe he used to run a chain of betting shops down in Essex, but he sold up and moved north. I think he lost his wife, and wanted a fresh start. Anyway, he has one outlet in Market Melbourne, and he's looking to take on a shop in Scarborough for some reason.' He frowned. 'It's strange, really. Wouldn't you think that someone with that amount of experience in the gambling industry would realise that Leo's business was going down the pan?'

Beverley gathered up the notes and coins and shoved them into the familiar grey drawstring bag. Fifty-seven pounds and forty-eight pence wasn't much to show for a full day's takings, even if it was only a Monday. It might have been more if Harry Tennant hadn't backed an unexpected winner in the 3.30 at Plumpton, but no one who had seen the delight in the old man's rheumy eyes would have begrudged him the victory, not even the irascible Leo if he'd been around to witness it.

She dropped the bag lightly onto Leo's desk, and then sank into the plush leather chair behind it with a sigh of resignation. It hadn't come as a surprise to hear that Leo had done a disappearing act. There was hardly any income coming into the shop at all now, and most of what they had been taking had been laid across the counter by the unlucky and now elusive Neil Redfern.

She wrapped her thin, pale arms across her chest and hugged herself, and wondered what could have happened to Evie Green's brother. He hadn't been in today, and she was sure that Evie would have called to let her know if he'd been found, propping up the counter in another gambling den, or drowning his sorrows and his losses over a meagre half pint of bitter in some spit-and-sawdust pub.

It was strange, really, the way he'd just vanished into

nothing. Both she and Evie had long since realised that Neil's addiction had reached the point where, as long as there was air to breathe, he'd be found somewhere close to a betting terminal. It had been cruel of Leo to go on advancing him credit, and given the state of the business she couldn't really see the point. Why go on offering credit to a punter that was never going to be able to clear his slate?

She laughed softly under her breath. Of course, by Friday Neil's ability to repay his slate would be someone else's problem. And she couldn't imagine the shop's new owner being anywhere near so charitable to a problem punter.

She snuggled back into the chair and thought about Benny Bradman. If the sale of the business went through on Friday, nothing would ever be the same again. He had promised investment, a turn-around plan, job security for her and the other girls, even an improvement in their contracts. And he really seemed to understand the business. But the business – this business – was in trouble. Had Leo Pearson really reeled Benny Bradman in? Or was he going to back out of the sale? Was that why Leo had gone to ground, because he knew that the sale would fall through and the writing was on the wall?

It was a sobering thought. She lowered her head and let out a sigh. She might have known it was all too good to be true. The sale would fall through, the business would fold, there probably wouldn't even be enough money left in the accounts to cover the outstanding wage bill. That was probably the real reason the police were looking for Leo.

She slipped her hand into the pocket of her blue nylon blouse, and pulled out a small, neatly printed business card. Perhaps she should have been more honest with Detective Inspector Mulligan. Perhaps her hint about Mrs Pearson hadn't been heavy enough for him to spot. According to Leo, Verity wasn't just supportive of the sale, she wanted the sale. She wanted Leo to give up the shop, and take her abroad for a fancy retirement. Women like that, she mused with a disparaging shake of the head, don't know when they're lucky. A fancy house in Kirkby Park, a swish convertible motor to drive around in, holidays to the Maldives, and no need to go to work because she had a husband to pay for it all ... none of that was enough for a woman like Verity Pearson, was it? Even now, when the business was under pressure, she couldn't tighten her belt and encourage Leo to invest in the shop. She had to persuade him to cash in their chips and arrange a fancy retirement to Portugal to top it all off.

If would serve the arrogant mare right, Beverley thought, if Leo Pearson really had done a runner. Maybe he knew that Benny was going to back out of the sale, and he'd left her behind to sort out the mess. Or maybe he knew that the sale was going through, but he planned to pocket the cash and sail off to Portugal without her.

The possibilities brought a glow to Beverley's thin, pale face. Maybe he even had another woman tucked away somewhere. Maybe Verity Pearson would have to get off her toned and pampered backside and work for her own living. Maybe she'd even have to come here, and get used to running the shop.

The thought struck a chord, and Beverley lifted her head and turned her gaze towards the small grey safe in the corner of the office. No one but Leo knew the combination of that safe, and someone was going to have to take care of today's takings, scant though they were. And since Leo had gone missing, and no one else in the shop was trusted to take the responsibility, it would have to be Verity Pearson. Poor Verity, having to drive out from Kirkby to Scarborough to collect a meagre fifty-seven quid.

A smile of smug anticipation began to play around Beverley's pale, thin lips. She stretched out a hand to the phone on Leo's desk and dialled the Pearson's home number from memory, and then settled contentedly back into the chair while she waited for Verity to pick up.

5

Rose Bennett pulled her jacket a little closer around her shoulders. It was cold in the small windowless meeting room on the top floor of the Kirkby office, but it was the worrying implications of the case she'd been given that were really causing her to shiver. Now, on a call to Clive Barden, she was taking her time and choosing her words carefully.

'You needn't worry about your processes and controls. Toby Dugdale rolled over without a fight. He's admitted that he helped the customer to borrow more money than he could afford to repay, but he hoped that the customer's business would be sold before the next review was due. He expected the sale proceeds, along with some additional funding from the customer, to settle the outstanding debt before anyone noticed.'

'Why on earth would he do that, Rose?'

'The customer was having trouble with cash flow. Toby agreed to the additional lending to give him time to get his affairs on a better footing, and he trusted the customer to be good to his word that the debts would be settled before the next review in November.' She paused, and then said 'I know you won't like this bit, Clive. Toby Dugdale is the customer's cousin.'

'You mean there is a personal relationship between the two of them?'

Rose smiled to herself. 'Yes, I think that's what I'm saying. The last time I thought about it, being someone's cousin was pretty much a personal relationship.'

'Please don't trivialise the issue, Rose. This is a serious matter.' Clive's disdain was evident in his tone. 'All personal relationships must be declared to avoid a conflict of interest. You know that. Had we known, we would have taken immediate steps to move the Pearson accounts to another manager. It's an open door for fraud to be committed.' He clicked his teeth. 'Where on earth was Julia Spencer in all of this? Why didn't the relationship come to light when Toby was considered for the job?'

'I don't know, Clive. I haven't discussed it with her yet. That wasn't a part of my brief.' Rose blew out a sigh, and felt the pain to come for Julia. 'As I recall, you asked me to dig around and find out how and why Toby had advanced the money to the customer. He did it because Leo Pearson was his cousin, and he wanted to help him. As to how he did it, I don't have the full details yet, but I understand there may be some issues around a false statement of accounts.'

'False accounting?' Clive groaned at the end of the line. 'So we have a dishonest customer making use of a personal connection at the bank, to borrow money that he cannot afford to repay, for purposes that are completely unknown to us?'

'Well, I don't think the purposes are completely unknown to us. I have no reason not to believe Toby when he says that Leo Pearson was having cash flow issues. We can take a look at the business account to see what funds have been drawn from it. We can trace his cheques, and any direct transfers or payments. I can't imagine he has drawn any of it as cash. I've already asked Toby to run me off a full print of transactions, going back to last November.'

'We must take steps now to arrange for Leo Pearson to come into the bank and discuss this, Rose.'

Rose winced. 'That's not going to be possible, I'm afraid.' She lifted a hand to her face and rubbed at her forehead. 'Toby has informed me this afternoon that Leo Pearson has gone missing. But his car has been found. Burnt out. With a body in it.' She waited for Clive to respond, but heard only an ominous silence. 'We're assuming that the body is Leo Pearson until someone tells us otherwise. We haven't had any sort of official notification. It's just come from Toby. We have no idea of the circumstances, and whether the death is suspicious.' She hesitated, aware of the continuing silence, and then asked 'are you still there, Clive?'

There was a cough at the other end of the line, a strangulated clearing of the throat. 'Am I to understand that as well as a dishonest customer, a disingenuous member of staff, and a set of fraudulent accounts, we now have the possibility of a suspicious death?'

'I know, Clive.' Rose bit her lip, and tried to sound sympathetic. 'I'm finding it hard to get my head around it, too. Given the circumstances, I have to warn you that it's unlikely the ENB will recover everything that was loaned to Leo Pearson. Even when his business is sold there will be a substantial shortfall. I know Toby is certainly worried about the possibility. He believes that Leo Pearson had a solution in mind to cover it, but it's unlikely now that we will find out what that was. His wife, Verity, is a co-director in the business, so in the light of his supposed death she may technically be liable for any outstanding debts. But obviously we will have to tread carefully and treat the case sympathetically. I would suggest that we have a meeting with her as soon as possible, to see what we can do to help.'

'Agreed. And we must take immediate steps to support the sale of the business and ensure that it does not fall through.'

'Ah.' Rose closed her eyes and winced again. 'That's the other thing that I haven't shared with you yet. I've discovered this afternoon that the prospective buyer of Pearson the Bookmaker is a friend of mine, Benny Bradman.'

'The name is familiar to me, of course.' He fell silent for a moment, and then asked 'although he is a friend, you didn't already know that he was buying the business? I do hope, Rose, that this new development is not going to prove a test of your loyalties.'

'I don't believe so, Clive. My loyalties lie with honesty and with the truth. I'm not going to dissuade Benny from buying Leo Pearson's business, if that's what you're worried about. Benny will make up his own mind. But if I continue with this investigation on your behalf, and I do find evidence of criminal activity somewhere along the line, something that affects the sale of the business, then it's very likely that he will find out.'

'So what would you propose?'

'Well, if you really want me to dig deeper into Leo Pearson's affairs, I will. But there are two conditions. One, I would like you to leave Toby in his role as commercial account manager while I conduct the investigation. He could be useful. He's close to Verity Pearson, and if he thinks there's a chance that he won't be fired he will try to be helpful.'

'It will be against my better judgment, given his relationship to the customer. But if that is your advice, then I will agree. Providing you monitor him closely.' He clicked his teeth. 'And what is the other condition?'

'Give me your approval to tell Benny Bradman about my investigation. If Leo Pearson is dead, Benny will have to make his own decision about whether to proceed with the purchase of the business or not. But if I can persuade him to delay that decision, he may be willing to help us. He will have access to Leo Pearson's business from outside the bank, and might uncover information that we couldn't possibly hope to acquire in any other way. It might even give him an opportunity to reaffirm that this is the right business for him to purchase.'

'We are in this mess because Toby Dugdale has failed to declare a personal connection to a customer. Are you proposing, Rose, to investigate the case by using an undisclosed personal connection of your own as a mole?'

'Well technically, Clive, it's not an undisclosed personal connection, because I've just revealed it to you. And if you're not comfortable with it, we can always pretend that I didn't suggest it, and you can find someone else to do the investigation for you.'

The sting of her words hung crisply in the air. And then Clive barked a final, brusque instruction. 'I will take a further update from you in the morning, then.'

There was a click as he disconnected the call, and Rose slumped back in her seat and looked up at the ceiling with a fading smile. 'Don't mention it, Clive. As always, it's been my pleasure.'

Evie Green rested her elbows on the kitchen table and took another sip of lukewarm instant coffee from a garish mug emblazoned with the words "World's Best Mum". It was an accolade she didn't feel she deserved.

She had been glad to let Liam get out of the house, and relieved beyond words when a neighbour had offered to take the boy out with her own brood for an impromptu treat of burger and chips. The disappearance of his uncle was clearly unsettling him, and Evie was running out of answers. He'd already lost a father and a step-father in his seven short years, one to a shattering car accident, and the other to a cocktail waitress who was too young to vote. The loss of the uncle who unfailingly stepped into the breach would be more than his young heart could bear.

She glanced up at the clock on the kitchen wall. Liam had been out for two hours now, and in those one hundred and twenty minutes she had become almost an expert in what did and didn't constitute a missing person. She had scoured the internet on her ailing, second-hand laptop for anything that might help her to track Neil down, only to learn that he might not be missing at all.

It had never occurred to her before that someone may just drop out of sight because they wanted to. Because the pressure of work had become too much, or relationship issues had got the better of them, or because financial difficulties had driven them to the brink.

She had tried to convince herself that Neil wasn't the type, but there was no denying that two years of forced unemployment had certainly taken its toll. His wife had walked out on him, taking the kids, his job had gone west, and as for financial difficulties – Evie knew only too well that any spare cash Neil had was handed over to Leo Pearson to wipe off a gambling slate that he would run up again within days.

But would any of that be enough to make Neil take a walk, to disappear from his life without leaving any reassuring word for her, or a gentle word of goodbye for the nephew that she knew he adored? She took another sip of the fast-cooling coffee. Of course it wouldn't. Neil wouldn't just disappear from view, leaving them to worry, leaving them to mourn.

Unless …

She lifted her head. What if that disappearance was a cry for help? What if he wanted Evie to go looking for him? He must know that she wouldn't just forget him. Perhaps he just needed to be rescued. Perhaps the gambling had got too much, or the stresses and strains of the life that was happening to him – the life he hadn't chosen for himself – had just become too much to bear.

She put down the mug of coffee and picked up her mobile phone. It had been just over thirty minutes since she had last tried to call him. It was worth giving it just one more try. And if he didn't answer the call, then she wouldn't waste any more time.

The next call would be to the police. The next call would be to report Neil Redfern as missing.

6

Benny Bradman placed a pint of bitter and large glass of Pinot Grigio down on the table in the corner of The Feathers' snug, and pulled a packet of pork scratchings from his trouser pocket, crinkling the bag with his fingers. Mac, curled up on a rough wooden bench next to Rose, twitched an ear in Benny's direction, and then raised his head hopefully. They both turned their eyes towards Rose.

'Don't even think about it. Either of you.' Rose gave a shake of the head. 'Mac needs to get some of that weight off, and he can't walk as well as he could, so it's going to take more than exercise. And that means no more pork scratchings.' She held out a hand to Benny. 'And you can give those to me for safe keeping. I know what will happen when my back is turned.'

Benny dropped the packet into her outstretched hand, and sank onto a chair at the other side of the table. He tilted his head towards the terrier. 'Blimey, Mac, I don't know how you put up with that all day.'

'He doesn't have to put up with it all day. I'm back at work now. I started a new assignment this morning at the Kirkby office.'

'And where was Mac?'

'He stayed at home. He was fine. Jean and Dickie called in at lunchtime, and took him for a walk.'

Benny scowled his disappointment. 'He could have spent the day with me at the shop. You know I like to have him for company.'

'I know you like to feed him pork scratchings.' She picked up her glass and sipped on the wine. 'I have to go into the Kirkby office again tomorrow. If you promise not to feed him junk food, I'll drop him off with you in the morning.'

Benny chuckled, and winked at the dog. 'You're right, pal. She's all bark, and no bite.' He took a deep drink from his pint. 'I've been lookin' forward to this all day.' He savoured the taste, and then turned his dark eyes towards her. 'I hope you ain't gone back to work too early. You're lookin' a bit peaky.'

Rose glanced away, as if to banish the thought, and then turned back to him with a teasing smile. 'When you hear what I've been up to, you'll be glad I've gone back to work.' She leaned across the table and lowered her voice to a murmur. 'Does the name "Leo Pearson" mean anything to you?'

The dark eyes clouded, and Benny let out a low growl. 'Leo Pearson? Is that why you've invited me out for a drink?'

'Of course not.' She feigned an air of indignation. 'I'd already invited you before I'd even heard the name myself. Anyway, you're the one who's being secretive. Why didn't you tell me that you were planning to buy his business?'

Benny turned his face towards the bar. 'Because it was meant to be a surprise. A surprise for Michael, and for Vienna. I didn't want anyone to know until it was in the bag. That's why I kept it to myself. I didn't want to build Michael's hopes up in case it fell through. He's been through enough lately.'

Rose felt a sudden pang of sympathy. It would have been closer to say that Michael Spivey had been to hell and back in the last few months, and he'd taken his loved ones with him. The one-time petty criminal was Benny's right-hand man, and in the relatively short time that Rose had known them both she'd seen the hapless Michael grow in stature under Benny's guiding hand. He'd acquired himself a girlfriend, a pretty, intelligent creature by the name of Vienna Fielding, and Vienna had brought with her into Michael's lonely life a whole assortment of extended loving family, including two football-mad nephews and a mischievous niece who were the apple of Michael's eye.

It had been a cruel setback for them all just a few months ago, when what remained of Michael's own family had decided to make its presence felt. When the dying Jack Canning reached out to his son, hoping to build a bridge, no one could have foreseen the consequences. But then not many people could claim to have a contract killer for a father. Jack was gone now, and he wouldn't be coming back, but he'd taken innocent people with him, and left Michael to clear up the mess.

Rose sipped again on her wine, sober now, and tried not to think about how even she had come close to losing her life at the hands of Michael's father. 'Back in the summer, the day that Jack Canning came to Market Melbourne, you said you were thinking of expanding the business. That someone you knew in Scarborough was selling up, and you were thinking of making an offer. I suppose you were talking then about Pearson the Bookmaker?'

Benny stared thoughtfully into his glass. 'I backed off at the time. Michael had enough to contend with. But I heard on the grapevine that Leo Pearson was strugglin' to find a buyer, so I went back in September to take another look.'

'And you didn't see anything suspicious?'

He lifted his eyes sharply to look at her. 'Blimey Rose, what is this? Are you tryin' to tell me that there's somethin' dodgy goin' on?'

'I don't know. But I've been asked to find out. He banks with the ENB, and he's got himself rather heavily into debt with them on the business side. Possibly more debt than he can afford to repay. Clive Barden has asked me to find out how it happened.'

Benny placed his glass down on the table. 'I didn't notice anythin' when I went through the accounts. There are two commercial mortgages on the property, Leo didn't hide that. And there's a big overdraft. But that looked kosher. Nothin' for me to worry about, anyway. I'm not takin' on any business debt. When the sale goes through, I hand over the askin' price, and Leo pays off his debts. If he falls a bit short, that's his problem.'

'Not any more, it isn't. I take it that you haven't seen the evening paper?' Rose reached down into the bag at her feet, and pulled out a copy of the Kirkby Evening Press. She placed it on the table and pushed it towards him. 'Leo Pearson is front page news.'

Benny pulled the paper closer and skimmed his eyes over the headline. 'Body found on cliff top in burnt out vehicle?' For a moment the penny didn't drop. When it finally did, he lifted disbelieving eyes to look her squarely in the face. 'Please tell me this body ain't Leo Pearson.'

'I'm sorry, I can't do that. But I can tell you what I know.' She pointed to the pint glass in front of him. 'You work your way through that, and I'll nip to the bar and get you another. I think it's a good thing that I went back to work today. And when you hear what I have to say, I think you'll agree that one pint isn't going to be enough.'

Verity Pearson stared down at the mobile phone lying loosely in the palm of her hand. The phone was vibrating, and she glanced down at the screen, and then rejected the incoming call with a sharp jab of her thumb. There would be plenty of time tomorrow to speak to Toby Dugdale.

She tossed the phone casually to the other end of the generous lilac sofa, and then settled herself down against the pile of cushions arranged at her back, and resisted the temptation to yawn. The day had been quite exhausting enough. What she needed most now was some solitude, some time alone to think.

Somehow, in the peace of the evening, the events of the day seemed almost unreal. Leo assumed to be missing, his car burnt out in a remote location, a body discovered in the wreckage. She could hardly believe it herself, and yet all of the evidence was there. A visit from the police to break the news of Leo's death, a second visit from that charming young Detective Sergeant Scott to return her husband's gold chain, even an offer to escort her to Cayton Bay tomorrow so that she could see where the tragedy took place.

She let out a sigh, and rubbed at her temple with a manicured finger, seeking to ease a growing tension. Today had been only the beginning, though it had marked the end of a chapter. She had woken this morning as Leo Pearson's wife, and would be ending the day as his widow. Tomorrow would be the start of a new life, a different life, a life in which Leo Pearson would play no part.

A life in which the possibilities might be endless.

She closed her eyes and relaxed against the cushions, and tried to imagine how the day might unfold without him. There would have to be a meeting with the bank. That would probably be best in the morning. There was the funeral to arrange, a small unobtrusive affair, something tasteful and suitably discreet. There were her widow's weeds to choose, something dark green perhaps, or an inky shade of violet. Even Leo wouldn't expect her to schlep around in black until the funeral and mourning were over.

And at some point, she supposed, she would have to put in an appearance at the shop.

She shivered at the thought. Just four more days until that unspeakable money pit would become someone else's problem. Four more days of keeping up an appearance, of holding her head high, of steeling herself against the blame and disapproval of those girls. Who were they, to stand in judgment of her choices, to gossip about her behind her back? She gave an incredulous shake of the head. Had Beverley really expected her to drive all the way to Scarborough this evening, just to collect a sum of money so paltry that it wouldn't even pay for a tank of petrol? The girl obviously had no idea of just how difficult things had become. She certainly had no respect for the situation.

Friday just couldn't come soon enough. Friday, when Benny Bradman would hand over the cash, and the business, the mortgages, the overdraft, and those peevish, petulant girls would all become someone else's problem.

It was a liberating thought, and one that deserved celebration. She opened her eyes and allowed them to wander towards the coffee table close to her knees, and the large glass of chilled champagne that was resting there. She leaned languorously forward and stretched out a hand to the glass and then hesitated, her attention suddenly drawn to a slim fold of papers on the table beside it. Without another thought, her fingers drifted to the documents, and she took hold of them and lifted them up to her face.

By Friday the business would cease to be a problem. But then, she thought as she brushed her glossed lips across the paper with a contemplative kiss, by the time Friday came it probably wasn't going to matter that much to her anyway.

'So let me see if I've got this straight.' Benny folded his arms onto the table and regarded Rose with reproving eyes. 'You want me to poke about in Leo Pearson's business, and report back to you, so that you can tell Clive Barden whether or not the East & Northern Bank has put its foot in it and advanced too much money to a criminal?' He put up a hand. 'No, I missed a bit out, didn't I? As well as all that, you want me to go ahead and buy Leo Pearson's business, even though it might not be worth the price that

Leo Pearson put on it, just so that the ENB can get most of its money back?'

'I think you're being a bit harsh there.' Rose made a valiant attempt to keep her face straight, but she was fighting a losing battle. 'What I thought I said was "would you be prepared to ask a few questions, just to help me out?"' She bit her lip to stem her amusement. 'And just because Clive is keen that the sale of the business should still go ahead, that doesn't mean I'm suggesting you should go ahead and buy it. I thought you'd already made up your mind to buy it. Everyone is telling me that the sale is due to complete on Friday.'

'Don't get smart with me, Rose. I thought we were mates.'

'And so did I.' It was Rose's turn to reprimand. 'Of course Clive wants to make sure that the ENB recovers its money. But I've already told him that I wouldn't keep anything from you. If I turn up something at the bank that I think you ought to know, I won't hesitate to share that with you. And I just hoped that you would be prepared to do the same for me.' She tapped a finger on the table. 'You didn't even know that Leo Pearson was "missing presumed dead" until I brought it to your attention.'

Benny pursed his lips. 'Well I'm tellin' you now, the ENB shouldn't be countin' its chickens. I'll be takin' another look at Leo Pearson's accounts, and if I think there's a need to back out of this deal, I will. I already know I've offered to pay him more than the place is worth, but I was willin' to do that because the shop was right for Michael. But I can't take it on if we ain't goin' to be able to turn it into somethin' profitable.'

'I wouldn't expect you to. In fact, I'm going to prove that to you now by telling you something else that you need to know.'

'Which is?'

'You've already seen a set of accounts for Leo Pearson's business and based on those accounts you believed that the place was turning enough of a profit to service its debt to the bank?'

'So?'

'Toby Dugdale suggested to me that Leo Pearson had been tampering with the accounts, so I took a look at the overall position of the business for myself. And I would say that Pearson the Bookmaker was making a loss.'

Benny frowned. 'I took those books apart, Rose. They looked clean to me. Everythin' reconciled.'

'And yet Toby told me that when Leo Pearson offered to provide him with a new set of accounts for the quarter, he didn't bother to take them. Because in his words, they weren't worth the paper they were written on. Somehow Leo Pearson managed to make the set of books he passed to you look convincing. That in itself is a criminal offence.'

'That's all very well, but Leo Pearson is dead. He ain't goin' to be around to face any charges, is he?'

'Leo isn't, but Verity Pearson is. And she's a joint director of the company, isn't she?'

Benny gave a shrug. 'I believe so. But I think it's in name only. I don't think she has anythin' to do with runnin' the business. Leo reckoned that she hated the place. He was sellin' up because of her. She had some notion to retire abroad. Portugal, I think. I don't suppose she'll be doin' that now.' He stared into his empty glass. 'You know, that's a funny thing, Rose. I always understood that they were rollin' in money. Big fancy house, luxury motors, exotic holidays … I knew they couldn't be livin' like that on the income from Pearson the Bookmaker. I just assumed that they had other income. Maybe another business, or a legacy, or somethin'.'

'And maybe they do. But I think it's unlikely. They wouldn't be the first couple to live the high life on borrowed money, would they?' She stared down into her own empty glass. 'I'm supposed to be meeting with Verity Pearson tomorrow. What's she like?'

Benny considered the question. 'I've only met her once,

at a golf club dinner the year before last. She's a nice lookin' woman, young for her age.' He nodded to himself. 'She didn't have much to say for herself when Leo introduced us, but she was polite enough.'

'Was she happy?'

'Happy? I don't know. It's not somethin' I would have thought about at the time.' He turned his head away, trying to remember. 'That's a funny thing, because if I think about it now, I'd probably have to say that she was lonely. I didn't really see her mixin' with other people, just sittin' on her own at the table, workin' her way through a bottle of wine.' He nodded towards the empty glass in front of Rose. 'Talkin' of which, have you got time for another?'

'Go on, then. But after that I'd better be on my way. I've still got Leo Pearson's personal accounts to wade through this evening.' Rose watched as Benny got up from the table. 'At least I'll have one piece of good news for Clive in the morning. He'll be delighted that you've agreed to help us out. Even more so when I tell him that you're still going ahead and buying Pearson the Bookmaker.'

Already on his feet, Benny turned to her and raised a cynical eyebrow. 'I knew you weren't listenin' to me earlier. What did I say about the ENB not countin' its chickens?'

7

George Mulligan glanced up as DS Scott closed the office door behind him, and mumbled a greeting as the sergeant sank down onto the chair at the other side of his desk. 'Sorry about the early start, Scottie, but I'm hoping that we'll have a cause of death for Leo Pearson this morning.' He leaned back in his seat. 'At the very least I'm hoping for a view on whether the fire was started deliberately.'

'So you're satisfied that the body in the car actually *is* Leo Pearson?' Scott's cynicism was tinged with good-humour.

'I'm not satisfied, no. But I'm going with the balance of probabilities for now. I don't want to cause Verity Pearson any unnecessary distress, so I'm not going to suggest looking at dental records yet, but I reserve the right to change my mind on that one.' He shot a warning glance at DS Scott. 'As far as I'm concerned, this is a suspicious death until proven otherwise, regardless of who the victim turns out to be.'

'And how suspicious do you think this is, George? Are we talking "electric fault in the car" suspicious, or "somebody wanted him dead" suspicious?'

'I'll give you the answer to that question when I know whether the fire was started deliberately. Until then, it won't do any harm to put out a few more lines of enquiry.'

'Have you considered at any point the possibility that it might have been suicide?'

'Suicide?' Mulligan snorted. 'You don't take your own life by strapping yourself into the car and setting fire to it.'

'Why not? Surely anything is possible if you're desperate enough?'

'Why not just take an overdose?'

'Maybe he didn't have access to any medication. Maybe it was a spontaneous decision. Maybe,' Scott gave a dismissive shrug, 'he just wanted to make sure that he finished the job.'

'On a piece of waste ground, in the middle of the night?' Mulligan's brows beetled forward. 'Forget about the "how" for a minute, and think about the motive. Why does a man take his own life?'

'Because the balance of his mind is disturbed?' Scott took a moment to consider alternative possibilities. 'To avoid being found out? To avoid shame?'

'Shame of what?'

'I asked Verity Pearson about the meeting that her husband didn't want to attend. It was with his business manager from the bank. She said that the account manager was creating some difficulties for them, and Leo was running out of patience with him. I didn't push her for more detail, because she was upset. But maybe he owed the bank money, and was under pressure to pay it back?'

Mulligan grunted, and turned away to look out of the window across the Kirkby skyline. Then he nodded to himself, and turned back to his desk to pull a piece of blank paper from an in-tray. 'Let's find out who they bank with, and who this account manager is.' He slid a hand into a drawer and pulled out a ballpoint pen. 'I suppose if they had financial problems Leo Pearson might have taken his own life as a way out.' He scribbled the word "suicide" on the blank page in front of him, tapped on the paper absently with the pen, and then added a question mark beside it. 'What about the poker game she mentioned? Do you believe that story? I've always heard that bookies don't gamble, that they're too busy taking money from other suckers to risk their own. But what if this one did? That might have made his financial situation worse.'

Scott dismissed the idea with a shake of the head. 'I don't think that poker school exists, George. I think that "playing poker" was a euphemism for a very different sort of game. Verity hinted that her husband had a habit of playing away, so she didn't ask too many questions.'

'Does that mean we need to look around for another woman?' Mulligan added the suggestion to his fledgling list. 'I suppose that could be one of the staff, although I can't see Leo Pearson preferring any of those mousy girls in the shop to an attractive piece like his wife.' He put the pen up to his mouth and chewed thoughtfully on the end, and then discarded the idea with a low chuckle. 'Does Verity Pearson really strike you as the type to put up with that sort of behaviour?'

'Funnily enough, yes, she does. She has a nice home, a fancy car, she doesn't need to work … maybe she put up with it for the money. She was obviously lonely, so I'd argue she hasn't stayed with Leo Pearson because she loves him. She's stayed for the lifestyle.'

'But what if you're right, and that lifestyle was at risk? When you take her to Cayton Bay this afternoon, have a word about their financial situation. Find out why they were selling the business. They might not have been planning to retire at all. Maybe they needed the money. She didn't let on to either of us yesterday that the business was about to change hands. There must have been a reason she was keeping that quiet. And ask her what she's planning to do now. She's going to be a beneficiary of the death, so presumably she will inherit the business, and benefit from the sale.'

'Do you want me to call in at the business premises this morning?'

'No, you can leave that to me. I want to have another word with the manageress. I want to know more about Leo Pearson's movements yesterday. But you could take a look at this.' Mulligan dropped his pen onto the desk and reached to the left for another page of scribbled notes. 'It landed on my desk this morning.'

DS Scott took the paper from him and ran his eyes quickly down the page. 'A missing person?'

'His name is Neil Redfern. They only passed it my way because he was a regular in Leo Pearson's shop.' Mulligan swivelled gently to and fro in his seat as Scott took in the details. 'The call came in last night from his sister. He's not a high-risk case, but it might be worth having a word with her. See if you can find out how well he knew Leo Pearson. You never know, if we can track him down there might be a connection.'

'I have to admit, Rose, that this case has given me a sleepless night.' Clive Barden sounded tired, his voice low and enervated at the end of the phone line. 'I am definitely sensing something far beyond irresponsible lending. I think it may be fraud of some persuasion, but I cannot tell you why.'

Rose let out a sigh, and glanced down at the terrier tucked underneath her right arm. Mac returned her gaze with a look of resignation as she placed him gently back into his basket and stroked the top of his head. 'Clive, could this wait? I'm still at home. I was literally just on my way out of the door when you called. I thought we were scheduled to speak at ten o'clock?' She turned away from the dog and lowered herself onto a chair at the kitchen table, the mobile phone still pressed to her ear.

He gave an impatient click of the teeth. 'I would appreciate an update now. Have you been through all of the documents relating to the Pearson accounts?'

'Yes, I've been through the documents. And Toby was right to be worried. At the current price set, the sale of Pearson the Bookmaker won't realise enough to settle all the business debts outstanding to the ENB. As he suspected, there will be a shortfall of around forty thousand pounds. On top of that, it would appear that the Pearsons are overstretched financially on a personal level. They own a house in Kirkby Park which has an approximate value of five hundred and twenty thousand pounds, with an outstanding mortgage of around four hundred thousand. The mortgage repayments are around two and a half thousand pounds a month. Leo Pearson has also been covering monthly repayments for car finance on two premium vehicles, and for three credit cards, two in his own name, and one in his wife's. And that's all before we look at their day to day living expenses.'

'Have you found any further evidence of financial malpractice? Any evidence that he used the business account to cover these personal liabilities?'

'Not directly. But he appears to have been drawing a far higher salary from the business than his turnover would support. And he's made a significant number of cash withdrawals over several months, sometimes as many as four or five in a week, and always for the sum of five hundred pounds. I suppose he could have been paying that towards other debts, or into a personal account held with another bank.'

For a few moments Clive didn't respond, and then he said 'Leo Pearson must have been under a significant amount of financial pressure. How on earth do people get themselves into such situations, Rose? Borrowing far more money than they can afford?'

'How?' Rose smiled to herself, an incredulous curve of the lips. 'Well, I hate to be the one to point it out, but in Leo Pearson's case all roads seem to lead back to that disagreeable phrase "irresponsible lending". If appropriate affordability checks had been made by all the parties responsible for his debts, then I very much doubt that the situation would have arisen.'

If the admonition had been aimed at Clive, then it fell

far wide of the mark. 'So we have no evidence that he was using the cash drawn from the business to pay his bills. Perhaps we should content ourselves with closing down the company's accounts, recovering our outstanding liabilities, and simply getting this mess off our books.' He sounded unusually deflated.

Rose hesitated, and then said 'there is no easy way to tell you this, Clive, but I don't think you're going to find it that easy to shake this thing off.' She didn't have to see him to know that at the other end of the line his jaw was beginning to stiffen, and his broad brow furrow forward with concern. 'I uncovered something else yesterday evening, and I think you need to be prepared for a curved ball.'

'I'm not going to like this, am I?'

'No, not much. Leo Pearson took out a keyman insurance policy with the ENB just over four years ago. In the event of his death, and under the terms of the policy, the ENB is liable to pay out the sum of two hundred thousand pounds to the business known as L&V Pearson Ltd to enable them to continue trading as Pearson the Bookmaker.'

At the other end of the line Clive's voice crackled with displeasure. 'A keyman insurance policy is designed to cover any losses for the business which result from the death of a key individual.'

'You don't need to explain it to me, Clive. I know what it is.' Rose smiled to herself. 'Leo Pearson was a turf accountant. He managed the business, set its strategy, created its business model, was responsible for its debts … to all intents and purposes he *was* Pearson the Bookmaker. And in order to survive, the business needs a new turf accountant. This insurance policy is designed to cover any costs or losses while the business finds someone to replace him.'

'But the business doesn't need a replacement. Benny Bradman is buying the business. You told me so yourself.'

'Ah yes, but Benny doesn't take over until Friday. Technically, the insurance policy will still have to pay out.'

'Pay out?' Clive hissed the words angrily through gritted teeth. 'Pay out two hundred thousand pounds of the bank's money to cover any potential costs and losses for the next three days? To a business that's already failing to break even?'

'I know it's not funny, Clive, but you must see the irony. The sale of the business won't realise enough to repay everything that Leo Pearson owed to the ENB. But when the ENB pays out under the keyman insurance policy, as the remaining director of the firm, Verity Pearson will be able to use some of the proceeds to repay the shortfall. So the ENB will get its money back after all.' Rose bit on her lip and tried to sound grave. 'At least, the ENB's commercial banking division will get its money back when its insurance division has paid out on the policy.'

Clive Barden sucked in a deep breath. 'Was this Leo Pearson's intention all along, Rose? Is this a case of suicide for financial gain?' He blew the breath out again noisily. 'And why on earth didn't Toby Dugdale mention this yesterday? He must have known about this policy?' He was breathing heavily at the end of the line now, his anger growing. 'There is something about all of this that stinks, Rose. I want a thorough – and I mean thorough – investigation before we pay out a penny of the moneys due under that insurance policy. I hope I have made myself clear.'

There was a sudden click as the call disconnected, and Rose slumped back in her seat and lifted her eyes to the ceiling. Clive had developed such an irritating habit, a propensity to just disconnect a telephone call when he didn't like what was being said, and he didn't want to hear any more. On the plus side, it meant that his anger was cut short.

On the other hand, it made it all the more difficult to

pick up the threads of the conversation later, and tell him that there was more bad news to come.

Verity Pearson slipped off her dark green woollen coat and draped it over the back of a chair, then edged herself into the seat opposite Toby Dugdale with a quizzical look. 'Why on earth did you want to meet me in this mausoleum?' She gave a shiver of disdain as she dropped her sleek leather handbag to the floor. 'It's not even clean.'

'I chose it because it's close to the office, but no one from work would be caught dead in here.' He cast a glance around the Abbey Tearooms, taking in the dark, sticky furniture and greying lace tablecloths. 'I've ordered us a pot of coffee. They can't do much damage with that. It doesn't matter if you don't want to drink it, but we can't sit in here without buying something.'

'I don't understand why you couldn't just come to the house this morning.'

'Because people are watching me at work. I shouldn't really be meeting you at all. But I need to know about Leo.' He leaned across the table towards her. 'Has there been any more news?'

She put up a hand and pinched at the bridge of her nose. 'Leo is dead, Toby. He died in the fire. The police will confirm that today.' She gave a resolute sniff. 'I wish I could say that I'm sorry. But how can I?' She pulled a crumpled cotton handkerchief from the cuff of her cashmere jumper, and used it to dab at her nose. 'He was obviously having an affair.'

'An affair?' Toby narrowed his pale blue eyes. 'Leo wouldn't do that to you. He thought the world of you.' The idea was inconceivable. 'But even if he did, why on earth would that lead to his death? That doesn't explain what happened to him.'

'Well it couldn't possibly have been an accident, could

it? Can you think of any other reason that your cousin would have been up on that cliff top in the middle of the night?' Verity pouted. 'I know you thought a lot about Leo, Toby, but you have no idea what kind of life he subjected me to. Sometimes I would have no idea where he was. He would just stay out all night.' She sniffed her condemnation into the handkerchief, and then shook it out and recrumpled it into her fist. 'I think he was up on the cliff top with a woman, and that he was found out. I think the woman had a husband or a partner, and that they were followed. I really can't think of any other explanation.'

Toby let out a sigh, a soft doubting hiss. It didn't sound like the Leo he had known all his life. 'Do you know who the woman was?'

'No, of course not.' She gave him a withering look. 'He was hardly likely to tell me.' She tucked the handkerchief back into her cuff and stretched out a manicured hand to place it gently over his wrist. 'Toby, I need your help. Now that Leo is gone, I'm responsible for the business. And as you're my business account manager …'

'Verity, I can't help you outside the remit of my role at the bank.'

'But you're the business account manager.' She pushed out a petulant lip. 'It's your job to help me. And you seem to be forgetting that I'm bereaved. You're not showing very much sympathy and consideration, considering I'm your cousin's widow.' She tightened her grasp on his wrist. 'You know that I'm not business-minded. Leo took care of everything financial. And now he's gone, there isn't anyone else to help me. Only you.' She moved her head a little closer to his. 'You know it's what Leo would have wanted. He would want you to help me, to do your best for me, to act in my best interests. That's what family is about.'

He leaned away from her. 'I'm afraid it just isn't that simple any more. The bank is beginning to investigate why I advanced so much credit to Leo for the business. That's why I've been instructed not to meet with you without another manager present.' He drew his hand from her grasp, and pushed his chair backwards. 'The ENB know that Leo was my cousin, and that I didn't declare the conflict of interest. I haven't been fired yet, but if I step out of line again, it's the end of my career.'

'It doesn't have to be. In fact, it could be in the bank's interests for you to help me. It could be the solution to everyone's problems. Look.' She reached down to the bag at her feet and pulled out a long, slim fold of documents. She opened them up onto the table and smoothed her manicured hands across the paper. 'I found these documents in Leo's desk last night. His desk at home.' She spoke quietly. 'Leo was insured, Toby. You must have known that. I need your help to put in the claims. Then I can use some of the money to pay off the shortfall on the business debt, and you won't be in trouble any more.'

Toby stiffened, and then he muttered the word under his breath. 'Insured?' He put out a hand and pulled the documents towards him. *Insurance policies?* He'd known that Leo was insured, of course. But in his shock and grief at Leo's death, claiming on an insurance policy was the last thing on his mind. He would have expected it to be the last thing on Verity's too. But he had obviously misread that one. 'I wouldn't know how to go about claiming on these. I suppose you'll have to report Leo's death to the bank. Officially, I mean. I'll speak to Rose when I get back to the office. She'll know what needs to be done.'

'Rose?'

'Rose Bennett. She's the independent consultant looking into how I handled Leo's affairs.'

Verity's eyes became suddenly wary. 'Is she going to cause problems for us, Toby?'

'No.' He gave an almost-confident shake of the head. 'No, Rose is cool. I've been honest with her, and taken the blame for the lending. I'm sure she'll help us with this, especially if it means the debt will be settled.' He lifted up the top page and peered at the print underneath. 'They're going to ask you what happened to Leo, so the sooner the police can advise you on that the better.' He turned back to look at her. 'Verity, what are you going to do now? Now that Leo is gone, I mean?'

'What am I going to do?' Her green eyes glazed as she considered the question, and then she turned to him with a soft and almost diffident smile. 'I'm going to do what Leo would want me to do. I'm going to sell the business, settle his financial affairs, and then I'm going to start a new life out in Portugal. Just as we had planned to do together.'

'I can only apologise, Mr Bradman, but Mrs Pearson isn't available.' The young woman sounded sincere in her apology as she ushered Benny into the small office at the rear of Leo Pearson's shop. 'I'm afraid she's going to be tied up for most of the day, dealing with the investigation into Mr Pearson's disappearance.' She seemed reluctant to refer to it as Mr Pearson's death.

Benny offered her a sympathetic smile. 'I'm sure it's been a very difficult time.' He cast a nonchalant glance around the office. 'How is Mrs Pearson? I was hopin' to pay my respects.'

'I'm afraid I can't really say. I only spoke to her briefly on the phone this morning.' Behind her pleasant demeanour, the girl looked harassed. 'We're doing our best to carry on, but we're used to Mr Pearson running a tight ship. I've opened up the shop as usual, but I'm normally given a float to put in the tills at the start of the day. And I don't have access to the safe.' She gave a self-deprecating laugh. 'I've had to settle for putting yesterday's takings back in the till. It's not much, but it will have to do until Mrs Pearson shows up.'

Benny lowered himself uninvited into the plush leather chair behind what he assumed was Leo Pearson's desk, and studied the girl's face as she hovered at the other side. She was a pale, ethereal creature with natural blonde hair and worried eyes, and he couldn't help wondering if the worry came from knowing more than she felt at liberty to say. He pointed to the badge pinned to the shoulder of her blue nylon blouse. 'So you're Beverley? Leo didn't introduce us, did he, the last time I came into the shop? But he's been singin' your praises to me. You've been the manager for over a year now, is that right?'

Disarmed by his attempt at a charm offensive, she visibly relaxed. 'Yes, but I've worked here for three years in total.'

'Well that sounds hopeful. I hope that's goin' to continue when I take over the shop.' He rested his forearms on the desk. 'You know, if you're worried about keepin' the ship afloat today, I'd be happy to spend an hour or two here with you this mornin'.'

Her pale face clouded over. 'Oh, I'm not sure about that, Mr Bradman. I'm not sure if Mrs Pearson would be happy with that.'

'Well we don't really want to worry her, do we? Not with everythin' else that's goin' on. As it is, you're goin' to be workin' for me in a few days anyway. I might as well try out Leo's office for myself, and give you a hand while I'm here. It'll give us a chance to get to know each other a bit better.'

'I don't know …'

He leaned forward across the desk. 'I can see why you'd feel uncomfortable not followin' instructions, Beverley. But the thing is, you're only goin' to be workin' for the Pearsons for another few days, and then … well, to be blunt about it, you're goin' to be workin' for me. Always supposin' that you're not plannin' to surprise me by handin' in your notice.' He watched as she gave a nervous shake of the head. 'Well, that's good to know. Because I can always use good people, especially the ones who are keen to get on.' He leaned back again, and flicked a finger towards the empty seat at the other side of the desk. 'I don't think, under the circumstances, that it would do any harm for you and me to have a little chat, would it? I don't want to get in the way of your workin' day, but I really would appreciate ten minutes of your time to give me a bit of information about the shop, and how you like to work. And if you can spare another five minutes to introduce me to the other girls behind the counter, then I'll just tuck myself into the office here and let you all get on with it.' He tried to sound casually cheery. 'There'll be plenty of time for longer chats after I've taken over the business, but a few minutes now wouldn't do any harm, would it? I'll square it with Mrs Pearson later, if you like. I need to give her a call anyway. And you never know, I might even pop next door to the bakery afterwards and bring you a round of pastries to cheer up the mornin' coffee break.'

For a moment it looked as though she might demur. And then hope won out, and she gave a gentle smile. 'It seems odd to think that Mr Pearson won't be in charge after the end of this week.' She sank awkwardly into the chair opposite. 'But you're quite right, it wouldn't do any harm to tell you a bit about the shop.' She blinked at him, her face open now, her expression guileless, almost child-like. 'Where would you like me to start?'

Stacy Singleton ran a long red fingernail down the front page of the document in front of her, and nodded to herself. 'I haven't witnessed many claims on a keyman insurance policy, Rose. But I have seen one or two. On the face of it, I can't see any reason why the ENB wouldn't pay out on this one.' She looked up with an impish smile. 'Clive isn't going to like it, is he?'

They were sitting at a small table in the corner of the ENB's staff canteen, the same remote and sheltered spot where Rose had met with Toby the previous afternoon. They were well away from the inquisitive ears of colleagues ordering their mid-morning coffees and freshly-baked pastries, but Rose still felt the need to lower her voice. 'He already doesn't like it. I tried to speak to him about it this morning, and he hung up on me.'

Stacy giggled. 'Then it's a good job that he has you and me to take care of it for him.'

'Indeed it is.' Rose smiled at the girl with genuine warmth. She was unexpectedly relieved to see Stacy looking so well. The long, lustrous waves of chestnut hair that Rose remembered from their last encounter were looped efficiently up into an elegant topknot at the back of Stacy's head, the impossibly long legs, so immaculately tanned in the summer, now encased in sensible thick black tights, her feet still shod in vertiginously-heeled stiletto shoes, the collar of her white uniform blouse resting crisp and pristine against her faintly-tanned neck.

It must have been the best part of four months since their paths had first crossed, when Rose had come to Kirkby to investigate the affairs of a deceased customer and Stacy, the ENB's bereavement officer, had fallen prey to the practiced and rather hollow charms of his dishonest brother. Luke Kingsley, local sporting hero turned fraudster, had been instrumental in bringing about the death of his own brother, tried to defraud his late brother's fiancée of her inheritance, and narrowly missed being wiped out by a crime boss and his tame hit man. In the process he had broken the smitten Stacy's heart without as much as a second thought. But it was good to see that she had bounced back with gusto.

'I don't want to pry, but I take it that you're well and truly over the Luke Kingsley thing now?'

Stacy's cheeks lit with a guilty blush. 'Well, Clive has forgiven me for my faux pas. I should never have passed confidential information to Luke Kingsley, however handsome he was.' It was a regrettable lapse of judgment that almost cost Stacy her job. 'Did you know that Luke got four years for his part in that gambling scam?' She gave a coltish shake of the head. 'Can you believe that after everything he did to me, he had the nerve to send me a prison visiting order?'

'Funnily enough, yes, I think I can.' Rose picked up her cappuccino and sipped on it. 'I take it that you weren't tempted?'

The girl's blush deepened, and her voice hushed to a whisper. 'Between you and me, Rose, I'm afraid I was. It's hard not to feel sorry for him, when he has so few people in his life to care about him. But I know that Clive would never forgive me if I disgraced myself again, and my job is too important to me.' She fell silent, lost in a private thought. And then she lifted her head with a valiant smile. 'Anyway, I wouldn't want to miss all the fun of this Pearson case.'

'I get the picture.' Rose sipped again on her coffee, and then asked 'how much has Clive told you about the Pearsons?'

'Not much. They run a bookmaker's shop in Scarborough and they hold their business accounts with the ENB. There is some complication around the settling of a business debt.' Stacy frowned. 'And we've had a report that Leo Pearson may be deceased.' The frown deepened. 'When I spoke with Clive earlier he mentioned something about Toby Dugdale, and a possible disciplinary procedure, and the need for complete discretion.' Her face brightened. 'And then he said that you were investigating the case for him, and that you would give me all the details and let me know what I can do to help.'

'Well, I guess that almost sums it up. Leo and Verity Pearson are joint directors of a business called L&V Pearson Ltd, which trades as Pearson the Bookmaker. The trading style of the business has been sold to a third party, along with the business premises and goodwill, and contracts will be signed on Friday. But the sale won't realise enough capital to repay what is owed to the ENB. According to Toby, Leo Pearson had a solution for meeting the shortfall, but yesterday afternoon we had a report that Leo Pearson was missing, presumed dead. We'll have to meet with his widow, to discuss her proposals for winding up his business affairs and settling the debt. But there are a number of added complications. Firstly, we've discovered that Leo Pearson was Toby Dugdale's cousin, and the relationship wasn't disclosed. Then when I reviewed the Pearson's accounts, I discovered that they also hold a good deal of their personal business with the bank. And just to add the icing on the cake, I've turned up three insurance policies with the ENB. One guarantees the repayment of their mortgage should either of them die. The second is a simple life policy on Leo Pearson's life, with Verity Pearson as the beneficiary. That stands to pay out three hundred thousand pounds.'

'And the other is this keyman insurance policy?' Stacy tapped a finger on the document in front of her.

'Yes. It's not unreasonable for there to be a keyman insurance policy on Leo's Pearson's life, because he was wholly responsible for the success of the business. Without Leo, the business will suffer, and the policy should cover the cost of finding a replacement for him, and cover any operating costs and losses until that replacement is found.'

'But the business is due to change hands on Friday.'

'And that's just what Clive said when I told him about it. Which rather makes the timing of Leo Pearson's supposed death look … well, I hesitate to say it, Stacy, but don't you think it all looks rather convenient?'

8

Evie Green wrapped her arms around her slender body and swayed slightly in her chair. 'I've already given as much detail as I can to the officer who called round last night.' The presence of a detective sergeant in her living room, even one as personable and reassuring as DS Ian Scott, appeared to be making her uncomfortable. 'I haven't heard anything from Neil since then. I've continued to call his mobile, and the landline in his flat. He isn't picking up on either of the numbers.' She let out a sigh. 'My son, Liam, is on holiday from school. It's half term. And I don't want him worried by this, so I arranged for him to spend the day with a school friend's family. After they picked him up this morning, I went round to Neil's flat again to take a look. I knocked on the door as loud as I could, but there was no answer. The curtains were all drawn, but I couldn't hear anything inside, no radio, or the sound of anyone moving about.'

'How old is Liam?' There was an array of framed photographs on the mantelpiece, and Scott pushed himself up from the sofa to cross the room and look at them. Most of them were of a soccer-mad youngster in a red and white kit.

'He's seven. Football mad, of course.' She gave a sniff. 'A Kirkby FC fan, like his Uncle Neil.'

He picked up a large framed photograph that showed the boy standing next to a dark-haired man, both of them smiling broadly, red and white scarves raised above their heads. 'Like father, like son, eh?'

A flush of colour seeped into Evie's alabaster cheeks. 'That's his Uncle Neil in the picture. They're very much alike.'

'Ah.' Scott placed the frame gently back on the mantelpiece. 'Are they close, as well as alike?'

'Neil is Liam's godfather. They've always been close. And he's the nearest thing Liam has to a father-figure. Neil wouldn't just walk away from him.'

The policeman picked up another picture and examined it. 'But you have no idea what might have happened to him?'

'I think it might be a cry for help. But I don't know where to find him.' Her eyes were beginning to fill with tears, and she blinked to push them away. 'Neil hasn't had a very good time over the last few years. His wife left him. She had an affair with one of their neighbours, and the two of them moved away to Scotland. They took Neil's kids with them.' She swallowed hard. 'It was awful for him. The stress really got to him, and he started to make mistakes at work.'

'And where was that?'

'At Colliers, the fish processing plant. He worked as an accountant in the finance department. They were very understanding to begin with, but … well, he made quite a serious mistake and it cost them a lot of money. We were worried for a while that they might hold him responsible for the losses. But they didn't. Except,' she shook her head, 'they did force him into redundancy. They gave him a choice – go quietly, or face disciplinary action.'

'Could they do that? If he was suffering from depression, surely there were medical grounds to be considered?'

'He could have fought it. But he didn't have much fight left in him by then. They gave him a small redundancy payment, but it didn't last long, and he didn't seem to have any inclination to find another job. When Diane finally asked him for a divorce, he had to sell the house to cover the legal fees, and then what was left went to her for the divorce settlement.'

'And now?'

Evie gave a shrug. 'A shabby first-floor flat on the Barnfield estate. Life on benefits. And most of that goes on the horses.'

DS Scott bowed his head in understanding. 'When you reported him missing, you told my colleague that Neil spent a lot of time at Pearson's.'

'It's virtually his second home. That's when I got really worried, when they told me that he hadn't been in yesterday to place a bet.'

'Was he a lucky gambler?'

'Is there such a thing?' Evie considered the possibility. 'No, I don't suppose he was. I never heard him talk about being on a winning streak, or anything like that.'

'So how could he afford to gamble, if he was living on benefits?'

She opened her mouth to speak, and then closed it again. The question seemed to pose her a problem. Eventually she said 'I don't know. I never really thought about it. I know that he did some odd jobs for Leo Pearson now and again. I think Mr Pearson just paid him in cash for what he did. He probably just ploughed it all back into the tills at the betting shop.' She let out a self-conscious laugh. 'I shouldn't have said that to a policeman, should I?'

DS Scott gave her the warmest smile he could muster. 'Don't worry about it, Evie. I'm not here on behalf of the tax man. I'm just here to help you find your brother.' He jerked his head towards the photographs on the mantelpiece. 'Could I take one of these with me? I'll bring it back for you later. It will help with the investigation.'

'Of course.' She watched as he examined each picture in turn, and finally settled on the one that had first caught his eye, the large framed print of Neil and Liam standing outside the gate of Kirkby FC's football ground. 'That's Liam's favourite picture.'

'Then I promise I'll bring it back later today.' He tucked the frame under his arm. 'Just one other thing. You don't have a key for Neil's flat?'

'He wouldn't give me one. He's always been private like that.' The thought seemed to make her uncomfortable. 'There's nothing suspicious in his flat, if that's what you're worried about. I do go there regularly. I just don't have my own key.'

'And you're absolutely certain that he wasn't in the flat when you called round this morning?'

'Yes.' She paused, and then a fleeting realisation crossed her face. 'You don't think he was in there, and couldn't speak to me? You don't think that he was ill, or … or … something even worse?'

George Mulligan lowered his bulk onto the hard, wooden visitor's chair in Leo Pearson's office. 'Well I have to say that you were the last person I expected to find here.' He grinned across the desk at an acquaintance who was in danger of becoming a friend. 'What's all this Pearson business got to do with you?'

Benny Bradman folded his arms and leaned back in the plush leather seat that was fast becoming his own. 'Come this Friday it won't be Pearson the Bookmaker, George. It'll be Bradman the Bookmaker. At least it will be if the sale goes through.' Benny grumbled under his breath, but the ire was directed at himself, and not at the policeman. 'Since our paths usually only cross when there's trouble afoot, I'm guessin' that the rumours I've heard about Leo Pearson are true. Is he dead?'

'It's beginning to look that way. We've got a burnt-out car, and a body, and a tentative ID from his wife. She hasn't spoken to him since yesterday afternoon, and so far we haven't turned up anyone else who has seen him or heard from him. I called in here yesterday and spoke to Beverley, but she wasn't that forthcoming. I thought she might have warmed up overnight, and remembered something that might point us in the right direction'. The policeman smiled, a gentle creasing of shrewd eyes. 'But since you and I have got to know each other so well over the last couple of years, you'll do nicely instead. How well did you know Leo Pearson?'

'Apparently not as well as I thought I did. I've played golf with him more than a few times. He told me in the summer that he was plannin' to sell up, and I thought it might be an opportunity for me to expand the business.'

'Did you like him?'

'Not much. Between you and me, George, I found him hard work. Bombastic. A bit too full of himself. But I didn't need to like him to buy his business.'

'Is it true that he was selling up so that he could retire to Portugal?'

'That's what he told me. And I didn't see any reason to disbelieve him, at least not at the time. To be honest, George, I put in an offer for the place because I thought it had potential. I thought it was going to seed because he'd lost interest and wanted to move abroad. The books suggested they weren't makin' big money, but the shop was turnin' over. I thought there was scope to grow the business with a bit of investment.'

'But?'

'I don't think it's as profitable as Leo led me to believe. I've only been here twice before. The first time I was invited, and the second time I just turned up on spec. Leo was here to greet me both times, and he seemed happy enough to show me around. I can't say the place was buzzin', but there were enough customers to make it look viable. But now it feels different. Too quiet to be turnin' the sort of numbers that are shown in the accounts.' There was a page of scribbled notes and numbers on the desk, and Benny tapped a finger on it. 'On top of that, I think I've found a discrepancy in the books.'

'Evidence of false accounting?'

'Is that a fancy name for bein' on the fiddle?' Benny grinned. 'Now I look at it again, there are a few entries in the books that don't look right, but I was plannin' to talk to Beverley about it this afternoon, to see if she could shed any light.' Benny pondered the suggestion, then he said 'I'll be happy to let you know if there's anythin' relevant.' He chuckled under his breath. 'I'm already doin' undercover work for the ENB, I might as well add you to the list.'

'The East and Northern Bank? What's it got to do with them?'

'Leo Pearson owed them money, and they're keen to have it back.'

'And you've been asked to help them recover it?'

'Rose Bennett has been asked to help them recover it. I'm just doin' a bit of the diggin' for her.' Benny paused to let George Mulligan absorb the news, and then nodded his head. 'I thought that might bring a smile to your face.'

'I didn't know Rose was back in Market Melbourne. When did that happen?'

'She moved into Lu Aylesbury's cottage three weeks ago. But it's not as straightforward as it sounds. She's had to move out of her own place for a while.' Benny hesitated, reluctant to betray a confidence. 'She's had a bit of trouble with the ex-boyfriend. He took exception to findin' himself in the past tense, and decided to make things a bit heavy for her.' He narrowed his eyes. 'I hope you'll keep that bit to yourself, George. I just wanted to put you in the picture.' He brightened. 'Still, she seems to be on the mend, and Hertfordshire's loss is our gain, eh?' He sounded pleased. 'You might want to have a word with her about this Leo Pearson business. She's at the Kirkby office today, but don't let on that I told you so, or I'll never hear the end of it.'

'So how come you're helping her with the investigation? What's in it for you?'

'She heard I was buyin' the business from Leo Pearson, and asked if I would mind checkin' a few things out for her. And in return, she's tippin' me the wink on the real value of this place, so that I can work out whether the price I'm payin' is a fair one. But the main benefit is personal, of course. It means I get to spend a lot of time with someone warm and cuddly.' Benny winked as first surprise, and then incredulity, registered on the policeman's face. And then he pointed under the desk. 'You didn't see Mac dozin' in his basket under there, then, George? Surely when I said "someone warm and cuddly" you didn't think for one minute that I was talkin' about Rose?'

'I'm sorry to take up your lunch break. But I've uncovered something about Leo Pearson's business that I really need to discuss with you.' Rose rested her elbows on the table and fixed Toby Dugdale with firm but friendly eyes. 'What do you know about his insurance policies?'

They were in a small, windowless meeting room on the top floor of the ENB's Kirkby office, a hidden space so cramped it would have made a broom cupboard look capacious by comparison. The room was airless, and although they had occupied it for little more than a few minutes, Toby was already beginning to perspire. He flinched at the question posed, and ran a finger nervously around the damp inner edge of his collar. 'I believe Leo held a keyman insurance policy to protect the business.'

'And the mortgage and personal policies that he held with the ENB?'

'I didn't know about those until this morning. I only have sight of his business accounts.'

'So how did you find out about them?'

A flush of guilty colour seeped into Toby's handsome face. 'Verity mentioned them to me.' The colour deepened. 'I know you asked me not to speak to her yet, but I met her for coffee. I wanted to know if there had been any more news about Leo.'

'And has there?' If Rose was annoyed by his disloyalty, she didn't let it show. 'Do we know yet what happened to him?'

'No, not yet. I suppose it's too soon.' He looked a little sheepish. 'Verity has asked if I will help her to sort out Leo's financial affairs.'

Rose inclined her head as if considering the possibility. 'I'm not sure that that would be appropriate, Toby. You know that the bank doesn't like personal relationships mixing with business.' It was the mildest of reprimands. 'But we do have to speak to her about the sale of the business, and I don't mind helping her on your behalf. Would you be happy to invite her to come into the bank this afternoon?' The suggestion hung in the air between them, and before he could answer Rose asked 'are you close to her, Toby? I know she's your cousin's widow, and you feel you ought to help her, but do you really know her that well?'

'I thought I did. But now I'm beginning to wonder. I met her occasionally at family get-togethers. And I saw her at the house when I went over to visit Leo. But when it came to the business, she didn't really have anything to do with it. She left everything to him.'

'I see.' Rose looked down at her notebook, open on the table in front of her, and tapped her fingers thoughtfully on the page of scribbled notes. 'Do you know what she plans to do now?'

'She told me this morning that she's still planning to sell up and move to Portugal. It was what she and Leo had intended all along, to sell up the business and retire abroad.'

'Even though she's just been bereaved? And in such

distressing circumstances?'

'She doesn't seem distressed. If anything, she seems angry. She thinks that Leo was having an affair. That he may have been murdered because of it. I just can't take it seriously.' There was a sour note in his voice. 'She's trying to make out that Leo's had affairs before. That it's one of the reasons they were moving abroad. She wanted to make a fresh start.' His blue eyes clouded. 'I find that hard to believe. I know that Leo adored her. I think he would have done anything to please her.'

Rose leaned forward in her seat. 'I don't suppose there is any possibility that the body in the car wasn't that of her husband?' She tried to make the question sound casual.

'I can't really see how it could be anyone else. They found some of Leo's jewellery in the wreckage of the car, his gold neck chain and his wedding ring. Verity has confirmed they were Leo's, and she says the police are happy to take that as identification.'

'Are they?' Rose bit back an unbidden smile. 'The police might be happy with that, Toby. It could save them the cost of an expensive investigation. But when it comes to the insurance claims, I think it might take more than Verity Pearson's opinion on a few pieces of jewellery to persuade the ENB to hand over the best part of a million pounds.'

9

It was bleak on the cliff top at Cayton Bay, but at least it wasn't raining.

DS Scott drove the Audi cautiously across the scrubland, his attention focused on the plain white tent that still protected what was left of the crime scene. He brought the car to a halt with about ten metres to spare, and pulled on the handbrake without turning to look at the woman in the passenger seat.

Verity Pearson had fallen silent as they turned off the main road, and he could see out of the corner of his eye that her face had taken on a sober expression. He waited until she had taken off her seatbelt, and then said 'take your time, Verity. It's a lot to take in.'

She nodded without speaking, and then opened the door and got out. He kept his eyes on the tent as she opened the car's rear door to reach in and pull out a large bouquet of white lilies, and then watched as she picked her way carefully across the uneven ground towards a line of fluttering blue and white police tape that surrounded the tent. She was dressed in a dark green woollen coat, a soft blue shawl draped elegantly around her shoulders, and he had a sudden sense that she was playing a part, and playing it well.

She paused beside the tape, and then glanced

questioningly back over her shoulder at him. He nodded, and she turned away and gently placed the flowers down on the ground, as close to the tent as the tape would permit. But she didn't linger. The flowers placed, she turned on her heel and strode back to the car, shivering as she opened the door. She sank down in the passenger seat without looking at him.

'What on earth was he doing up here?'

DS Scott shrugged. 'We were rather hoping that you might be able to shed some light on that. There's nothing here that jogs your memory?'

'No.' She shook the burgundy curls.

'Is it possible he could have come here to meet someone?'

She gave a scornful laugh. 'A bit of slap and tickle in the back of the Jaguar?' She closed her eyes and gave the curls another shake. 'It wouldn't surprise me. Leo wasn't the most romantic of men.'

'I wasn't thinking of a woman.' DS Scott shifted awkwardly in his seat. 'When we spoke yesterday, you didn't mention to us that Leo was in the process of selling his business.'

'I didn't think it was relevant.' She pursed glossed lips into a pout. 'Leo's death can't be anything to do with that. There's nothing contentious about the sale. It's a straightforward business deal.'

'And will the sale still go ahead now?'

'Of course it will. Life must go on, Sergeant Scott. Anyway, I don't want to let the buyer down. And what would I do with the business? I know nothing about gambling or sport. I'm a director of Pearson the Bookmaker in name only. No,' she let out a sigh, 'once the sale has gone through I will be packing my bags and heading for Portugal. It will be tough, starting again out there on my own. But it's what Leo would have wanted me to do.'

'And will you manage financially?'

The directness of DS Scott's question brought a flush of colour to her cheeks. 'Is that relevant to your investigation, Sergeant Scott?'

'I'm afraid everything is relevant until we know how and why your husband died, Verity.'

'He died in a fire.'

'His car was destroyed by a fire, and a body was found in the car. We're assuming that the body was that of your husband, and you've confirmed that jewellery found with the body belonged to him.' He glanced away through the car's windscreen in the direction of the tent. 'But we're still waiting to hear whether the fire was set deliberately.'

'Deliberately?'

'Yes.' DS Scott shifted in his seat and turned to look at her. 'Don't you want to know why he died, Verity?' He studied her face. 'I know that your marriage to Leo wasn't perfect. And I know that you had your suspicions. You thought he was being unfaithful to you. And I know what that feels like.' He sucked in a breath. 'My marriage wasn't perfect, and my ex-wife was unfaithful to me. But I still care about her. And if I thought that she'd died a horrendous death, that she'd lost her life in the way we think your husband died, I'd want to know why.' He leaned a little closer to her. 'I'd want justice for her.'

Verity held her silence, and then her face crumpled. 'Of course I want justice for Leo. But I've already told you, I don't know who he was seeing. And even if I'd asked him, he probably wouldn't have told me.'

'You still think this is something to do with him having an affair?'

'What other solution is there?'

'He didn't have any enemies, anyone with a grudge against him?'

'I can't say that he didn't. I can only tell you that if he did, I didn't know about it.'

'And you can't think of anyone who would benefit from his death?'

'Of course not.' She pulled a small lace-edged handkerchief from the pocket of her coat and dabbed with it at her eyes. 'Sergeant Scott, would you mind driving me back to Kirkby now? Just before you picked me up, I had a call inviting me to the East and Northern Bank for a meeting. They're expecting me at four o'clock.' She forced a smile, and pushed the handkerchief back into her pocket. 'I'm very grateful to you for bringing me to the spot where Leo died. But I'm beginning to find it upsetting now. And I need to stay strong to put Leo's affairs in order. I still have a business to sell, and a funeral to arrange.'

Scott considered for a moment, and then he stretched out a hand and placed it on her arm. 'Of course.' He'd pushed her too far. And too soon.

He started the car's engine, and turned the wheel hard to point back in the direction of the main road. As the Audi began to trundle slowly back across the scrubland, gently navigating its way between gorse bushes and scattered lumps of rock, he risked a glance at Verity Pearson. Her face was a mask now, indecipherable. He grunted under his breath. There was a question that remained unanswered, a question she had swerved with considerable skill.

But DS Scott wasn't inclined to be misdirected, and the journey back to Kirkby would give him twenty-five miles of cross-country driving in which to ask her that question again.

Benny Bradman reversed his sleek, black Mercedes into the parking space and turned off the engine. The view through the windscreen was a dismal one, a grey and misty vista across Scarborough's North Bay. A relentless north-easterly wind had begun to throw drifts of insidious, bone-freezing drizzle across the windows of his car. And still there were hardier souls than himself braving the cold wet sands, walking dogs, wheeling pushchairs, brazenly striding out against the elements.

He released the clasp on his seatbelt, and then cast a glance over his shoulder to the back seat, where Mac was curled up on a blanket and quietly snoozing. 'You stay asleep as long as you like, pal, we ain't walkin' out in this.' Benny didn't like the cold, or the damp, any more than he liked the uncomfortable knot of tension that was beginning to form in the pit of his stomach. He still wasn't sure just what twist of fate had led him to road test Leo Pearson's business for himself that morning, but he couldn't deny that the experience had left him feeling distinctly ill at ease.

It wasn't as if there was anything wrong with the business itself. The premises were shabby, but they were tidy and clean. The tills and terminals were serviceable, and the girls behind the counter were as keen and cheerful with the punters as any prospective new owner could hope for. And it hadn't taken much effort to persuade Beverley to let him camp out in the shop for the best part of the morning so that he could get the feel of the place for himself.

He'd found the place to be friendly. There was a homely atmosphere that would make any regular punter want to sink into one of the soft leather sofas, kick off his shoes, and spend the afternoon watching the racing on the state-of-the-art home-cinema-sized TV screen that graced the rear end of the shop. Beverley had even convinced him that there was a small hard-core of happy regulars who didn't seem to care about the coming change of ownership just as long as Benny could assure them that the opening hours wouldn't change and the complimentary tea and coffee would keep on flowing.

So why did he feel so strongly that there was something about this business that he was missing?

He slipped his hand into the inside pocket of his jacket

and pulled out his mobile phone. There were no missed calls. He had left four voicemail messages now for Verity Pearson, and she had made no attempt at all to call him back.

He swiped at the phone's keypad, and then jabbed at it with his thumb to bring up Rose Bennett's number. The call went straight to voicemail. 'Rose, it's me. Can you give me a bell when you get this message? I'm in Scarborough.' He paused, and then added 'you were right about Leo Pearson's accounts. There's somethin' in there that stinks. I could do with some advice.'

He ended the call and dropped the phone onto the passenger seat. Rose was good at advice. If it hadn't been for Rose, he might never have made the move to buy this shop in the first place. He might have gone on living in the shadows, looking over his shoulder. He'd been carefully planning this for weeks now, keeping it quiet not just from Michael, but from Rose. He'd admitted to her that he'd been planning to surprise Michael with the acquisition, but he'd stopped short of confessing that he wanted to surprise her too. To show that he'd listened to her advice. How could he admit that he'd hoped to surprise her, pulling the new shop out of the bag like a rabbit out a hat, when it looked like the whole performance was going to collapse without mercy around his ears? It was a prospect that didn't bear thinking about.

He heaved out a sigh. He'd known all along what he'd been looking for - a tidy little business with a decent set of books and a lot of potential. And everything he'd seen so far had led him to believe that Leo Pearson's business was the one. But there was one thing he hadn't been prepared for.

That someone had been taking him for a mug.

He bent forward and wrapped his arms around the rim of the Mercedes' steering wheel, and stared out into the distance through the misted glass of the windscreen, pushing his gaze out across the sands and beyond, into the choppy waters of the merciless North Sea. More than once he had seen something as he combed through the sets of accounts that Leo Pearson had sent to him, and more than once he had brushed away a niggle that had plagued him every time he picked up those accounts and looked at them.

Over a period of four months, Leo Pearson had banked a number of large and regular deposits that he had recorded as simple cash receipts. Cash receipts in his trade were nothing new, even in these days of rampant online gambling. But there was something about these particular receipts that hadn't quite smelled right, something that had looked unusual to Benny's practiced eye. He had seen them, and he had smelled them, and he had been stupid enough to ignore them. Hell, he'd even deluded himself so successfully that he'd declared to Rose Bennett that there was nothing wrong with the accounts.

He bent his head forward and banged it gently off the steering wheel, and muttered under his breath.

Bradman, you're a muppet.

In his desire for this business to be the one, because in every other way it was perfect for his needs, he'd broken his own golden rule, and ignored his gut. And as if it wasn't enough that Leo Pearson had done a disappearing act, his calls to Verity Pearson were going unanswered, and Rose was ringing alarm bells that there was something rotten hidden among the trail of Pearson's financial affairs, now that shrewd and sardonic herald of doom George Mulligan was casting the spectre of a police investigation across the threshold of the shop.

There was only one thing to be done. He lifted his head from the steering wheel and stretched a hand behind his head to pull on the seatbelt, clicking it quietly into place before starting the car's ignition. It would only take him ten minutes to make his way back to the shop. And this time he was going to ask the questions that he should have asked this morning.

And he wasn't going to leave without the answers.

Verity Pearson followed Rose into a softly-lit, comfortable office. 'I thought Toby would be here.' She slipped off her dark green woollen coat and glanced around the room for somewhere to put it. 'I suppose this will just have to drape somewhere.' She selected a chair at the table and arranged the coat carefully over the back of it, and then lowered herself into the seat opposite Rose.

Rose waited until she was settled, and then offered her a friendly smile. 'Toby will still be assisting us in taking care of your business accounts, but I'm afraid he's currently engaged with another client. In any case, this meeting is really just an opportunity for you to meet with myself and Stacy. Toby has advised us that you would appreciate some help in settling your husband's business affairs.'

'My *late* husband's affairs.'

'Forgive me. Your *late* husband's affairs.' Rose gestured towards the colleague seated beside her. 'As I mentioned when we spoke earlier on the telephone, Stacy is the ENB's bereavement officer. Under normal circumstances, she would only be involved when we've been formally notified of a death. But given the context of Mr Pearson's disappearance, and the significant amount of business that you have with the ENB, I thought it would be helpful for her to join us for this meeting. Stacy will be able to advise you on putting in a claim under any insurance policies, and give any other assistance that might be helpful.'

Verity turned towards the girl sitting next to Rose. 'I wouldn't expect there to be any difficulties. Leo's business will transfer to a new owner by Friday, and then the business accounts can be closed. The proceeds of the insurance policies will be payable to myself, and I will settle any outstanding liabilities from the proceeds.'

'Perhaps if I might take a step back?' Stacy shot an anxious glance at Rose, and then turned back to Verity. 'Can I ask if your accountant and solicitor have been advised of your husband's disappearance?'

'You mean my husband's death?'

Stacy looked uncertain. Then she said 'if we could just put the matter of his death to one side for a moment …'

'Put his death to one side?' Verity hissed out the words. 'My husband is *dead* Miss Singleton. I have no intention of putting his death to one side.' A flash of anger lit up the green eyes, and she turned their full force towards Rose. 'I came here this afternoon on the understanding that you were going to assist me to put Leo's affairs in order.'

Rose raised a hand to placate her. 'With respect, Mrs Pearson, that is what we're trying to do. Your husband's financial affairs involve more than the business accounts and insurance policies that you've mentioned, and if we are to give you appropriate advice, we have to understand the picture of his financial affairs as a whole.' She turned to her colleague with an encouraging smile. 'Go ahead, Stacy.'

Stacy blinked, still unsure, and then reached into a slim document folder on the table to pull out a thin sheaf of papers. She slid the top page across the table towards Verity Pearson. 'I've listed out for you the various steps that the bank will take in settling your husband's business accounts, and also the various pieces of documentation that we will need from you in order to proceed.' She waited while Verity scanned her eyes over the list. 'We understand that we have to deal immediately with the business accounts, because it's in everyone's interests for the sale to complete on Friday. But that part of the process is relatively straightforward, and we expect most of the information to come from your solicitor and accountant.'

Verity sucked in her cheeks. 'It says here that I have to notify the ENB when the sale of the business is finally complete, and ensure that all outstanding liabilities to the bank are settled in full.'

'You are the sole surviving business partner, Mrs Pearson, and our paperwork shows that you signed a personal guarantee in respect of the commercial mortgages taken out with the bank. That makes you responsible for the business, and for the repayment of the mortgages.'

'But I've already explained that the business will no longer be my responsibility after Friday.'

Stacy drew in a steadying breath. 'As things stand, the business holds two commercial mortgages and a very significant overdraft with the ENB. In the light of your husband's disappearance …'

'You mean my husband's *death*.'

Stacy cast an imploring glance at Rose, and in reply Rose rested her arms on the table and mustered her most disarming smile for Verity Pearson's benefit. 'We plan to do everything we can to help you, Mrs Pearson. The terms and conditions of your commercial accounts with the bank are legally binding, and they will remain so until any outstanding borrowing has been repaid, even after the business has been sold and changed hands. They require certain steps to be taken in order for us to reach the end result. I'm afraid it's a bit like a game of financial snakes and ladders – we may have to slide down a couple of snakes before we can climb up the ladder to a satisfactory conclusion. Your husband died owing a substantial amount of money to the bank. We understand from Toby that he planned to sell the business and use the proceeds from the sale to settle his outstanding business debts, so we don't expect that to be an issue providing the sale goes through and the price realised is enough to cover the outstanding debt. In the short term, as the surviving director of the business, it will become your responsibility to ensure that all outstanding liabilities to the bank are settled in full.' Rose hoped she sounded convincing. 'It's just a matter of process. In a couple of days the business will change hands, the sale proceeds will come in, and the debts will be settled. After that, and assuming that the debts have been fully settled, the ENB will be happy to leave the business bank account open until either you or your accountant confirms that all other liabilities have been met and the account is no longer needed.'

'Other liabilities?'

'Yes. I'm assuming that there will be staff wages to settle before their employment transfers to the new owner, final tax bills to pay, and final utility bills for the trading premises.' Rose watched Verity Pearson's face, and noted a transient flash of bewilderment. 'I'm sorry, I'm sure this all sounds very confusing. Toby tells me that you haven't had a great deal of involvement with the running of the business. But I'm sure that your accountant will have everything in hand.' Her voice softened. 'You have spoken to your accountant, Mrs Pearson? And your solicitor?'

'Not yet. It's all been rather sudden.' Verity's voice had become small and flat, her anger momentarily subdued.

'Then I strongly recommend that you do so, and as soon as possible.'

There was a protracted silence as Verity appeared to consider the suggestion. And then she sucked in her cheeks again and narrowed the green eyes, and turned her attention back to Stacy. 'How long will it take you to process the insurance claims?'

Stacy started, and turned to glance again at Rose. Rose, sensing her discomfort, graciously accepted the baton's return. 'If I understand correctly, there are three individual policies in place on your husband's life - one as an indemnity for the mortgage on your property in Kirkby Park, a simple life policy, and a keyman insurance policy to protect the business. Before any claim against those policies can be considered, the bank will require a copy of your husband's death certificate.' She kept her voice low and calm. 'Once we have that, then work will begin on assessing the claims.'

'Assessing the claims? How long is that going to take?' Verity Pearson began to rock gently in her seat. 'I have a funeral to arrange, and bills to pay. How am I supposed to deal with those?' Her mouth twisted suddenly into an anguished snarl. 'How am I supposed to know what to do? Leo always dealt with everything. I don't know anything about running the business or paying the bills.' There were unexpected tears in the green eyes now, and she brushed them away with the cuff of her jumper.

Rose stretched out a hand and placed it gently on Verity's arm. 'We're very sorry for your loss, and for the distress this is causing you. But we are going to do everything we can to help you. The keyman insurance policy carries a "sudden death" clause, which entitles you to an immediate payment of ten per cent of the proceeds to ease the business cash flow. Normally we would require the death certificate to release this, but because we understand that it may take some time for the necessary paperwork to come through, I've outlined your case to one of our senior insurance assessors, and I've been given permission to provide you with that amount as an advance against the policy.'

'An advance?' Verity Pearson blinked her bemusement. 'And how would I access that?' She sounded calmer, but still unconvinced.

'Well, Stacy will help you to prepare the claim form today, and we will hold that ready for processing until the death certificate is available. Then, in anticipation of the claim being agreed, we'll arrange for an interim payment of twenty thousand pounds to be made to the business account for Pearson the Bookmaker. That should be available within twenty four hours, and provide you with sufficient cash flow to draw a salary payment for yourself, to settle the final wage bill, and to deal with any outstanding business expenses after Pearson the Bookmaker transfers to its new owner. I'm sure that your accountant will be able to advise on the details. I have to stress that I will require your signature on an indemnity document which will guarantee the bank against any losses should your claim against the insurance policy fail.'

'And how will I settle the final wage bill? I mean, how do I pay the girls their wages?'

'I'll speak to Toby, and ask him to help you. I'm sure if he speaks to your accountant we can sort something out. In the meantime, in order for the insurance claims to be processed, we need to obtain a copy of the death certificate.'

'And how do we do that?'

Stacy leaned forward. 'Again, that might be something for you to discuss with your solicitor. But if it helps, I can explain a little. Someone will need to register your husband's death, and that would normally be yourself or another family member.' Her voice was gentle. 'Unfortunately, due to the circumstances of your husband's death the coroner will have to be informed. If that's the case, then you won't be able to register the death until after the coroner's investigation has been completed.'

Verity let out a tiny gasp, a sharp intake of breath that brought with it an unmistakable squeal of distress. 'However long is that going to take?'

'I really can't say, Mrs Pearson. It depends on the circumstances of the case. I'm afraid that's a question you will have to put to the police officers investigating your husband's death.'

George Mulligan placed the phone's receiver gently down on the cradle and reclined into his office chair with a quiet, self-satisfied smirk. The forensic report had come in later than he'd hoped, but he couldn't deny it had been worth the wait. Much as he'd expected, it was impossible to give an accurate cause of death for the poor sod whose remains had been found in what was left of Leo Pearson's Jaguar. But accelerants had been used to set the car alight.

No real surprise, then, that his initial suspicions were

right on both counts. But suspicions weren't enough to launch a murder case. You needed facts to turn a suspicious death into a malicious one, and now he had the facts he could insist on a formal identification of Leo Pearson's remains, and a thorough investigation into the businessman's private and professional life.

Someone wanted Leo Pearson dead, wanted it enough to leave him strapped in the driver's seat of his car, spread petrol all around him, and light the match to start a conflagration that would leave him nothing more than a pitiful heap of smoked and charred remains.

The policeman swivelled on his chair, turning his attention to the computer screen on his desk, and tapped at the keyboard beneath until a grainy image filled the screen. He rested his forearms on the edge of the desk, and peered at the bleak image, his nose almost touching the screen. His eyes moved slowly, almost pixel by pixel, over the image of the scrubland at Cayton Bay.

There must have been somebody with him.

It was absolutely inconceivable that Leo Pearson would have driven himself off the main road, over the gorse and the heather, parked up, got out his vehicle, saturated himself and the Jaguar in petrol, climbed back into the driver's seat, fastened himself in with the seatbelt, and then struck a match to start the blaze. Inconceivable that he would sit there, conscious and suffering, and wait for the flames to engulf his own body. Inconceivable that he would have consumed some sort of drug or medication to render himself unconscious before the pain became too much.

More likely, then, that someone had travelled in the car with him. Someone in the passenger seat. Someone who had … what? Drugged him first, then set the car alight? Someone he trusted? No, not just someone he trusted. Someone he trusted enough to drive out with them to such a bleak and desolate spot. A friend, a relative, a lover … a wife?

He leaned away from the screen. Whoever it was, that second person had to make their own way back to the main road. There had been no other tyre tracks, so it must have been on foot. Someone had made their way on foot, probably in the dark, back to the main road ... and then what? He closed his eyes and tried to visualise the stretch of road in question.

A quiet road, a long and dreary stretch between two roundabouts, parallel to the main coast road, and deserted by comparison. No houses, no shops, just the occasional passing car cutting through. Leo Pearson's companion had walked coolly back to this deserted road, and somehow made their way back to civilisation. On foot? Unlikely. By car, then?

There was a notebook on Mulligan's desk and he flicked it open, and then reached into a nearby drawer for a pen. *Sightings of killer on road?* He scowled as he scribbled down his thoughts. Sightings were unlikely, but they would have to at least ask the question. *Where was the killer going?* Home? Some other safe spot? Wherever he went, he would be stinking of petrol. The fumes would be on his clothes, his skin, his hair. *What was the killer's motive?*

He let out a sigh, and dropped the pen onto the soft surface of the notepad. Wasn't that always the question? *Why did the killer kill?* Why this death? Why this method? Why this place?

Who wanted Leo Pearson dead?

There was only one obvious answer to that question, and it wasn't the disgruntled husband of some fictional mistress. If Leo Pearson really was playing away, then his wife had as good a motive as anyone to see him wiped out. She wouldn't be the first woman to want her revenge, and something to compensate her for the pain. If Scottie was right, and she was a lonely woman who suspected her husband of being a serial philanderer, then Leo's death would bring an end to the suffering and a sizeable financial benefit to support a new start in life. Leo would have trusted her enough to drive with her to that remote spot, and wouldn't have suspected for a minute that she could do him any harm.

The idea of the pretentious Verity Pearson, carefully picking her way in the dark across the cold, wet gorse on the cliff top in expensive waterproofs and designer wellington boots, hell bent on making her way daintily home undetected, to enjoy her freedom and her ill-gotten gains almost - just almost - made it into the detective inspector's mind. But reality got there first.

George Mulligan felt his chest begin to rise as the laughter began to bubble in the pit of his ample stomach, and he pulled a crumpled handkerchief out of a trouser pocket, and dabbed with it at his eyes. Sometimes in an investigation, he thought, you have to consider the improbable.

The skill for a detective was to know just where to draw the line between the improbable and the downright ludicrous.

Benny Bradman watched as Beverley's eyes dropped slowly to her hands. There was a gold signet ring on the middle finger of her left hand, and she rested the fingers of her right around it and began to twist it back and forth. Eventually she looked up and smiled at him. 'I'm afraid I don't really know anything about it. I don't have anything to do with the accounts.'

'Well, that's a shame, and no mistake.' They were sitting in the small office at the back of the shop, Benny now firmly in possession of Leo Pearson's plush leather chair, while Beverley perched uncomfortably on the edge of the hard, wooden seat at the visitor's side of the desk. 'I was hopin' that you might have at least some of the answers. Because without those answers, this deal is over for me.'

'You'll back out of buying the shop?'

'I don't really see that I'll have a choice. I've been over the books again, and there's somethin' in there that just don't look right.' He rested his elbows on the desk. 'You're the manager here, Beverley. You might not have anythin' to do with drawin' up the accounts, but you supervise the cashin' up. You know what cash is goin' through those tills.' He jerked his head in the direction of the door, and the counters beyond.

'If you back out of the sale, what will happen to us?' The penny was beginning to drop. 'Mrs Pearson doesn't want the business, and it might be weeks, even months, before another buyer is found.'

'It won't be easy, I'll grant you that. This place needs a lot of investment. Still, I suppose if Verity Pearson can't find someone to take it on as a goin' concern, she can always just sell the freehold. A double-fronted shop, with two empty flats upstairs? It's just possible she might get more for the place as a development opportunity than she would as a bettin' shop.' Benny let her think about it, and then said 'I used to dabble in property a bit myself, Beverley. I'm not sure I'd want to do another development in Scarborough, but someone might.'

She tilted her head, her brow furrowed, and looked into his face. 'I thought the contracts were going to be exchanged on Friday? You wouldn't back out now?'

'I'd have every right to back out, if I thought the value of this business had been overstated.' He lowered his voice to a growl. 'And I'd have every right to report it to the police as fraud if I thought that the people who ran this business had colluded with the people who worked for them to create a false set of books to do it.'

Panic flashed across Beverley's pale blue eyes. 'I haven't done anything wrong, Mr Bradman. I told you, I don't have anything to do with the accounts.'

'I've found entries in those accounts that show regular healthy sums of cash comin' in. Now you and me both know that there's nothin' strange in that for a bettin' shop.

Most punters come in with cash. And it usually happens when there's a big sportin' event. Wimbledon. The Grand National. The Grand Prix. Maybe a juicy Premier League soccer game.' He folded his arms across his chest. 'But these sums of cash I'm talkin' about, they all came in against the horse racin' calendar. And not against big race meetin's.' He lifted his left hand and began to count across the fingers. 'Wetherby, Market Rasen, Beverley … small meetin's, family courses. And the sums that came in across the counter always added up to just about the same amount every day that it happened. Just shy of five hundred quid.'

'I don't really understand what you're getting at.'

'You've got a problem punter at this shop.'

Beverley started, and her eyebrows lifted in an incredulous arc. 'How …?'

He slumped back in his seat. 'I've been too long at this game.' He'd grilled the girl enough now, it was time to stop playing with her. 'Who is it?'

'His name is Neil, Neil Redfern.' She spoke with a quiet reluctance. 'He comes in just about every day. Sometimes he doesn't have much to stake. But over the last few months there have been days when he's rolled up with about five hundred pounds in cash.'

'Where's he gettin' that sort of money, then? He's not winnin' it back here. I can't see any evidence of big pay-outs in the accounts. So he must be earnin' it somewhere.'

She gave a non-committal sniff. 'He's unemployed. He lives on the Barnfield estate on his own. I heard that his wife left him a while back, and he lost his job.' She looked unhappy now. 'I don't know where he gets the money from, Mr Bradman. I only know how he loses it. I've tried to persuade him to stop, but you know how it is with some people. They're just too far gone to be helped.'

'No one's too far gone to be helped, Beverley. Just because it's a struggle for them is no reason for us not to have another go.' He reached into the pocket of his jacket and pulled out his wallet. He took a twenty pound note from it and handed it to her. 'Nip next door to the bakery and get us a round of cakes in, and get one of the other girls to put the kettle on. And when you get back, we'll have another chat about this Neil. If he's in today, I want you to introduce me to him.'

'I wish I could.' She pushed herself to her feet, and rolled the twenty pound note carefully around between her fingers. 'But right now nobody seems to know where he is.'

'He's stopped gamblin' at this shop?'

'He seems to have stopped gambling at any shop. His sister has been trying to find him, but last night she gave up and reported him to the police as a missing person.' She turned to leave the office, and then looked back over her shoulder at Benny. 'Will you still be buying the shop, Mr Bradman?'

The question fell on deaf ears. Benny had stopped listening at the words "missing person".

10

DI Mulligan eased himself into the passenger seat of DS Scott's Audi, and gingerly handed over a cardboard cup of coffee. 'I didn't think it was worth dragging you back to the station when we were both going to be heading out again. No point in wasting time in the rush hour traffic.'

They were parked up in a layby on the outskirts of Kirkby, a convenient meeting place on the bypass with the benefit of a mobile coffee van and easy access to their onward destinations. Mulligan carefully levered the plastic lid from the top of his own cup and sipped on the murky brown liquid inside with a grimace. 'At least it's wet and warm.' He swilled the coffee around thoughtfully. 'How did you get on with Verity Pearson at Cayton Bay?'

Scott gave a shrug. 'I couldn't get her to admit to any financial difficulties. But apart from that, she behaved pretty much as I expected. She gave a fair impression of the grieving widow, and laid an extravagant bouquet of lilies close to where the body was found.' He laughed. 'Then she dried her eyes, told me she couldn't think of anyone who would benefit from her husband's death, and coolly asked if I would drive her back to Kirkby so that she could go to the bank and discuss claiming on his insurance policies.'

The inspector chuckled under his breath. 'Is there a will?'

'Yes. I asked her about that on the way back to Kirkby.

According to Verity, she inherits everything.'

'Well, at last we're moving forward. We have a body we believe is Leo Pearson. We have evidence that the fire in his car was started deliberately. And we have a not-quite-grieving widow who benefits from his death. Whether she has financial difficulties or not, that sounds like a possible motive to me.' He sipped again on his coffee. 'On top of that, we have a possible person of interest in the shape of a missing gambler who used to do odd jobs for the Pearsons.' He nodded to himself. 'This is shaping up quite nicely. What sort of odd jobs are we talking about?'

'According to his sister, he helped out with the garden – cutting the grass, trimming hedges, that sort of thing. And he valeted the car now and again. She thinks Pearson paid him cash in hand, although at times Neil Redfern also had a significant slate at the betting shop, so it's possible that he did some of the work to offset what he already owed in gambling debts.'

'If he did odd jobs around the house and garden, he must have come into contact with Verity Pearson. Is he a good-looking sort? Could his role as odd job man have extended to keeping Verity Pearson company?'

DS Scott reached into the back of the car and retrieved a wooden picture frame wrapped in a crumpled carrier bag. He shook off the bag and handed the picture to Mulligan. 'I reckon he was younger than Leo Pearson by about ten to fifteen years. I don't think the age difference would have bothered Verity.'

Mulligan rested the frame on his knee and looked down at the picture. A tall, slim man with thick dark hair was standing next to a young boy who was smiling happily into the camera. The man's eyes were troubled, his own smile evidently forced for the benefit of his nephew. 'He's a good-looking bloke. I could see Verity Pearson being interested. Could you see him doing away with Leo Pearson so that he could wipe his slate clean? Was there a grudge over these gambling debts?'

'His sister didn't mention one. I suppose we'd have to ask the staff in the betting shop.'

'If he valeted the car, he would have had access to Leo Pearson's car keys, possibly even had hold of a spare set himself.' The inspector frowned. 'Would that be too thin a motive? Would you really murder someone to get rid of your gambling tab?' He doubted so himself. 'What about lust? Could you see him doing away with Leo Pearson so that he could make off with his wife?'

Ian Scott snorted. 'Could you really see Verity Pearson with the odd job man?'

'He wasn't always an odd job man. I thought his sister said he was an accountant? He's an educated and professional man who has landed on hard times.' Mulligan was warming to the idea. 'And there might be a twist. What if Verity was in on it? What if Verity arranged for Neil to murder Leo so that she could be free? You said she suspected her husband of having an affair. What if she'd had enough?' He shook his head. 'I think it's worth questioning her about how well she knows Neil Redfern. Even if there isn't anything personal going on between them, there could be a business arrangement. She could have paid Neil Redfern off in return for getting rid of her husband. There's no denying that he needed the money.'

'Do you want me to go back and question her now?'

'No. I think you should stick to the plan. Go back and talk to the sister again. See if you can find out anything else from her about the jobs he did for Leo Pearson, and how well he knew Verity. We could do with his mobile phone records. And up the ante in the search for him. Get someone out to try his flat again, and any other betting shops in the area. Someone has to know where he is.'

'Do you want to come with me?'

'No, I'm going to dig a bit deeper into the Pearsons' financial affairs to see if there is a motive there. They banked with the ENB, and I've heard on the grapevine that there were issues with their bank accounts. I think that's why their account manager from the bank was keen to meet with Leo Pearson, and why Pearson himself didn't want to attend the meeting.'

'You're a bit late for the bank, George. They close at five.'

Mulligan hesitated, and then turned towards the sergeant. 'Are you still harbouring a thing for Rose Bennett?'

'Is that how you say it now, George? "Harbouring a thing"?' Ian Scott wrinkled his nose. 'I heard a rumour that Rose was back in Market Melbourne.' He stared wistfully down into what was left of his coffee. 'Sometimes you have to know when to back off. I'm chalking her up as my one that got away.'

'And is that new-found pragmatism anything to do with Verity Pearson?'

'The black widow? No, she's definitely just a line of enquiry that needs a bit of special attention.'

Mulligan nodded, but he wasn't convinced. The torch that Ian Scott had carried for Rose Bennett had burned too bright to be extinguished by little more than common sense. Mulligan knew his sergeant well enough to know there would be another romantic prospect in the background. If it wasn't Verity Pearson, then perhaps it was Neil Redfern's sister. There would be a time and place to ask the question, he supposed.

But this one wasn't it.

Benny Bradman perched awkwardly on the edge of a lilac armchair and regarded Verity Pearson with the most sympathetic gaze he could muster.

She was sitting opposite him on a large and comfortable sofa, her slim legs folded along the edge of the seat, the large green eyes watching him closely from beneath a mop of tousled burgundy curls. 'I'm sorry if I seemed a little vague when I answered the door, Benny.' Her voice was honeyed. 'It's been a while since we met, and I'm afraid I'm not very good with faces and names.'

'That's alright, Verity. It was only a very fleetin' introduction. At the golf club dinner, a couple of years back.'

'Of course.' She gave a gracious bow of the head. 'You were there alone. I remember asking Leo about you after we'd been introduced, and he said you hadn't been in the area very long.' She looked thoughtful. 'Leo was so pleased when you put in an offer for the business. He'd been hoping to sell to an old-school turf accountant. He really didn't want to sell out to one of the big anonymous chains.'

Benny took the compliment in good part. There would have been more chance of hell freezing over than a savvy multinational betting outfit buying Leo Pearson's ailing business. But this wasn't the time to call it out.

He licked his lips, reluctant to speak until the right words had come. Eventually he said 'I wanted to come and pay my respects, Verity. I was sorry to hear about Leo, and I'm very sorry for your loss. But I'm pleased that you've mentioned the business. I've spoken to your accountant this afternoon, to ask if the sale is still goin' ahead. He suggested that I check in with you.' He hesitated, and then added 'he's been tryin' to reach you. To ask for instructions.'

Verity put a hand up to her face and pulled on a burgundy curl beside her cheek, wrapping the strand of hair thoughtfully around a manicured finger. 'I know I should have spoken to him today. And the solicitor. I'm afraid I'm rather useless when it comes to business affairs. Leo always dealt with everything. I'll speak to them tomorrow. But yes, the sale is going ahead. At least I hope it is. I'm relying on you to take it over, Benny. I don't know what I would do if I had to try to find another buyer. It's bad enough just dealing with the investigation into Leo's death.' She let go of the curl with a snuffled laugh. 'You know, I don't think that I've really accepted yet that he's gone. I keep expecting to hear his car pull up on the drive, or his key turn in the lock.'

'That will pass in time.' He felt a fleeting pang of sympathy, along with an acute reminder of a pain he'd almost dared to believe was buried. 'I lost my wife four years ago. That was one of the reasons I moved up to Market Melbourne from Essex. I wanted a fresh start. I still think of her every day, but there comes a point when you have to accept that they're just not comin' back.'

'I can't imagine what that will feel like.' She cast a glance around the room. 'I can't stay here, of course. I don't want to live here without Leo.'

'But you won't be goin' to Portugal now?'

She arched a precisely-drawn eyebrow. 'Won't I?' She pushed out her lips in a practiced pout. 'No, I think I will. Once the business is sold, and the rest of Leo's affairs are settled, then I plan to fly out to look for a property. It's what Leo would want me to do. And there's nothing to keep me here now.'

'I suppose Portugal must hold happy memories for you. Leo told me that you used to holiday there every year.'

'It was certainly a happy place for me. It was the one place that I knew I had my husband's undivided attention. It wasn't so easy for him to be unfaithful to me on holiday. Perhaps if he hadn't been unfaithful to me at home, he might still be here.' She drew in a breath. 'I hope I haven't shocked you, Benny. But the police seem to be quite at a loss as to how my husband came to meet his maker. They haven't said in so many words that his death is suspicious, but that is the only conclusion we can draw. No one seems to be interested in my opinion on the matter.'

'Which is?'

'Leo told me that he was planning to stay out late and play poker with a few friends. I've always assumed that "playing poker" was a euphemism for "playing away", that he had one little tart or another on the go.' She laughed softly under her breath. 'If that was the case, then Leo has been "playing poker" for the entire thirty years of our marriage.' The laugh subsided, and made way for a loud sniff of disdain. 'Perhaps this time he picked the wrong woman. Perhaps this time there was a husband to consider. And perhaps that husband didn't like Leo messing around with his wife.'

Benny put up a hand and scratched at his ear, a self-conscious gesture that did little to mask his discomfort. 'I can see that you have a lot on your mind. Would it help if I gave you a hand with the shop for the rest of the week? I called in there today and had a word with Beverley. I hope you don't mind? I could give you a couple of hours a day until the end of the week. It would give me a chance to get to grips with the place before we exchange contracts.'

Verity blinked, and her lips curled into a smile. 'Benny, you wouldn't just have my blessing, you'd have my eternal gratitude.' She sighed out her relief. 'I have more than enough to deal with. If I thought you would be happy to take over the shop now ...'

He put up a hand. 'I'm happy to help out, but it would just be an informal arrangement. Just to keep the place tickin' over.' He hesitated, and then placed his hands purposefully on his knees, ready to push himself to his feet. 'I think I've taken enough of your time. I really ought to be makin' a move now.'

Her smile began to fade. 'Are you sure you wouldn't like to stay a little longer? I'd be glad of the company.'

He looked down at his hands. 'I'd better be on my way. I've got a friend's dog in the car. He's gettin' on a bit in years. I don't like to leave him for too long if I can help it.'

'Then don't leave him in the car. Bring him indoors.' There was a persuasive edge to her voice now. 'You're not really going to leave me here alone this evening, are you? I can't begin to tell you what a dreadful day I've had. I could rustle up some supper. It wouldn't be much, maybe a lasagne from the freezer.' She looked suddenly vulnerable. 'I don't have anyone else I could ask.'

Benny tried valiantly to hold his ground, and groaned inwardly as old-fashioned chivalry won out. He offered her a smile of capitulation. 'Well it's very kind of you to ask me, Verity. If you really don't mind, I'll bring Mac in from the car. He's well-behaved and his paws are clean. He won't be any bother.'

Out in the hallway, he drew in a measured breath. Spending the evening with Verity Pearson was the last thing he wanted to do. But on the other hand, Rose had asked him to get closer to Leo Pearson's widow in pursuit of the truth, and an invitation to stay for supper was about as close as he could possibly get. At least there were two thoughts to comfort him. One - he would have Mac as a four-legged chaperone. And two – there was no question that Rose was going to owe him big time for this one.

'This is the second evening on the trot that I've been in The Feathers. I'm beginning to feel like part of the furniture.' Rose raised a toast to DI Mulligan with a small glass of Pinot Grigio. 'Here's to a successful investigation for both of us.' She watched as he sipped on a modest half pint of shandy. 'It was quite a surprise when I got your call. How did you know I was looking into Leo Pearson's accounts?'

The policeman grinned. 'I'm not supposed to tell you that. Benny Bradman will never let me forget it.' He placed his glass down gently on the table. 'I went over to Leo Pearson's shop this afternoon, and found Benny in the manager's office. He reckons there have been some irregularities with Leo Pearson's business accounts. Could that have something to do with his death?'

'We're not sure. When Clive Barden asked me to

investigate this case, Leo Pearson was still very much alive. Clive had discovered that Pearson's account manager at the bank, Toby Dugdale, had bent the rules to lend more money than the business could afford to repay. Clive wanted to know why it had happened.' She hesitated, and then added 'I think he thought Toby may have colluded with the customer to defraud the bank of the money borrowed.'

'Does Clive Barden usually get involved with a case as small as this? I would have expected the bank's Head of Risk to have bigger fish to fry.'

Rose gave a whimsical smile. 'This *is* a big fish for Clive. He's interested in the case because he's responsible for the amount of risk the bank can take when it lends money. If it turns out that fraud has been committed, and it's down to a gap in the lending process that he's approved, then he'll be taking on a new role as the bank's ex-Head of Risk.'

Mulligan let out a low whistle. 'So what do you think, Rose? Is some kind of fraud taking place?'

'I don't know. I think it's too early to say. What I can tell you is that the Pearsons have been carrying a significant amount of personal debt as well as their business debts, and there isn't much in the way of income to make the repayments. But there is a significant amount of insurance in place to cover the debts if anything happens to Leo.'

'There was nothing fraudulent in Leo Pearson taking out the policies in the first place?'

'No, he had every right to. In fact the bank would have insisted on at least one of the policies, the one that would indemnify his domestic mortgage.'

'And will the ENB pay out on those policies? Will Verity Pearson benefit from her husband's death?'

Rose gave a shrug. 'As things stand, we are assuming so. We've already approved an interim payment against one of the policies, pending receipt of her husband's death certificate. If all three policies pay out, then she will stand to benefit significantly. The mortgage will be paid off, she'll pick up the proceeds of a simple life policy, and any remainder from a commercial policy designed to compensate for Leo Pearson not being around to run the business.'

'So how much does that amount to?' Mulligan looked down at his hand and began to count through his fingers. 'The house?'

'Worth about half a million.'

'The life policy?'

'Three hundred thousand.'

'And the commercial policy?'

'Probably about another hundred and thirty thousand pounds after outstanding liabilities have been deducted.'

Mulligan was thinking now. 'There is no reason for the bank not to pay out all these monies?'

'Not at this stage, although Clive very much wishes that there was. If the body turns out not to be Leo Pearson after all, or if it transpires that his death was brought about deliberately in order to benefit from the insurance policies … well, that would be a different matter altogether. If there were any suggestion of foul play, then the bank would be within its rights not to pay out on any of the policies. Clive has already suggested that this may have been suicide for financial gain.' Rose hesitated, momentarily awkward, and then asked 'I don't suppose you have anything you could share with me about the cause of Leo's death that might help?'

'Well I'm pretty certain that you can discount the suicide theory. The manner of death doesn't lend itself to that.' Mulligan leaned in closer. 'This is completely off the record, you understand? But we don't believe the death was accidental, either. We've found evidence that accelerants were used to set the fire. I can't give you official confirmation of that yet, but I will as soon as I can.'

'That would be much appreciated, Mr Mulligan. And if there's anything that I can do to assist with your investigation …'

'You've already been a great help, Rose. The thing we're struggling with is motive, but it's beginning to sound to me like our thoughts are moving in the same direction.'

'I've heard it suggested that Leo Pearson may have been having an affair, and that he fell foul of a jealous husband or partner.'

'Yes, I've heard that rumour as well. Verity Pearson seems keen for that story to do the rounds. But I'm not buying it.' He shook his head. 'This is beginning to look like murder for financial gain. It's down to me to test that theory now.' He stared down into what remained of his shandy. 'Have you met Verity Pearson yet?'

'Yes, I have.'

'Did she strike you as a killer?'

'Are you asking if I think she could have murdered her husband for financial gain?' Rose blew out a breath and contemplated the possibility. 'She claimed that Leo had always dealt with their financial affairs, and that she didn't even realise she needed to consult with his solicitor or accountant. I couldn't tell if it was an act.' She sipped on her wine. 'She seemed ill-informed, and rather vague. And yet when I hinted that the bank might not just roll over and pay out because she expected it, she seemed to lose her cool. She almost panicked.' She paused, unsure whether to ask a question that was troubling her, and then courage won out. 'I wonder, can I ask … has Leo Pearson's body actually had a formal identification?'

The question brought an unmistakeable twinkle to DI Mulligan's eyes. 'His widow has identified certain items that were found with the body. We'd hoped that was going to be enough. But now that we know the fire was set deliberately, we'll be taking a look at his dental records to make absolutely certain.' He stared into his glass, and then drained off the dregs of his shandy. 'As far as I'm concerned, the sooner we know for certain that body is Leo Pearson's, the better it will be for all us.'

11

DS Scott placed the framed photograph of Neil Redfern and his nephew gently down on Evie Green's mantelpiece. 'I told you I would bring it back today.'

A shy smile crossed Evie's face. 'I didn't expect you to be working so late.'

'Well, officially I'm off duty. But I like to keep my promises. And I had a couple of extra questions I wanted to ask you about Neil. If you wouldn't mind answering them, of course?'

'I'll answer anything if you think it will help you to find him. I take it there's still no news?'

'Nothing so far. We sent a couple of uniformed officers back round to his flat this afternoon, but the place was empty. At least as far as they could tell from the outside. No one came to the door when they knocked, and they can't just force their way in without good reason.'

'I still can't believe that he would walk away from us without a word. But I understand that you have to follow the rules.' She pointed in the direction of the kitchen. 'Would you like a coffee while you're here?'

'I'd love one.' It was an invitation he'd been hoping for. He slipped off his jacket and draped it over an armchair, then followed her through into the kitchen. 'Where's Liam?'

'He's playing with the kids next door. They're a bit older than him, but they look after him.' She set about filling the kettle. 'Do you have kids yourself?'

'Yes, two. A boy and a girl.' He took a seat at the kitchen table. 'I see them as much as I can, but it's difficult when you work police hours.'

'It must be difficult on your wife, too, I suppose?'

'It was.' He gave a self-deprecating laugh. 'That's probably why she's my ex-wife.'

'I'm sorry, I didn't mean to pry.' She sounded awkward.

Ian Scott gave a shrug. 'It's all water under the bridge now.' He relaxed into his seat. 'What about you? It must be difficult raising Liam on your own.'

'It will be a damn sight harder if Neil doesn't show up. He's been a Godsend for both of us. I need him to look after Liam on the evenings I work, and Liam just plain adores him. He's the nearest thing he has to a dad.' She turned towards Scott. 'So what are these questions you wanted to ask me?'

'It's about Leo and Verity Pearson. When we spoke earlier, you mentioned that Neil did odd jobs for them. Did he talk about them much? Mention anything about whether he got on well with them?'

'Not really.' Evie frowned, trying to remember. 'Nothing in particular.' She tilted her head to one side. 'What has that got to do with Neil going missing?'

'You must have seen the news in the last twenty-four hours? Leo Pearson's car was found burned out, up on the cliff top near Cayton Bay. It's possible that Neil might have spoken to him yesterday.'

An uncomfortable silence settled between them, and then Evie turned away and lifted a single clean coffee mug from the kitchen draining board. 'I thought you were helping me to find Neil. Because he's vulnerable.'

'I am.'

'So what does that have to do with Leo Pearson?' Her was voice calm, but there was an inflection that suggested a growing suspicion.

'Evie, you have to admit that it's a coincidence. Your

brother has disappeared, and Leo Pearson's body has been found. There may be some connection.'

'Are you telling me that you suspect Neil of having something to do with what happened to Leo Pearson?'

'I'm not saying that at all. Apart from anything else, I want to make sure that nothing bad has happened to your brother.'

She didn't appear to be listening. An angry flush had appeared across her cheekbones, and she was glowering into the empty coffee mug. 'My brother is a good man. He's not a criminal, or a thug. He's a victim.'

He'd aggravated her now, and it was going to take some effort get her fully back on side. But since that was the case, and since he had every intention of taking however long it would take to win back her trust, he figured he had nothing to lose by asking the other awkward question. 'You never heard your brother talk about Verity Pearson? He didn't say anything about working with her in the garden, or talk about any other odd jobs he might have done for her? Driving her around, maybe?'

'No.' It was a definitive answer.

'And he never said anything about her relationship with Leo? You never heard him say that she was lonely, or that her marriage wasn't a good one? Did he ever talk about forming any sort of friendship with her?'

Evie slammed the coffee mug down on the kitchen counter. 'You know, I thought that you were alright. I thought that you were going to help me find my brother.' She spun around to face him. 'But I think you'd better go now.'

'Evie, I do want to help you find your brother. I have to ask these questions.'

'You're just using me to get information about Neil.'

'That's not fair.'

'Well, welcome to *my* world. Very little in my life has been fair, Detective Sergeant Scott. But I wouldn't expect you to know what that feels like.' Her eyes were glistening now, tears forming beneath her long dark lashes. 'Now if you don't mind, I think we're done here. I'm quite happy for you to stop searching for my brother. Now I know why you're looking for him, I can't help thinking that I'd rather he just stayed out of sight. At least then he can't be blamed for something that I know he didn't do.'

Rose flicked the remote control in the direction of the television, and the screen went blank with an almost inaudible click as she mumbled under her breath. 'About time, too.' Her mobile phone was skittering across a nearby coffee table with the vibration of an incoming call, and she scooped it up with an impatient hand and swiped at the screen with her thumb to answer. 'Have you any idea what time it is?'

The voice at the end of the line was an unexpected one. 'I believe it's just after eleven o'clock.' Clive Barden sounded contrite. 'I can only apologise for the lateness of my call, Rose. But I've spent the entire evening in executive meetings, and this is the first opportunity I've had to return your call.'

She closed her eyes, and gently rested her head against the wing of the armchair. 'Clive, I'm so sorry. I thought … well, I was expecting a call from someone else.'

'I see.' He sounded vague, as though he didn't really see at all. 'I hoped that you had some news for me regarding the Pearson case.'

'Yes, I do.' She tucked the phone into the crook of her neck and settled back into the chair. 'Stacy and I met with Verity Pearson this afternoon. We tried to explain her position regarding Pearson the Bookmaker's outstanding debts, but her primary concern seemed to be how to claim on her husband's insurance policies.'

'Has there been any news yet regarding his death?'

'Yes. I met with DI Mulligan this evening. I didn't think you would mind, as it was in the bank's interests. He's in charge of the investigation.'

'Of course we are always happy to assist the Inspector, especially when it is to mutual benefit.'

It was certainly to the bank's benefit this time. 'He's unofficially confirmed that the circumstances around Leo Pearson's death are suspicious. The fire was started deliberately.'

'Indeed?' There was a pause, and then Clive said 'I read your email, Rose. Regarding the additional insurance policies.' There was a hint of remorse in his voice. 'I should not have been so quick to hang up on you this morning. It appears that Verity Pearson stands to benefit significantly at our expense from her husband's death.'

Rose smiled to herself. It was the nearest she would get to an apology. 'Mr Mulligan seems to be keen on the idea of financial benefit as a motive for Leo Pearson's death. He thinks we can discount the idea of suicide. But he certainly sees those insurance policies as a motive for murder.'

'Then we must put a block on them until the police investigation is complete. I will deal with that as a priority in the morning. I suggest that we continue with the advance under the keyman policy, though. I wouldn't want us to tip off Verity Pearson, that we suspect any wrong-doing on her part.' He thought for a moment, and then asked 'did she mention the sale of the business?'

'Yes. She made a point of reminding us that the business would change hands on Friday, and I honestly think she was naïve enough to think that the outstanding debts had nothing to do with her. I broke the news to her as gently as I could, that she would be responsible for ensuring that any business debt due to the ENB would be settled. It was obviously a surprise. She doesn't seem to understand the process of closing down the business. I don't think she's even spoken to her accountant or solicitor.' Rose frowned. 'You know, Clive, I can't tell if she really is that innocent, or whether it's all an act. But I do know that we'll have to deal with her carefully. Whatever the case, she is still potentially a bereaved customer. We have to assume that it was her husband who died in the fire. And we have to treat her with respect.'

'With respect, yes. But we must be careful not to let our sympathies cloud our judgment. I am not inclined to believe that Leo and Verity Pearson have been anywhere near as innocent in all of this as you would seem to think.'

'Perhaps. But have you stopped to think what the worst case situation would be for Verity Pearson? If the body in that vehicle is her husband's, and the ENB pay out on those insurance policies, she's home and dry. She can settle any outstanding business and personal debts and have more than enough left over to begin a new life in the wake of her husband's death. If they don't ... well, she'll be up to her neck in unmanageable debt. And if Benny decides to back out of buying the business, she'll also be responsible for Pearson the Bookmaker's commercial debts.'

'She will still have control of a viable business, the freehold of the commercial premises, and the equity in her home. If she sold her house in Kirkby Park, she could release a hundred and twenty thousand pounds in equity.'

'Yes, if she could find a buyer. But even if she did, she would still need somewhere to live. And there are outstanding debts to be serviced or settled. From where I'm standing, that looks like a significant overdraft, two sets of car finance, and three personal credit cards. According to Toby, Verity has never worked and has no private personal income. She would have no idea how to run Pearson the Bookmaker until they find another buyer.'

At the other end of the line, Clive fell ominously silent. Eventually he said 'I think you are tired, Rose. You are sounding uncharacteristically mawkish this evening.'

'Perhaps I am. But there are times, Clive, when I

wonder why we do this job. It isn't just money we're dealing with, is it? It's people's lives.'

'Surely not just their lives, Rose. In the case of Leo Pearson, we are dealing with someone's death. And perhaps on this occasion, though it pains me to say it, someone's unnecessary and untimely death.'

DS Scott leaned back against the Audi's passenger door and stared up at the corner windows of a shabby concrete block of maisonettes. He still wasn't sure what he was doing on the Barnfield estate. It wasn't exactly a sensible place for an off-duty policeman to hang out on a dark October night, especially at an hour so close to closing time. But some instinctive urge that evening had pushed him irrationally in the direction of Neil Redfern's grubby second-floor flat. He still hadn't worked out if it was down to a detective's need to ferret for the truth, or simply the desire to show the untrusting Evie Green that he was trying to do his best to find her brother.

It had done him little good to try the door. He'd used both the doorbell, and the tarnished brass knocker that hung beside it on the doorframe, but no one had responded. He'd tried peering through the letter box, an ill-advised manoeuvre that had done little more than expose him to a nose-full of pungent smells from within, a heady mix of strong bleach with hints of chicken curry. The place was in darkness, the curtains drawn, and silence prevailed.

And yet there was something. Some intangible feeling, some suspicion, something that he couldn't quite pin down. It wasn't that he was convinced the place was still inhabited. It just didn't feel deserted.

He cast a glance about him. The street was empty, there was nothing to be learned here, no point in hanging around any longer. He rolled off the side of the car and walked around to the driver's door, and fished in his pocket for his keys. He had barely unlocked the door when a movement to his right caught his attention, and he spun instinctively around and braced himself against the side of the car.

'By, lad, you're a bit twitchy, aren't you?' An elderly man in a threadbare Crombie was strolling across the road towards him, his hands deep in his pockets, his eyes lit merry with a hint of ale, or perhaps something a bit stronger.

DS Scott relaxed. 'I didn't hear you coming.'

'Aye, well, I'm always light on my feet when I've had a few. It was the only way I could stop the wife from waking up and nagging at me when I came in late.' The old man chuckled softly to himself. 'God rest her soul.' He shook his head as he passed. 'He's not in there, you know. Neil Redfern. I told those other coppers who came at teatime.'

'Other coppers?'

'You all look the same to me, lad. You might not be in uniform like they were, but you still look like a plod.' The old man stopped on the edge of the pavement and turned with a wry smile. 'They came near six o'clock.'

DS Scott stepped forward. 'Do you live in this block?'

'Ay, I've lived here forty years. He hasn't, mind. Not Neil. Just a year or two.' The old man chewed thoughtfully on his lip. 'He's a decent enough sort. A bit of a loner, but he's never done me any harm. He has a sister, you know? And a nephew who comes to visit him, a nice little lad, keen on football.'

'So when did you last see him?'

'The night before last. He was on his way out to meet someone. He said he was going out for a few pints.'

'Did you see him come back?'

'No, but I heard him moving about. I live in the flat next door, and those walls are paper thin. I can even hear the kettle going on and off when he's making a brew.' He frowned. 'I wondered if he was a bit under the weather, you know. I sometimes see him down at Pearson's, I like a flutter now and again, and so does Neil. But he's not been in the past two days.' The frown turned to a grin. 'He had a visitor this evening, just after five o'clock. They went out at half past five. I heard the door go.' He glanced up at the darkened windows. 'It doesn't look like they've been back since. Happen he's found a new interest in life to take his mind off the horses. It sounded like a lady.' He turned back to DS Scott with a knowing wink. 'And I'm not talking about his sister.'

12

Verity Pearson pulled her silk-pyjama-clad legs up onto the plush lilac sofa, curling them to the left, and then wriggled a little to find the most comfortable position. She stretched out an arm to a small side table to retrieve a deep china bowl filled with yoghurt, and then set about enjoying the contents. At least she had recovered her appetite.

Looking back, the events of yesterday had been enough to put anyone off their food. Braving the cold and damp of Cayton Bay to lay flowers beneath a fluttering line of police tape was one thing. Squeezing out crocodile tears to meet Detective Sergeant Scott's expectation of grief had been quite something else. And why did he have to have such an intrusive line of questioning? He seemed to like asking questions just for the sake of it, almost as much as she herself preferred not to answer them.

She scowled at the thought, and licked at the back of her spoon, a reflective flick of the tongue. They had liked asking questions at the ENB, too. How was she supposed to know anything about running Leo's business? It hadn't been her responsibility to settle the wages, or deal with the accountant and the solicitor. That had been Leo's job. Her own role was far less demanding.

She narrowed her eyes, and cast her mind back to the meeting, and the delicate matter of Pearson the Bookmaker's debts. It had never occurred to her, until Rose Bennett suggested it, that any business debts in Leo's name might pass to her after his death. He'd always led her to believe that being a director in the company was simply a matter of routine, a nice little tax dodge that gave her a salary from the business. Why give the money to the tax man, Leo had said, when they could use it to fund her convertible? All she had to do in return was sign a few documents now and again. It had never crossed her mind that Leo might have been wrong, let alone that he might have been economical with the truth.

Both of those possibilities troubled her. She'd asked Benny Bradman, the evening before, if Rose Bennett might have been right. The question had made him uncomfortable, and he'd waffled without giving her much of an answer, other than to suggest that she speak to the accountant. Perhaps she should take his advice. Perhaps the accountant could answer the other question that Benny had evaded. How was she supposed to know what a personal guarantee was?

She blew out a sigh. In the big scheme of things, did any of this really matter? Once the sale of the business went through, and the insurance policies paid out, there would be plenty of cash to go round. In the meantime all she had to do was come up with a death certificate for the bank, and keep Benny Bradman on side until Pearson the Bookmaker changed hands.

Her face brightened at the thought. The unexpected appearance of Benny Bradman had been the one thing to cheer up her day. Until yesterday, Benny had been nothing more than a name, the intended purchaser of Leo's ailing business, a vague and fleeting memory from a less-than-exciting evening at the golf club. It had never occurred to her that Benny in the flesh would be so charming, nor so solicitous. But then neither had she remembered that he was so fit or so handsome. It had been kind of him to stay to supper, and a disappointment that he wouldn't stay for longer. The evening could have ended so differently, if not for that dribbling and moth-eaten mutt that Benny insisted on returning to his friend.

She puffed out another sigh, a deeper one this time. It was all well and good thinking about missed opportunities, but there were things to be dealt with today. She would have to let Beverley know that Benny would be spending more time at the shop. And she needed to speak to the estate agent, and the accountant. And, most important of all, she needed to come up with a death certificate.

She was looking forward to procuring that death certificate. She was looking forward to presenting it to the bank, and to watching as it unlocked the door to a succession of well-deserved riches. It was difficult to believe that a simple piece of paper would set her well on the way to a million pounds.

She dug her spoon back into the yoghurt with a confident hand. She would have to re-engage with the inquisitive Sergeant Scott. He was bound to be able to help, if only he could be called upon to do it without asking any more of those tedious questions. She leaned across to the side table, and swapped the bowl of yoghurt for her mobile phone. She swiped at the screen with a sticky thumb, searching for a newly-stored number, and then tucked the phone neatly under her chin and waited for the unsuspecting policeman to answer her call.

'You'll have to forgive me this morning, Stacy. I'm not really firing on all cylinders yet.' Rose Bennett nudged the door of the small meeting room with her shoulder, and waited for it to swing shut behind her. She regarded her colleague ruefully as she took her place at the table. 'Last night was a late one for me.' There was no need, she thought, to mention the reason. It was no-one's fault but her own if Benny had spent the whole evening with Verity Pearson, but she would have preferred him not to dognap Mac in the process.

Stacy gave a whimsical smile. 'I hope you weren't working all evening?'

'No, nothing like that. But at least I was still awake when Clive called for an update.' She let out a laugh. 'I don't think that man has an off-switch. He called after eleven to ask how we were getting on.' She opened her soft leather notebook to a page of neatly-written notes. 'Anyway, I wanted to give you an update on the Leo Pearson case. The police have confirmed off the record that Leo Pearson's death was suspicious. They have evidence that the fire was started deliberately.'

'Heavens, what does Clive make of that?'

'He's still worried that this is insurance fraud.' She gave a dismissive shake of the head. 'You know what Clive is like – "let's panic now, just in case, and worry about the facts later". He's going to freeze all three of Leo Pearson's insurance policies this morning, pending further advice on the cause of death.'

'And what do you make of it, Rose?'

'Truthfully? It might not be anything to do with insurance fraud. It's perfectly feasible that Leo Pearson met a sticky end for reason or reasons unknown, and that Verity Pearson will just get lucky with the insurance pay out as a result. But if Clive wants us to assume insurance fraud until further notice, then that's the line we'll have to take.' Rose thought for a moment. The investigation was moving a long way now from the reason that Clive brought her in. 'My original brief was to look at the way Toby manipulated the lending process, and whether or not he'd been involved in any crime. He's already admitted to failing to disclose his relationship to Leo Pearson, and to knowingly advancing his cousin far too much credit. I suppose if there is a possibility of insurance fraud, I need to consider whether Toby might have known about that too. But I can't really see that he would have a motive. And even if I could, I haven't had a great deal of experience with this type of fraud. If there were more evidence at this stage I would be tempted to just hand the case off to the Fraud Team and leave it with them.'

Stacy eyed Rose with a serious concern. 'I have to admit that I don't know much about insurance fraud either, Rose, but I do know that what will matter most to the bank is who killed Leo Pearson, and why. Under most circumstances there would be no reason not to pay out on those policies, even if he was murdered, providing the motive had nothing to do with financial gain. But if it turns out that someone killed him to benefit financially from his death … well, that would be another matter altogether.' Her deftly-pencilled brows knitted forward. 'Extending too much credit to a customer is an internal matter for the bank. So is not disclosing a personal relationship with a customer. If the bank failed to train Toby properly to follow those procedures, that is down to the ENB. But involvement in insurance fraud? Now that's a serious crime. One that Toby might do time for, if it turns out to be true.'

Rose tilted back her head and stared up at the ceiling, contemplating the possibility, and then she turned back to Stacy. 'How well do you know Toby?'

'Not that well. We have a sort of nodding acquaintance, because I helped him with a bereavement case some years back when he worked as a complaint handler. I've always thought of him as … well, just normal, really. I mean, he's worked here for years. I just couldn't see him as a fraudster, somehow. Any more than I could see him be involved in someone's death.' She looked away, battling some inner thought, and then she turned back to Rose. 'He isn't just normal, isn't he? He's one of *us*.'

'Yes, he's one of us. But we're none of us perfect, are we?' Toby Dugdale certainly wasn't. He'd already lied about his relationship to Leo Pearson, and admitted to Rose any number of misdemeanours at work, not least of all knowingly advancing credit to a customer when he knew that the customer didn't have the means to repay the debt. Rose shook her head. 'Like it or not, we have to consider the possibilities.' She reached down into her bag and pulled out a pen. 'If insurance fraud has been committed, then there must have been a motive.' She began to scribble in the soft leather notebook. 'Leo and Verity Pearson had a pressing need for money. We know that their financial situation was more precarious than Toby had led us to believe, and we know that selling the business wasn't going to be the answer to all of their problems. But claiming on the insurance policies might be.'

'Surely you don't think that Verity Pearson could have murdered her husband for the money?'

Rose sounded uncertain. 'I know it sounds unlikely, but the police are certainly keeping an open mind on that one. She is the beneficiary of those policies, after all. And isn't it possible that she might have had an accomplice? Someone close who was prepared to commit a fraud – possibly even murder – for Verity to benefit?'

'Toby?'

'Frankly, I hope not.' Rose tapped on the open notebook with her pen. 'But we have to acknowledge the possibility. He was close to Leo Pearson, and we only have his word for it that he isn't equally close to the person who stands to benefit from Leo Pearson's death.' She let her pen drop softly onto the open notebook. 'At the very least, don't you think we should try to reassure ourselves that Toby *wasn't* involved?'

George Mulligan rapped on the glass wall of his office to attract Ian Scott's attention. Scott, sitting behind his own desk at the other side of the glass, looked up with tired eyes and rose almost reluctantly to his feet to make his way towards the Inspector's open door.

'Is it true, then? Someone's confirmed that Neil

Redfern has been moving around in his flat?' Mulligan could hardly contain his excitement. 'I knew that beggar was involved in this Pearson business somehow.'

Scott closed the office door behind him, and leaned against it. 'Don't be jumping to conclusions, George. I've only been told that someone was moving around in that flat. We haven't had a confirmed sighting.'

'But there's been a woman there.' Mulligan lowered his bulk onto the chair behind his desk. 'The neighbour you spoke to confirmed that?'

'Yes, Harry Tennant confirmed that. And he confirmed that it wasn't a voice he recognised. It wasn't Redfern's sister.'

'It was Verity Pearson. It has to be.' The inspector sat back in his seat and folded his arms across his paunch. 'It's a damned shame that he only heard her. A positive sighting would have been better.' He stretched out a hand and tapped his fingers on the desk. 'Come on Scottie, you have to admit that it's the most obvious solution? Leo Pearson's business is going down the pan, and Verity Pearson can see that luxury lifestyle that she enjoys so much coming to an abrupt end. Add to that the fact that she's had enough of her old man's philandering ways, and she can see a way to rid herself of an unhappy marriage, and pick up the scoop at the same time. Along comes Neil Redfern, younger than her husband, better looking, but down on his luck and up to his neck in gambling debts. Verity spots an opportunity and persuades Neil Redfern to collude with her in her husband's murder. Redfern sets fire to the car and finishes off her old man, and then makes his way back to his flat and lies low. She picks up the insurance money and the rest of her husband's estate, Neil Redfern has his gambling debts wiped out and maybe picks up a bit of cash on top. Maybe he even picks up Verity Pearson as a bonus prize.'

'And how does he get away? You've already marked him as an obvious suspect. How is he going to evade investigation? He can't stay holed up in that flat forever.'

'He's not in there all the time. He's obviously confident moving around at night. And soon he'll have to make his move and bale out to another location.'

'Why hasn't he done that already?'

Mulligan shrugged. 'Maybe he *is* having an affair with Verity. Maybe she wants him close until she can make her own move.'

'Forgive me, George, but you don't think this is all a bit *too* obvious? We don't really know anything about Neil Redfern. We don't know if he was the sort of man to commit a murder. We don't know his whereabouts on Monday evening, or whether he even had much of a relationship with Verity Pearson.'

'Not yet we don't. But we will. Didn't that neighbour tell you that Redfern went out for a pint on Monday evening? Someone must have seen him.' Mulligan rested his elbows on the desk and fixed his colleague with a resolute stare. 'I want Leo Pearson's dental records as soon as possible, so that we can get a confirmed ID on that body in the car. I want phone records for all three of them – Verity and Leo Pearson, and Neil Redfern. And I want a warrant to search Neil Redfern's flat. We've got little hope of getting forensic evidence to prove that he was at the crime scene, the fire will have put paid to that. But there's every chance we could find something of either Leo Pearson or the crime scene deposited somewhere in Neil Redfern's flat. If we're really lucky, he'll be in there when we arrive with the warrant. And if we aren't, at least we might find something in there to incriminate him.'

'You seem quite keen to stick this crime on him, George.' DS Scott sounded less than convinced. 'You know, I spoke to his sister again yesterday evening. She doesn't believe that Neil had anything to do with Verity Pearson, beyond doing a few odd jobs.'

'Well she would say that, wouldn't she? She's his sister.'

'Evie's a nice girl. She has a good relationship with her

brother. If there was anything going on between him and Verity Pearson, she would know about it.' The sergeant sounded suddenly defensive.

Mulligan picked up the cue, and his face folded into a frown. 'So it's "Evie" now, is it?' He tried to sound avuncular, and fell slightly short of the mark. 'Is this Evie the same girl who claimed that Neil wasn't in his flat, and reported him missing? She's got you in her pocket already, hasn't she?'

'That's not fair.'

'Very little is in this game, Scottie. You know how much I value your opinion, but I don't want this investigation jeopardised by your fancy for a key witness.'

'Don't worry, it won't be.' Scott's jaw began to tighten. 'I'd like to tell her that Harry Tennant heard Neil moving around in his flat. I can't see it would do any harm, and it will put her mind at rest.'

'That's out of the question.' Mulligan peered at Scott over the top of his spectacles, and then added 'and I suppose you're going to tell me that that's not fair, either. But this is a murder enquiry now. Nothing is fair until we've nailed the killer.'

Chastened, Ian Scott blinked. 'So you want me to get hold of Leo Pearson's dental records, the phone records, and apply for a warrant for Redfern's flat. Anything else?'

'I want to talk to Verity Pearson again. Now that we know the fire that destroyed her husband's car was set deliberately, I want to break that news to her myself and see her reaction. And I want to get to the bottom of her relationship with the odd job man. Let me know when you've started the ball rolling for the paperwork, and we can go over to Kirkby Park together. I might need some of that famous Welsh charm that you've been using to your advantage this week.'

DS Scott stepped forward and opened his mouth to reply, and then thought better of it. He turned on his heel and opened the door, stepping through into the outer office without a word, and letting the door bang shut behind him. Mulligan watched him go and then slumped back in his chair with an unmistakeable pang of remorse. He'd known his sergeant long enough to recognise when Scottie was developing a thing for a woman. There had been plenty of occasions in the past, a uniformed WPC, a comely assistant in the pathology lab, even the redoubtable Rose Bennett had caught his partner's eye, come to that. But it was one thing for an officer to have a healthy interest in someone on the right side of the law.

And it was another thing altogether for that interest to alight on the sister of a prime suspect in a murder case.

13

'It's alright for you, sittin' under there in your nice warm basket. It's not you that's in the dog house.' Benny Bradman pulled at a corner of the half-eaten bacon sandwich in front of him, and then reached down under the desk to offer the morsel to Mac. The dog regarded him with dispassionate eyes and took the titbit with a skilful flick of the tongue. 'And don't be tellin' Rose that I gave you that, or we'll be gettin' that lecture about pork scratchin's again.'

He pulled a handkerchief from the pocket of his trousers, and wiped his fingers on it. It wouldn't be so bad, he mused, if he hadn't been following instructions. Perhaps he'd been a widower for so long now that he'd forgotten how a woman's mind works. Perhaps the mistake had been to think that when Rose said she wanted him to get as close to Verity Pearson as he could, he'd actually thought that she meant it.

It wasn't as if he'd enjoyed the experience, nor that he'd learned anything that was going to be of any real use to their investigation. He hadn't wanted to stay and have supper with Verity, because he already had the answer to his own question within five minutes of arriving at her home – yes, the sale of the business was still going through. As to whether the business was worth the price she was asking - well, that was still up for debate. He was pretty sure now that Pearson the Bookmaker's income over the last few months had been inflated by the large sums of cash that Neil Redfern had been throwing over the counter. It was where that cash came from that was troubling Benny.

He'd tried fishing for the answer with Verity Pearson, but it hadn't brought him a catch. She'd spent most of the evening bemoaning her marriage to a serial philanderer, complaining of Leo's infidelity one minute, and weeping into her lasagne the next at the thought he was never coming back. A charitable onlooker might have put her erratic behaviour down to the grief. The cynic in Benny was more inclined to think it was an act.

He couldn't help wondering if it had been a mistake to offer his help at the shop. He'd been happy to suggest a few hours a day for the rest of the week. It was in his own interests to keep a hand on the rudder, an opportunity to make sure that the business stayed afloat until the details of the sale were concluded. But Verity had taken the opportunity to completely misinterpret his offer of support, and he'd arrived that morning to find Beverley waiting for him and ready to hand over both the keys for the shop and the combination for the safe. There was no doubt that Verity was jumping the gun, and trying to palm the place off on him before the ink on the contracts was dry.

He swivelled back and forth in Leo Pearson's plush leather chair, troubled by a transitory thought. There was no doubt in his mind that the avaricious Mrs Pearson was expecting to become a wealthy, if not a merry widow in the wake of her husband's demise. So why had she seemed so troubled by the idea of inheriting her husband's business debts before the sale of the betting shop went through? He was about to give the conundrum the consideration it deserved when the door to office creaked gently on its hinges, and he looked up to see Beverley's pale face appear in the gap between the door and its frame. 'I hope you don't mind, Mr Bradman. I've brought you a coffee. I always used to bring one for Mr Pearson before we opened up for the day.'

He threw her an appreciative smile. 'Well, then you'd better bring it in, Beverley. I never turn down a coffee.' Nor, he thought, the opportunity to ask a question. 'While you're here, come and tell me what else you know about Neil Redfern. Has he turned up yet?'

She stepped closer to the desk and placed the mug of coffee gently down on its edge. 'I don't think so. I've heard on the grapevine that the police are looking for him in connection with Mr Pearson's disappearance.'

Benny raised an eyebrow. 'Is that a new development?'

'I suppose it must be.' She looked perturbed. 'It's awful if it's true. But they do say you can never really know someone, don't they?'

'Do they? Maybe they do.' He snuffled a humourless laugh. 'There was somethin' I meant to ask you yesterday. If you knew that Neil Redfern was livin' on the Barnfield and down on his luck, didn't it ring alarm bells when he started rollin' up with fistfuls of cash?'

The girl looked suddenly sheepish. 'Of course it did. The first time it happened I didn't think much about it. I thought maybe he'd had a bit of luck at another shop, and brought the winnings over to us to stake. But when it happened a second time, and then a third, I spoke to Mr Pearson about it. He told me to stay quiet, and just take the cash. He said it wasn't our responsibility to ask where the cash came from. It's a free country, he said, and if Neil wanted to spend it in here then why should we stop him?'

It sounded like the sort of thing that Leo Pearson would say. 'You mentioned his sister yesterday. Do you have a way of gettin' in touch with her? Because if you do, I wouldn't mind a word.' He pulled thoughtfully on his ear. 'I'd like to have a chat about her missin' brother, and see if there's anythin' I can do to help her find him.'

DI Mulligan balanced his bulk on the edge of Verity Pearson's generous lilac sofa, and regarded the newly-bereaved woman with an appraising eye. There was something different about her today that he couldn't quite place. She was dressed in a petrol-blue knitted sheath that hugged at the contours of her curves, and there was something about her, a hint of almost smug self-satisfaction buried beneath the unconvincing grief, that made him feel slightly uneasy.

She was perched on the edge of an armchair directly opposite, and as she bent forward to speak to him, she cast a cloud of musky perfume around his face. 'I'm so pleased that you've come. I didn't expect you to be here so quickly. I only left the voicemail message for DS Scott twenty minutes ago.'

'We haven't come in response to your message, Verity. We were already on our way here.' Mulligan gave a shake of the head. 'I'm sorry to tell you that we've come to break some difficult news. We've confirmed that the fire that led to your husband's death was started deliberately. We're treating Leo's death as a murder case.'

'Of course you are.' She cast bemused eyes towards the man sitting next to George Mulligan on the sofa. 'I've always known that Leo was murdered. I told you that again yesterday.' She put up a manicured hand to brush a wayward burgundy curl away from her face. 'Leo was conducting an affair. If it led to his death, then he had no one to blame but himself.'

DS Scott answered her quietly, his gentle Welsh lilt surprisingly stern. 'Do you have any evidence of that, Verity? A name, for example?'

She let out a tiny gasp. 'Of course not. You don't think he would admit it?' She pouted. 'Why don't you try the girls in the shop? They might be able to tell you. It might even be one of them. Anything was possible with Leo.'

The atmosphere was cooling rapidly, but Mulligan's eyes were still on her face. 'We've applied for your husband's dental records this morning, to assist in identifying the body found in his vehicle.'

'I've already told you that it was Leo. I've identified his jewellery.'

'I'm afraid that's no longer enough. In the meantime, it would help if you could answer some further questions for us.' He cast a glance at DS Scott, a prompt to produce notebook and pen. 'Why didn't you tell us that your business was up for sale?'

'As I explained to the sergeant yesterday, I didn't believe it was relevant.'

'Like you didn't believe it was relevant to tell us he might be having an affair? I seem to recall that you originally told us he was playing poker on Monday evening.'

She pursed her lips. 'I told you that Leo was playing poker because that's the story that Leo had given to me.'

'But you didn't believe it.' Mulligan narrowed his eyes. 'And I don't believe it either.' He leaned forwards towards her. 'How well do you know Neil Redfern?'

'Neil who?' She whispered the name under her breath. 'Who the hell is Neil Redfern?'

'Well, to the best of my knowledge, he's the man who mows your lawn and valets your car.'

She flicked the green eyes sharply from Mulligan to Scott, and then back again. 'Is that his name? Redfern? I didn't know that.' She wrapped her arms across her chest in a loose hug. 'I just know him as Neil. In fact, I hardly know him at all. I think he's a punter at the shop. Leo felt sorry for him, so he gave him some odd jobs. It wasn't really anything to do with me.' She frowned. 'What's this got to do with Leo?'

'That's what we're trying to establish.' Mulligan exchanged another knowing glance with Scott. 'You see, I agree with you, Verity. I don't believe that your husband was playing poker. But I also don't believe that he was having an affair. I think that he was with Neil Redfern, and although I don't know why, I can promise you now that I will find out.'

Verity let out a laugh. 'What on earth would Leo have been doing with Neil? He's just some down and out, some loner who lives on the Barnfield estate and wastes his benefit money on the horses.'

'I'm surprised that you would know that much about him, Verity, considering you've just told us that you hardly knew him at all.' It was DS Scott who spoke. 'In fact, Neil Redfern is far from being a down and out. He's a professional man who has had a run of bad luck. And as to being a loner, he has a sister that's worried sick about him, and a nephew who adores him.'

The colour drained slowly from Verity Pearson's cheeks. 'A sister and a nephew?' She looked suddenly deflated. 'I didn't know that. Leo didn't say.' She turned her attention back to DS Scott. 'Surely if you believe that Leo was with this Neil, you could just track him down and ask him?'

'We'd love to ask him, Verity. But just like your husband, he disappeared on Monday evening. He told a neighbour he was going out for a pint or two, and he hasn't been seen since. We think he was going to meet Leo.'

She gave a bewildered shake of the burgundy curls. 'I'm sorry, I'm not quite sure I understand where all of this is leading. What has this got to do with me? Or with Leo? Have you done anything at all about trying to find the woman that Leo was having an affair with?'

'The other woman?' Mulligan's tone was incredulous. 'I'm not interested in this fictional other woman, Verity, or her fictional husband. I'm interested in the other man. I don't think your husband was being unfaithful. I think you were the unfaithful one.'

'How *dare* you?' Colour suffused back into Verity Pearson's face, and she flashed infuriated eyes at DS Scott. 'And do you believe that too? After everything I've told you?'

The sergeant's face was inscrutable. 'Neil Redfern is the

subject of a missing person case. And he's also a person of interest in our investigation into your husband's death.' He drew in a breath, and then quietly said 'if you know where he is, Verity, now would be the time to tell us.'

'I know this isn't the best of places to meet, but I wanted to get out of the office, and what I have to discuss with you is confidential. I don't think there's any risk of us being overheard, because no one from the office would be caught dead in here.' Rose cast a glance around the drab interior of the Abbey Tearooms. 'I can't imagine you've ever been in here before?'

'Actually, I have. This is where I met with Verity yesterday morning. I can only say that she wasn't impressed with my choice of venue.' Toby sounded weary. 'What is it that you want to discuss?'

'I want to talk to you about my meeting with Verity yesterday afternoon.' Rose stared down into a cool and insipid cup of coffee and resisted the temptation to drink it. 'I have to admit to being rather concerned about both the situation that Verity is in, and her understanding of it. I thought that she seemed rather ill-informed about her own financial situation. She didn't seem to understand that she was responsible for running the business now that Leo is gone, even though she's a director of the company. She's signed a personal guarantee for the commercial mortgages that are held on the business premises, without really understanding what that means. And she certainly didn't understand that the bank wouldn't just pay out on the insurance policies simply because she had turned up to make a claim.' Rose lifted concerned eyes to Toby's face. 'She didn't even seem to understand that she needed to consult with her solicitor over the circumstances of Leo's death.'

Toby put up a hand to rub at his forehead. 'Leo always

said that she didn't have a head for business, so there was no point in trying to explain it to her.'

'And it didn't trouble you, as their account manager, that you were dealing with a company director who didn't understand her responsibilities?'

He gave an indifferent shrug. 'She was more of a sleeping partner in the business. Leo used to joke that she was quite happy with the way things were – he earned the money, and she spent it for him. She certainly didn't have any difficult spending the money he earned. Or even the money that he'd borrowed. I think the two of them have always lived beyond their means, but somehow Leo just had the knack of being able to juggle it.' He muttered under his breath. 'I think, to be honest, that Leo was just as bad as Verity. That's why he wanted me to advance the business more money – he wanted to maintain his lifestyle until he'd found a buyer for the business. It would never occur to him to sell the house, or trade down to a smaller, less expensive car.'

'I see. And you, of course, were happy to help him live like that. Even if it meant disregarding banking regulation.' Rose watched as an unmistakable flash of indignation lit colour into Toby's cheeks, and she put up a hand to placate him. 'Oh, it's OK. I know that you've admitted to that, Toby, and I do appreciate your honesty. But there is something else I'd like to know. About the personal financial statement that Leo Pearson submitted to you along with his request to borrow more funding.' Her soft leather notebook was on the table in front of her, and she licked at an index finger and used it to turn the page. 'Back in February, when Leo put in an application to extend the business overdraft, did you run a formal credit check on him to verify that the numbers in his personal financial statement were true?'

Toby sucked in his cheeks. 'I don't understand what you're driving at.'

'No? Well, you've already admitted to me that the set of

business accounts Leo presented to you wasn't worth the paper it was printed on. I'm just asking if the same was true of the personal financial statement? Did you attempt to secure any kind of external verification on Leo Pearson's personal financial standing? Did you attempt to gain any kind of *internal* verification on the personal accounts that he held with the ENB? Because if you did, I couldn't find any evidence of it in the files.'

The blush in Toby's cheeks deepened to a guilty crimson. 'No, I didn't run a credit reference check. I'd already guessed that Leo was being economical with the truth.'

'And you weren't interested to know just how economical?'

'No. I thought, under the circumstances, it would be best not to know.'

'I'm sure you did.' Rose nodded to herself. 'Given the suspicious circumstances of your cousin's death, Toby, Clive has decided to freeze the proceeds of Leo's three insurance policies. Pending confirmation of how and why he died, the ENB will be taking steps to confirm that his death wasn't in any way engineered in order for his wife to benefit from the proceeds of the insurance policy.'

'You think that Leo might have committed suicide?' He sounded surprised.

'Or that he was murdered.' She spoke the words softly, and let him think about them before adding 'the bank will take a very dim view if there is any suggestion of insurance fraud. But that will be nothing compared with the view the police will take.'

Now the heightened colour drained back out of his cheeks, leaving a tell-tale pallor. 'Verity thinks that Leo was murdered.' His voice was low. 'She thinks he was murdered because he was having an affair. What could that possibly have to do with insurance fraud?'

Rose gave a shrug. 'Nothing, unless Leo changed the terms of the policies to enable a mistress to benefit from the proceeds.' She raised a mischievous eyebrow. 'Which he didn't, by the way. I've already checked.'

'Verity has done very well out of Leo's death, hasn't she?' Anger was growing in Toby's voice. 'She's accused him of having an affair, and tried to make out that it led to his death. But Leo adored Verity. He got himself into debt trying to please her. He was even selling the business because she wanted to retire abroad.' He swallowed hard, but the bile wouldn't be suppressed. 'It doesn't seem right, Rose. She's accused Leo of being unfaithful, she benefits financially from his death, and she doesn't even seem to be grieving.'

'She might not appear to be grieving, Toby, but we still have an obligation to her as a customer. Even though the circumstances of her husband's death are suspicious, we still have to ensure that we act in her best interests. Stacy is going to meet with her again this afternoon to discuss her financial position. In the meantime, you and I are going to work on a checklist of what needs to be done to complete the sale of Pearson the Bookmaker, and to settle its outstanding liabilities.'

Toby considered the suggestion, and then leaned back in his seat and folded his arms across his chest. 'Do *you* think that Verity was somehow involved in Leo's death?'

Inscrutability settled firmly across Rose Bennett's face. 'I think your cousin died so that someone could benefit from his death. Someone who benefitted so much that they were prepared to help him on his way. As to whether that someone was Verity Pearson, at this stage I couldn't really say.'

14

Benny Bradman raised his glass to George Mulligan with a cheerful smile. 'Well, this is an unexpected pleasure, George. I weren't expectin' lunch in the Crown and Anchor today. Is this goin' on your expenses?'

Mulligan snorted. 'I shouldn't think so. But I'm happy to put my hand in my pocket and stand you a pie and a pint if it means you can help move my investigation forward.' He rested his arms on the edge of the table. 'Leo Pearson's death is a murder case now. I've spoken to Verity Pearson this morning to let her know.'

'How did she take it?'

'Not very well, because I left her in no doubt that she was a person of interest in the enquiry.'

Benny let out a low whistle. 'Well I hope if you feel the need to arrest her you can see your way to holdin' off until the sale has gone through. I don't want my business plans in limbo.' He thought for a moment, and then said 'I had supper with her yesterday evenin', George. She doesn't strike me as a grievin' widow. I was lucky I had the dog with me, else I might have ended up as the dessert.' He chuckled at the thought. 'Mind you, me and Mac are in the dog house with Rose anyway. I wouldn't care, but it was her idea for me to talk to Verity Pearson in the first place.'

'And does it bother you if Rose Bennett's nose is out of joint?' The policeman sounded amused. 'You're a brave man if you're harbouring ambitions in that direction, Benny. The women in that family don't take any prisoners.' His voice took on a wistful note. 'You know I had a thing going with her aunt, back in the day? She was a career woman like Rose. There was no chance of her sitting at home waiting for a junior plod to come in for his supper.' He snorted a self-deprecating laugh.

'Well, Lu Aylesbury is a one-off, George. I reckon you had a lucky escape there. Some women are just made to be worshipped from afar.' He put out a hand and nudged at the policeman's arm. 'You've had a good life with Mrs Mulligan, would you really have wanted it any other way?'

'No, I don't suppose I would.' Mulligan nodded to himself. 'Which is probably why I'm having trouble getting my head around this case. Verity Pearson has been married for well over thirty years, by all accounts, but she doesn't seem to give a damn that her old man has been fried to a crisp. Scottie had her down at first as a bored and lonely housewife, but if that was the case I'd expect to see some vulnerability. She strikes me more as the man-eating type.' A smile began to tug at the corner of his mouth. 'Did she try to make a pass at you yesterday evening, then?'

'I didn't give her the chance, George. But I can't say the question surprises me. She asked me to stay and have a bite to eat because she was lonely, and I had my orders from Rose to take any opportunity to find out a bit more about her, and about the business, so I accepted. And then I had the pleasure of listenin' to her moan on about what a terrible husband Leo had been, but how she was goin' to struggle without him even though their marriage hadn't been a happy one.'

'Did you believe her?'

'Not a word of it. I don't know what kind of a husband he was, but I know real grief when I see it. I've felt it, George. It eats away at you. When I lost Catriona it was like someone had turned off all the lights, like I was going to spend the rest of my life livin' in the dark. Verity Pearson ain't strugglin'. But she's makin' a good show of it.'

'Do you think it's all an act?'

'Let's just say she's still got her wits about her in some respects. I offered to spend a few hours in the shop each day this week until the sale goes through, and she's already tried to palm the shop keys and the combination of the safe onto me this mornin'. I think she wants the place off her hands so much that she'd hand it all over to me now if she could, even though the contracts aren't signed.'

'So you're still going ahead and buying the place?'

'I don't see why not, but I'm not going to be payin' what she's askin'. Rose has done me a big favour there, drawin' my attention to the accounts. I've done a bit of diggin' for myself, and it turns out that Leo Pearson has been nursin' what I would call a sick punter.' Benny took a long drink from his glass. 'He's been takin' big cash bets from a bloke who couldn't afford to place them. Those bets made Pearson the Bookmaker look a lot more profitable as a business than it really was.' He placed the glass back down on the table. 'I don't like to see people sufferin', George. I want to have a word with this bloke.'

'Will you be able to get him some help?'

Benny grunted. 'That's a part of it. But it ain't all altruism with me. I don't like bein' taken for a mug, either. The cash behind those big bets must have been comin' from somewhere. And I think I've spotted a pattern in Leo Pearson's accounts that suggest there was somethin' very dodgy indeed goin' on. Those big cash bets always added up to around five hundred quid. And they always came in just a day or two after Leo Pearson had made a cash withdrawal from his business account.'

'Also for five hundred quid?'

Benny winked. 'You're catchin' on fast, George.'

'So what would be the point of that?'

'Leo chalks up the cash he's taken out of the account as part of his salary, or a director's loan, or whatever. There are plenty of ways an accountant can dress up cash goin' out of the business. But in reality, he gives the cash to this punter to spend how he likes in the shop. The punter comes in and blows the lot. That makes the takin's look good, so the shop looks more profitable.' He jabbed at his chest with his thumb. 'And muggins here is taken in by the scam and offers the askin' price.'

Mulligan tilted his head with a frown. 'That's a bit obvious, isn't it? Wouldn't it have been better if the punter had spread the bets over a number of days?'

'Have you ever tried givin' a problem punter five hundred quid and tellin' him to spend it slowly? In the punter's head, that's five hundred opportunities to win more cash. He'll tell himself that he can stake the lot in one day, win at least the five hundred back, and be back in the shop for another go tomorrow. The reality is that he stakes the five hundred, and probably a bit more on top of that, and walks away with nothin' until he gets the next hand-out.'

'Does Rose know about this? Would it be of interest to the bank?'

Benny growled. 'She'd know about it if I weren't in the dog house. I've been tryin' to tell her all mornin', but she ain't returnin' my calls. I'll be tryin' again after lunch. Maybe if I try bribin' her with dinner at Umberto's she'll think about it.' He let out a sigh. 'Anyway, this bloke has gone to ground, so I'm tryin' to have a word with his sister. She knows about his addiction, and she's worried about the fact that he's gone missin'.'

Mulligan's eyelids flickered. And then he said 'and I think that's where I came in, Benny.' He placed his glass down on the table. 'I'll lay odds that your sick punter is a bloke called Neil Redfern.'

'How the hell did you know that, George?'

'Because off the record, Neil Redfern is the other person of interest in our enquiry into Leo Pearson's death.'

DS Scott brought the Audi to a halt halfway down

Mulberry Avenue, and pulled on the handbrake with a heavy heart. There were times that he hated his job.

Granted those times were few and far between, or he would never have made it to detective sergeant. It had always been his way to err on the side of optimism, and he'd worked hard over the years not to let the rigours of the role sour his soul. But there was no denying that the last twenty-four hours had been a challenge.

He turned to look through the car's window at Evie Green's neat little two-up-two-down, with its spotless white net curtains and gleaming brass door knocker, and a sudden knot of tension began to build in the pit of his stomach.

For God's sake, man, will you pull yourself together?

He drew in a deep breath to calm himself. All he had to do was remember that he was on duty. He was here to tell Neil Redfern's sister that her brother had been heard moving around in his flat. That rather than missing, he appeared to have gone to ground. That a woman's voice had been heard in his flat. And that her brother was now a person of interest in the investigation into Leo Pearson's death.

But it wasn't really going to be that easy, was it? Because Evie Green wasn't just a suspect's sister. And Ian Scott wasn't just here on duty.

He closed his eyes and gritted his teeth. He wished that he could prove George Mulligan wrong. George was more than a senior officer. He was a friend. There had never been bad blood between them until now. And that blood was turning bad because Mulligan had designated Neil Redfern a suspect, and tasked Scott with the job of tracking him down. No, more than that – he'd tasked Scott with the job, and then accused him of dragging his heels because he'd taken a fancy to the suspect's sister.

There was only one way to resolve this. To carry out his duty, to let Evie Green know they'd applied for a warrant to search her brother's flat, and to offer her one last opportunity to come clean if she knew more than she'd already shared. Like it or not, George Mulligan was right – Neil Redfern had to be found, and he had to be questioned. They had to establish where he was on Monday evening, whether he saw or spoke to Leo Pearson, and whether he had any sort of relationship with the dead man's wife. And if Neil Redfern was the man his sister claimed, a good man fallen on hard times, then being questioned by the police about his whereabouts on Monday evening shouldn't pose him with any kind of a problem. He should be pleased to be eliminated from their enquiries.

Scott opened his eyes and turned to open the car door. The sooner he got this out of the way, the sooner the drama would be over. He swung his body out onto the pavement, and as he did so a movement at the window caught his attention, a twitch of the spotless white curtains. She was watching him get out of the car.

He slammed the door behind him and turned towards the house with an unwelcome sense of foreboding. He had to know now that Neil Redfern was innocent, that everything Evie had said about her brother was true.

And not just because he wanted to prove George Mulligan wrong.

'Toby? Whatever are you doing here?' Verity Pearson regarded the young man with a suspicious eye. 'I thought you weren't meant to meet with me unless it was on ENB premises?' Her suspicion gave way to a cautious smile. 'Well, you'd better come in, since you're here.' She stepped back from the door and turned on her heel without waiting for an answer. 'Has Rose Bennett decided that you can be trusted again?' She threw the words over her shoulder.

'I've been speaking to your accountant about the sale of the business. I thought I would come over and give you an update.' He followed her meekly across the hall, and paused in the kitchen doorway to watch as she lifted the kettle from its base, and set about filling it with water. 'The advance that Rose promised you against the keyman insurance policy has been deposited to your account. Your accountant has agreed to deal with the final salary calculations for you, and he's happy to sort out the utility bills if you forward them to him. But he'll need you to sanction the payments from the business account.'

'Will you be able to help me to do that?'

'Of course.' He nodded. 'I've been thinking, too, about what you said yesterday. About family looking after each other, and what Leo would have wanted me to do.' He cleared his throat. 'How have things been for you today?'

She rattled the kettle back onto its base and flicked at the switch with a furious finger. 'How have things been?' Her tone was mocking. 'Well frankly, Toby, they've been beastly.' She reached up into a cupboard to pull out a jar of coffee. 'The police have confirmed that Leo died under suspicious circumstances. I mean, for heaven's sake, tell me something that I don't know.'

He moved away from the doorway, and hoisted himself up onto a stool next to the breakfast bar. 'So if they think it was a suspicious death, they must know how Leo died?'

'They said that the fire was started deliberately. That Leo was probably unconscious in the car when the fire was set.'

'And do they have any idea who was responsible?'

'Oh, they've come up with some utterly ludicrous suggestion, some person called Neil Redfern.' She set the jar of coffee down on the counter and pushed herself away from it, then turned to glide towards the breakfast bar until she was close enough for his breath to be caught by her cloying, musky perfume. 'I don't suppose you ever heard Leo mention him?'

Toby leaned back a little, uncomfortable with her closeness. 'No, I've never heard of him. Why would the police think he had a reason to hurt Leo?'

'I don't know. I've been asking myself the same question.' She hoisted herself up onto an empty stool beside him. 'I know this Neil. Leo brought him to the house once or twice. He did some odd jobs for us around the house and garden, cutting the grass, cleaning the cars, that sort of thing. I think he had a problem with the gambling, and he'd run up a big slate with Leo at the shop. Leo told me that he felt sorry for him, that it made him feel better putting a few pounds back in the man's pocket to make up for his losses.'

'That doesn't sound like a reason to commit murder. It's sounds as though Leo was trying to help him.'

'I know. But I can't help wondering whether there was more to it. I mean, Leo said that he was quite a heavy gambler, and they were always having to extend him credit at the shop. I suppose they could have got into an argument about it? What if Leo had asked him to pay back what he owed, and the man turned nasty?'

'Is that what the police think happened?'

She flicked the green eyes away from him. 'I don't know what they think. I mean, I've tried to explain to them about Leo always having his little affairs on the side, but they don't want to know about that. It seems the most obvious solution to me. That if they can track down whichever little tart Leo had been spending his spare time with these days, then they'll have the motive for the murder, and they'll find the man behind it. I still think he was probably attacked by a jealous boyfriend or husband.' Her eyes were beginning to fill with tears, and she lifted them up to the ceiling. 'I know you were fond of him, Toby. But you never saw Leo's dark side. There was always another woman, just like there was always another financial crisis.' She fished into the pocket of her woollen dress, but there was nothing to be retrieved.

'It doesn't sound to me like the Leo I knew.' Toby sank a hand into his own jacket pocket, and pulled out a clean cotton handkerchief. 'How could we both know him so well, and yet see someone so different?'

'How?' She took the handkerchief from him with a tearful sniff. 'Because he was a liar.' She dabbed at her eyes. 'You don't really think he had any intention of paying that money back to the bank, do you? He didn't have a solution for repaying that shortfall. That was just something he was saying to keep you quiet while he worked out a way to wriggle out of it. Why do you think he didn't want to meet with you on Monday evening?' She didn't wait for an answer. 'It wouldn't have surprised me to learn that he was planning to run out on both of us.'

'But you said he was on his way to see me. You thought that he was stuck in traffic.'

'Because that was what I'd been told to say to you. Leo asked me to lie to you.'

'He asked you to lie to me?' He repeated her words, as if hearing them again would make them somehow a bit easier to believe. But it didn't work. 'Verity, I'm sorry, I still don't understand what that has to do with Leo's death? And where does Neil Redfern fit into it?'

'Leo disappeared on Monday evening. I knew that he wasn't coming back to the house straight away, because he didn't want to meet with you. According to the police, Neil Redfern also disappeared on Monday evening.' She coughed out a laugh. 'I know that this is going to sound utterly ridiculous, but the police have concocted some ridiculous notion that I was having a fling with this Neil Redfern, behind your cousin's back. And they think that Neil Redfern murdered Leo in order to get him out of the way.' She settled a hand on his arm. 'Of course, that's too ridiculous for words. We both know that I would never dream of being unfaithful to Leo, however badly he treated me. But,' she squeezed his arm gently, 'that doesn't mean that Neil Redfern might not have been responsible for Leo's death, does it? I mean, what if I was wrong? What if this time Leo wasn't having an affair at all, but he'd had some sort of argument with Neil Redfern about money?' She tightened her grip. 'What if Leo died because of something that happened at the shop?'

15

Evie Green looked uncomfortable perched on the hard wooden visitor's chair in front of Leo Pearson's desk. 'I had a visit from the police earlier this afternoon. DS Scott said that a neighbour heard Neil moving around in his flat, talking to a woman.' Her voice expressed confusion. 'He said he's become … what's that phrase? A "person of interest"?'

'Well, I'm sorry to hear that.' Benny spoken as gently as he could, hoping to put her at ease. 'I can't say I'm too bothered about what's happened to Leo Pearson. But I am interested in what's happened to your brother. I'm buyin' Leo's business, and I want to make sure that I'm not inheritin' a problem gambler at the same time. The girls here tell me that Neil spends a lot of time in this shop, stakin' money that he can't really afford to stake.'

She didn't seem surprised. 'I knew it was turning into a problem, but I didn't know how bad. To be honest, I've been worried that he's done something stupid. Or maybe that his disappearance is some sort of cry for help. But if I can't find him, I can't help him.'

'Has Neil always been a gambler?'

She considered the question with a frown. 'No more so than anyone else. He used to have a flutter on the Grand National, and that was about it. But after his wife left him, and he lost his job, he seemed to lose hope somehow. And then he started to gamble at Pearson's. When I asked him about it, he said it was nothing to worry about. That it was just a way for him to get out of the flat and pass the time while he was looking for work.' Her frown deepened. 'But I think the addiction took hold quite quickly.'

'Has he ever tried to get help?'

'No. Because he's never really acknowledged that he has a problem.' A look of distrust made its way across her face. 'Anyway, why would that be of interest to you? You make your living by taking money from gamblers.'

Benny felt a familiar pang of disappointment. She wasn't the first person to suggest that his business model was built on taking other people's money from them, and this wasn't the first time he'd felt the need to justify his own behaviours. 'I got into this game because I've always loved sport.' He swivelled slightly in his chair. 'For me, sport is about human achievement – runnin' faster, swimmin' further, showin' that you've got a greater level of skill than your opponent.'

'You don't have to throw money down the drain to enjoy sport.'

'And neither you do, Evie. I don't disagree with that. But for some people, it adds to the entertainment. My old mum, she used to love an afternoon at the races. At least once a year I'd take her to an afternoon meetin' somewhere quiet. She'd dress up in her best gear, treat herself to a new hat, and buy a copy of the Racin' Post on her way to the course. I'd treat her to a cream tea in the restaurant, and she'd go through the race card like a pro.' It was a happy memory. 'I can see her now, lickin' the end of her pencil and tickin' off the horse that she fancied in each race. And she always had a flutter. A pound each way on every race. Never a penny more or less. If there were any winnin's at the end of the day, she'd spend them on a box of chocolates on the way home. The bigger the win, the bigger the box.' He chuckled under his breath. 'And if she lost all her stake money, I'd buy her a box myself to make up for it.'

'You make it sound so simple. But it's not like that for Neil. It's ruining his life.'

'I know it is, girl.' He knew there were no words to console her. 'My old mum, she gambled for fun, and she knew when to stop. Your Neil? If he's gone through a bad patch, then it sounds to me as though he's started gamblin' to take his mind off things, and it's escalated out of control. That can happen when you start losin' money. I've seen it all before. It's not so much that the punter wants to win, they gamble because they can't bear to admit how much they've lost. It's the drive to win it back that fuels the addiction.' He shook his head. 'I run my business for the folks that enjoy a flutter, Evie. I'm not in the game to ruin people's lives.' He looked away from her for a moment, and then turned back and said 'I've heard that your brother was gamblin' large amounts of cash at Pearson's. Would you have any idea where he was gettin' the money from?'

Evie looked bemused. 'He only has his benefits to live on, but I know that Leo Pearson used to put odd jobs his way.'

'Odd jobs don't pay five hundred quid a pop.'

'How much?' The shock on her face was genuine. 'He couldn't possibly have been gambling that sort of money.' She looked worried now. 'Where on earth was he getting that from?'

'My theory was that he was gettin' it from Leo Pearson. I think Leo Pearson was givin' him that cash to gamble, as long as he spent it over the counter at Pearson the Bookmaker. And I think he was doin' it to make the business look more profitable before he sold it to me. And I think that's a pretty shabby thing to do, if I'm honest, to put that pressure on a problem punter, knowin' that he won't have the strength to say no.' Benny swivelled gently in his chair. 'The question is, Evie, did your brother know that's why he was bein' given the cash? And supposin' that he did, is that why no one can find him now?'

George Mulligan grumbled under his breath as the wall clock in his office chimed the arrival of four o'clock. The afternoon was almost over, and there was still no sign of the mobile phone records he'd requested, Leo Pearson's dental records, or the warrant that he needed to search Neil Redfern's flat. He raised himself out of his seat and cast a glance through the glass wall at the other side of his desk. The normally-busy outer office was empty, save for the presence of DS Ian Scott. Even with the glass between them he could feel the sergeant's discordant energy, Scott's frustrations still evident in the tense set of his jaw and the stiffness in his shoulders as he hunched over a computer keyboard.

Mulligan sank back behind his desk with a regretful sigh. At least Scottie had come to the right conclusion, that duty came first before inclination. He just wished it hadn't been necessary for him to call out the behaviour in the first place.

He stretched out a hand to the in-tray on his desk, and pulled two large pieces of paper from the top shelf. He placed them down on the desk side by side, the one on the left a paper copy of the photograph of Leo Pearson that Scottie had procured from his wife, the one on the right of Neil Redfern with his nephew. Mulligan stared at the two, his eyes moving back and forth from one to the other, and muttered to himself under his breath.

One of them dead, one of them missing.

Both of them tall, both of them slim, but where Leo Pearson had let himself go and developed a mid-life gut and a jowl at the jaw, Neil Redfern was still trim, still youthfully handsome. There must have been ten years between them at least. Redfern's hair was still thick and dark, while Pearson's sandy locks were thinning at the crown. Pearson looked smug, supercilious, and self-satisfied, while Redfern just looked unhappy, the hollow smile on his face forced for the benefit of the child at his side.

If only a picture could talk.

Mulligan's brows beetled forwards. He knew there was some vital point he was missing, some critical piece of the picture that still eluded him. The links between the two men were undeniable now. Leo Pearson paid Neil Redfern to do odd jobs, and in return Neil Redfern obligingly spent all his available cash in Pearson's betting shop. And if Benny Bradman's hunch was right, the two of them had colluded in a scam to inflate the value of Pearson the Bookmaker until a suitable buyer had been hooked.

But why would that lead to Leo Pearson's death?

Was that where Verity Pearson came in? Did Neil Redfern provide the means, and Verity Pearson the motive? Did she ask Neil Redfern to murder her husband, to set her free from an unhappy marriage? Did Leo Pearson have to die so that his wife could benefit financially from his death? And was she planning to take Neil Redfern with her, to start that new life in Portugal not with her husband, but with her lover? Was that why he'd been holed up in the flat, just waiting for the right time to make his move? Was he waiting for Verity to pocket the cash, so that the two of them could disappear from view, leaving the police to scout around for a mistress that didn't exist, forlornly hoping that they might turn up some aggrieved and violent fictional husband or boyfriend who would carry the blame for Leo's death?

Mulligan bent forward and pulled the two pictures closer to him, sliding them across the desk with his forefingers. He wasn't even sure what he was looking for. He just hoped that if he kept on looking, he would find it.

One of them missing, one of them dead.

One of them barely lamented by his wife, one sorely missed by his sister. He put up a hand to rub at his temple.

Why did Verity Pearson seem so surprised when DS Scott mentioned Neil's sister? Did she think she was the only woman in Neil Redfern's life? Had it come as a surprise to learn that there was a family, a sibling, a nephew, another claim on his time, another player who might add to the risk of their duplicity being uncovered?

Frustrated by his blindness, Mulligan lifted his hands to his face, and rubbed at his eyelids with his fists. He knew it was there, the answer, he knew it was in open sight but he just couldn't damn well see it.

Leo Pearson was dead. His body – or at least what was left of his body – had been found in his burnt out car. Found with his jewellery, a wedding ring and a necklace that his wife had identified as belonging to her husband. Funny, he thought, how gold always survives the flames. How a conflagration can destroy a body, and yet still not reach the heat required to melt the trappings and adornments of a man's simple human vanities.

Simple human vanities?

He opened his eyes and turned them down to re-examine the photograph of Leo Pearson on his desk. And then he laughed under his breath, a quiet inward chuckle of satisfaction, and stretched out a hand to the phone.

Rose Bennett let the door to Julia Spencer's office swing closed behind her, and sank onto a chair at the small meeting table, her mobile phone still pressed to her ear. 'I'm still here, Clive. I've just popped into Julia's office to get a bit of privacy. I wouldn't want our conversation to be overheard.' She had carried her soft leather notebook with her, and she opened it out onto the table with her free hand. 'Yes, I have quite a bit to share with you. But I don't think you're going to like it much. I still haven't received official confirmation from the police that Leo Pearson's death was suspicious, so with Stacy's help I've been trying to get a better picture of the Pearsons' overall financial situation.'

'I see.' Clive's tone was wry. 'I can't imagine that the view from the bridge was a good one.'

That would be putting it mildly. 'Stacy ran a credit reference check for me, and it's turned up a whole pile of additional credit card debt. The Pearsons have been teetering on the brink financially for months now. I'm guessing that they were trying to sell the business to cut short their losses, but I have no idea what their fall-back plan was going to be for the rest. Without the business there would be no income. They wouldn't have been able to afford their mortgage, let alone any other commitments. Even selling the house would have left them with sizeable personal debts.'

'Perhaps, Rose, they didn't have a fall-back plan. The business was up for sale for many months. I suppose it's possible that they tried to sell it prior to liquidating any other assets, but were unable to find a buyer until now. Perhaps they even planned to just post the keys of the house back through our door and skip to the continent. They wouldn't be the first couple to run away from their debts, and they most certainly won't be the last. Have you spoken to Toby Dugdale about this?'

'Not as such. I spoke to him this morning, before I knew how bad things were, and he admitted that he didn't make any attempt to validate the personal financial information that Leo Pearson had given him. He accepted a statement from Leo that declared the mortgage, three credit cards with a combined outstanding balance of eight thousand pounds, and their car finance.' She ran a finger down a meticulously scripted list in her notebook. 'According to the credit check that Stacy ran, Leo and Verity Pearson had fourteen credit cards between them, with an outstanding balance of close to a hundred thousand pounds, and some of the accounts had already fallen into arrears.'

'Why on earth is this only coming to light now?'

'Because Toby knew that things were bad, but he also knew that if he ran a credit reference check to confirm how bad they were, then the bank's lending process would have prevented him from advancing any further credit to his cousin.'

Clive's voice grew terse. 'Am I to understand that our computer systems don't make it mandatory for such a check to be carried out on a business customer?'

Rose smiled to herself. 'No, they don't make it mandatory, Clive. Because you yourself wanted the decision to rest with the account manager. You said that if we coded the check into the system, the ENB would lose the ability to take a bespoke approach to every business customer, and end up with that "computer says no" situation that you're always telling me you're so keen for the bank to avoid.' She waited for the message to land, and then added 'which is why I think we've ended up here in the first place. You originally wanted me to investigate whether the lending process was too lax, or whether Toby Dugdale had committed a crime. And I think the answer is that the process is as lax as you wanted it to be, and whilst it didn't necessarily lead Toby to commit a crime, it certainly gave him the opportunity to advance more credit than he should have done.'

There was a dry silence at the other end of the line, and then Clive asked 'putting your opinion of my personal failures to one side, Rose, may I ask why you've been unable to discuss the full situation with Toby Dugdale?'

'Well, mainly because I haven't been able to find him. I've been trying to track him down since early this afternoon, but he isn't answering his phone, and he hasn't been back to his desk. According to Julia, he told one of his colleagues that he was going out to visit a client, and he hasn't been seen or heard from since.'

'This is most troubling. I'm sorry to overrule your advice, but I think the time has come to remove Toby from the investigation and begin disciplinary procedures against him.'

'I don't see how you can. If you do that, and Toby is guilty of involvement in either a fraud or a suspicious death, you'll be tipping him off. You'll be letting him know that we're onto him. Don't you think it would be better for us to keep him close? It's only a matter of time before the police want to speak to him.'

16

George Mulligan swung his aging green Toyota onto the slip road, and accelerated down towards the Kirkby bypass without a word. He eased the car onto the carriageway behind a slow-moving saloon, and cursed impatiently under his breath as he waited for a gap in the adjacent lane. 'Where the hell are all these people going anyway?' The car jolted as he pulled hard on the wheel, and then swerved right into a shrinking space between a lorry and a transit van.

'It's called the "rush hour" for a reason, George. And you didn't have to drive. I would have been happy to take you in the Audi.' DS Scott turned his head to look out of the passenger window at the passing darkness. 'I don't see what difference it would have made.'

Mulligan curbed his irritation. 'Your car has already been seen outside Neil Redfern's flat. It's possible that whoever is in there would recognise it. You might have been seen yesterday evening, when you were standing in the street talking to the neighbour.'

'Well, whoever it is who's in there – always assuming that there *is* anyone in there – isn't going to open the door to us anyway.' Scott turned to look at his senior officer with weary eyes. 'Just what is it that you're hoping to find in there, George?'

'The answer to the problem.' Mulligan gave an irascible shake of the head. 'I don't know for certain, but I've got a hunch.' He glanced at the sergeant, his eyes flicking from the road to DS Scott's face and back again. 'You've seen the pictures of Leo Pearson and Neil Redfern. When you examined those pictures, didn't something strike you about the two of them?'

'Nothing much. Apart from how different they are. Leo Pearson was middle-aged, flabby, past his best. His hair was thinning, his face was lined. Neil Redfern is younger, fitter, better looking. A man still in his prime.'

Mulligan's eyes were still focused on the road ahead. 'What about how similar they are? What about height? Or build?'

'Well, I suppose they're about the same height. And they would be the same build, if Leo Pearson hadn't let himself go. But there's a good ten to fifteen years' age difference between the two of them, and Neil Redfern has a head of thick, dark hair. Leo Pearson's hair wasn't just thinning, it was a different colour.'

'And does that matter when you're looking at a burnt-out corpse?' The inspector permitted himself a momentary grin. 'Come on Scottie, I know you've got the hump with me, but put your brain into it. Differences like age and hair colour and muscle tone don't matter so much when you're dealing with the victim of a fire.' He cast another glance at the sergeant. 'Until we get hold of Leo Pearson's dental records, we have to make the best deductions we can about the identity of the remains for in his car. Agreed?'

DS Scott frowned. 'Agreed. But I still don't really see where you're going with this.'

'So think it through. What assumptions have we made about the identity of those remains?'

'We've assumed that the remains are those of Leo Pearson, because they were found in Leo Pearson's car, and no one has heard from him since he left the shop on Monday afternoon. And because his jewellery was found in the wreckage. His widow has confirmed that the gold neck chain and wedding ring belonged to him.'

'And what was missing?' Mulligan grinned as he flicked on the car's indicator. 'What else would you have expected to find in that car, amongst the victim's remains, if the victim of that fire was Leo Pearson?' He guided the car up the exit lane, and braked at the approaching junction. 'What else do we know about Leo Pearson? What else should we have found in that wreckage, that we would have expected Jimmy Miller to point out in the forensic examination? What else do we know about Leo Pearson that might distinguish him from any other potential victim of that fire? Even before we get his dental records?'

DS Scott turned his head away, and scowled through the window into the early-evening darkness. 'I have no idea what you're driving at, George. Hell's teeth …' He stopped, and blinked, and then slowly turned back to the chief inspector. 'Bloody hell, George, you're right. There *was* something missing from those remains. Leo Pearson had a gold tooth. And there was no gold tooth found with the remains.'

Mulligan gave a triumphant snort. 'It might only be a small distinction, Scottie, and we might not know yet who did die in that fire. But we know how damned thorough Jimmy Miller is. And if he didn't find a gold tooth with the remains of that body, then there was no gold tooth to be found. And that says to me that the body in the car wasn't Leo Pearson.'

'So the burning question now, if you'll pardon the unfortunate pun, is "just whose body was that in the car?"'

'Is it?' Mulligan pulled the car away from the junction and pointed it in the direction of the Barnfield Estate. 'I thought the burning question now was "if that wasn't Leo Pearson's body in the car, then where the hell is Leo Pearson?"'

Benny Bradman lifted the bottle of Chablis from a

tarnished ice bucket at the edge of the table, and topped up Rose Bennett's glass. 'I still can't believe you passed up dinner at Umberto's in favour of this.' He cast his eyes around him in a good-humoured attempt to feign indignation.

'That is because you haven't yet worked out that I'm a woman of simple tastes.' Rose lifted her glass and sipped on it. 'And because Umberto's won't let Mac sit underneath the table, while a pub like The Feathers doesn't mind the odd four-legged customer.' She looked down towards her feet, where the terrier was curled up awaiting his supper. 'He'll be happy with a spoonful of casserole, although it's more than he deserves after staying out all night with you.' She turned back to Benny. 'Anyway, I am planning to order all three courses from the most expensive end of the menu, and I'll be looking for a large liqueur with my coffee, so you're not getting away with it that lightly.'

'I wouldn't expect anythin' less.' He topped up his own glass from the bottle, before pushing it back into the bucket. 'If I'm honest, Rose, I ain't disappointed with the comfy choice of venue. I don't know what your day's been like, but I hope it was better than mine.'

'I wish I could say yes, but I very much doubt it. I spent most of the day working out just how much debt Leo and Verity Pearson had been carrying, and trying to second-guess whether Verity Pearson is as scatter-brained as she tries to make out. On top of that, I've lost Toby Dugdale – I'm supposed to be keeping him under observation, which is a bit difficult when he absents himself from the office in the middle of the working day, and refuses to answer his phone.' She rolled her eyes heavenward. 'Oh yes, and I've had an excruciating conversation with Clive, during which I had to heartlessly point out that his flexible approach to business lending had landed the ENB with an unacceptable level of risk.'

'Was that all?'

Rose pondered the question. 'No, I forgot one. After my conversation with Clive, I amused myself by spending two hours staring at Pearson the Bookmaker's bank statements, trying to work out why Leo Pearson kept withdrawing fistfuls of cash from his business account. I did manage to identify a strange repeat pattern, though, between the cash withdrawn and the amount of cash receipts taken back in over the counter. If I didn't know better, I'd say that someone was gambling that cash back in over the counter.' She turned her eyes towards him. 'Did you really miss those cash withdrawals when you examined the accounts, Benny? Did you really not spot that there was something dodgy going on?'

'If I'm honest, I spotted them. I just didn't want to believe it.' Benny pushed his wine glass to one side, and folded his arms onto the table. 'I suppose the fact that we both came to the same conclusion means it's pretty indisputable. I reckon that Leo Pearson was givin' that cash to a punter in the shop, and lettin' him gamble it back in over the counter to make the business look more profitable. I even think I know who that punter was. I think I've traced it back to a bloke called Neil Redfern, a regular at Pearson's shop.' His brow furrowed. 'At least, he used to be a regular at the shop. But now he's gone missin', just like Leo Pearson. I've been speakin' to George Mulligan about it today. He's lookin' for Neil Redfern in connection with Leo Pearson's death. And I've been speakin' to his sister. We're all beginnin' to think that if we can track down Neil, we can find out what happened to Leo Pearson.'

Rose ran a contemplative finger around the rim of her wine glass, and then ventured a provocative question. 'So if everyone thinks that Neil Redfern had something to do with Leo Pearson's disappearance, and what we assume to be Leo Pearson's death, then where does Verity Pearson fit into all of this?'

An unbidden smile began to flicker around Benny's

lips. 'I wondered when Verity Pearson's name would come into it. You know, I can't help thinkin' that you ought to be standin' me dinner tonight, rather than the other way around. I was on dangerous territory last night. It was a good job that I had Mac with me for protection. I don't think you realise just how far I stuck my neck out for you.'

Rose fought back a smile of her own. 'And did it do us any good? Did you learn anything about Verity or Leo Pearson that might be useful to the investigation?'

'I doubt it. She spent most of the evenin' bangin' on about what a terrible husband Leo was, and then contradictin' herself by sayin' how much she was goin' to miss him.'

'Did she sound genuine?'

'George Mulligan asked me the same question. It just looked like an act to me.' He shook his head. 'I don't know what you expected me to find out. She's still plannin' to sell the business, and she's still plannin' to retire abroad. She's talkin' about sellin' the house, collectin' on the insurance, and then disappearin' to Portugal, just like she and Leo had planned to do together.'

Rose picked up her wine glass and sipped from it, eyeing Benny over the rim. 'Well I have to admire her optimism. It isn't a given that the insurance policies will pay out. And not just because the circumstances of Leo Pearson's death were suspicious.' She gave a gentle shake of the head. 'We're picking up signs of insurance fraud.' She watched Benny's face and waited for the words to sink in. 'Until we know for certain that the body in the car was definitely Leo Pearson, and we're able to confirm that Verity had nothing to do with his death, Clive won't part with a penny of that insurance money.'

'But Verity Pearson will need somethin' to live on, Rose. If the sale of the business goes through, she won't have any income at all. How will she manage on a day to day basis? She was dependent on Leo for everythin'.'

'I don't disagree with that. But the way I see things, it

doesn't really matter whether the sale of the business goes through or not. If it turns out that she *did* have something to do with her husband's death, how she will manage on a day to day basis might be the least of her problems.

17

Toby Dugdale knocked back the remains of his whisky and soda, and banged the empty glass down onto the table. On any other day, in any other establishment, the resulting clatter might have drawn some attention. In the Jug and Ferret, on a busy Thursday evening, the sound simply dissipated into the deafening competition between an over-loud jukebox, a rattling fruit machine, and the overexcited chatter of a boisterous Kirkby clientele.

He pushed the glass away from him with a finger and then pulled a second drink towards him, staring down into the barely-fizzing liquid before lifting it to his lips and draining half the contents in one bitter, indignant gulp. *You think you know someone. You think you can trust them.* He was breathing heavily now, and he sipped again on the whisky in an attempt to calm his nerves. *But you can never really know someone, can you? And you can never really be sure that you can trust them.* He held the glass close to his mouth, ready to sip again. *When was he ever going to learn? That there's only one person you can trust in life, and that's yourself. Screw everybody else. Screw them. Screw the whole, bloody lot of them.*

'Toby? Is everything alright?'

He barely heard the familiar voice above the hum of the music, and he turned his head slowly to the left to see where the words had come from. He saw the legs first, long and slim, then he raised his eyes gradually past a tightly-fitting navy blue mini-dress to the slickly-glossed lips that had spoken. Stacy Singleton was peering down at him, her eyes concerned, her mouth turned out in a solicitous pout. She was holding a half-finished gin and tonic in one hand, and pointing to the empty seat beside him with the other. 'May I?'

He swallowed hard, and gave a reluctant nod. 'If you must.'

She sank onto the chair. 'This place is just awful, isn't it? I don't know why we come in here.' She cast a glance around her, and gently jerked her head in the direction of a small group of girls standing drinking at the bar. 'It's my friend Lydia's birthday today, so we're just having a quick one in here before we go for a bite to eat.' She swept her eyes back to his face. 'You know that Rose has been looking for you all afternoon?'

'I'm sure she has. No doubt I'll hear all about it tomorrow. She can tell me all about it when she tells me that I've lost my job.'

Stacy hesitated, and then she placed a reassuring hand on his arm. 'Rose isn't like that. She's worried about you. We both are. We know that you're caught up in this Leo Pearson thing. And nobody is blaming you.'

'Nobody is blaming me? After everything I've done?'

'For heaven's sake, Toby, it's only a job. You went out on a limb to help your cousin when he was in trouble. Do you think that no one else has ever broken the rules at the ENB? Do you think that no one else has ever let their heart rule their head?' She squeezed his arm. 'You must have heard about me? About what I did? It's common knowledge in the office that I broke the rules when I was dealing with Luke Kingsley's affairs.' She spluttered out a laugh of her own. 'I nearly lost my job because I had the hots for a second-rate footballer. How pathetic is that? But I'm still here, aren't I? I'm still at the bank, and I'm still on the way up.'

'Luke Kingsley wasn't a member of your family, though, was he?'

'No. But I don't see the relevance of that?' Stacy thought for a moment, and then said 'Look, you've been honest with Rose. You've told her what you've done, and you've admitted your mistakes. She played fair by me when I stepped out of line, I don't see any reason why she wouldn't play fair by you.'

'Maybe that's because you don't know what it is that I've done.' He stared into his glass, and then lifted it to his lips to down the scant remains of whisky and soda in one courage-inducing gulp. He turned back to look at her. 'That thing that you did, when you broke the rules - did you break the law as well?'

Stacy blinked, and considered the question. 'I don't know. I revealed confidential information to a customer about another customer's affairs. I know I broke the bank's rules, and I know I breached data protection regulations.' She looked perplexed. 'But even if I didn't break the law, I broke a code of conduct, didn't I? And that's what you've done. You've broken a code of conduct. I mean, it's not like anyone died, is it?'

Her words hung in the air, and then she lifted a hand to her mouth, and her eyes grew wide with a momentary shame. 'Oh Toby, I'm so sorry. I mean, I know that someone died ... that Leo died ... but that wasn't your fault, was it?'

'No, it wasn't my fault.' He spoke almost too quietly for her to hear. 'It wasn't my fault that someone died. But that doesn't take away the fact that he *did* die, does it?' He sounded weary. 'Do you trust Rose Bennett, Stacy? Do you trust her to do the right thing?'

'Of course I trust her.' Stacy moved closer to him, until her face was so near to his that he could feel her warm breath on his cheek. 'Why don't you speak to Rose in the morning?' She drew back a little and studied his face. 'And if you don't feel that you can speak to her alone, why don't we speak with her together? Whatever it is that you've done, I'm sure that talking about it can only make it better.'

DI Mulligan pressed his ear to the front door of Neil Redfern's flat. 'I can't hear anything.' He swivelled his eyes towards DS Scott. 'You'll have to just trust me on this one, Scottie. If we have to, we're going in without the warrant.' He depressed the door handle with a gentle pressure, and the latch gave way without a struggle. 'Well, at least we won't have to break in.'

He pushed gently on the door, and then recoiled as the smell of stale curry and unwashed linens hit his nostrils. He steeled himself against the stench, and called out through the gap in the door. 'Mr Redfern, are you at home?' He tilted his head, and listened for a reply. 'Mr Redfern?' Louder, this time. 'It's the police. Detective Inspector Mulligan and Detective Sergeant Scott. We'd like to come in, and ask you some questions.' He pushed the door inwards and stepped into the hall. There was nothing inside but silence. Silence, and a drab, unlit hallway.

He turned to look over his shoulder at DS Scott. 'There's a light coming from underneath one of the doors.' He kept his voice low.

Scott listened, and stepped forward to join him. 'Let me go first, George. If he's in there, he might try to make a run for it. I'd have a better chance of stopping him.' He edged past the senior officer and rapped on the interior door. 'Mr Redfern?' He pressed down on the handle, and slowly eased the door open. 'Mr Redfern, we'd like to have a word with you.' He paused, and took in the dimly-lit scene, and then he turned his head slowly a fraction to speak to DI Mulligan over his shoulder. 'How in God's name did you know, George?' He hesitated, bracing himself against the doorframe, and then pushed the door harder, and stepped forward into the room.

Mulligan watched in silence as Ian Scott crossed the

floor to a grubby, greying sofa. The body was sitting upright in the centre, shoulders slumped forward, the head lolling slightly to the left, the thinning hair matted thick with shimmering blood where some sharp and heavy object had come into contact with the skull beneath. 'The blood's still wet.' Scott turned his head, his face pale now, and hissed through his teeth. 'If we'd got here earlier ...'

Mulligan let out a growl as he walked through the doorway. 'I didn't expect him to be dead.' He leaned against the wall, and cast his eyes around the living room of Neil Redfern's flat. One end of the room held a small kitchen, an L-shaped arrangement of cupboards with a grease-splattered free-standing cooker and an antiquated fridge. At the other end, the sofa bearing the corpse almost filled the available space. There was no room for armchairs, but a small, square table had been pushed against the wall, and a flat-screen television hung precariously from a badly-fitted wall-bracket above the mantelpiece. A drab pair of heavy linen curtains covered the windows, blocking out the light from a streetlamp outside. The policeman swallowed hard. 'How the hell do people live like this, Scottie?'

'Because they haven't got a choice.' DS Scott straightened his back. 'You still haven't told me how you knew.' He sounded tense.

'I didn't know. It was a hunch.' Mulligan crossed the room to the kitchen and picked up a bottle from the counter. 'Lagavulin?' He held the bottle away from him, and squinted at the label. 'He certainly liked his whisky.' His whisky, and his other sundry home comforts, Mulligan thought. Anything to make his time in this stinking pit of a place more bearable. He pulled on the door of the fridge, and skimmed his eyes across the shelves inside, taking in the packaging of high-end convenience foods, luxury meals for one, strawberries and cream, a bottle of Veuve Clicquot. He slammed the fridge door shut. 'Any sign of a murder weapon?'

'There's something poking out from under the sofa. It looks like … I dunno. I think it's glass, maybe an ornament, or a statue, or something? I don't want to touch it.' DS Scott rubbed angrily at the back of his neck. 'I don't buy that it was a hunch, by the way. I know you too well for that, George. Did you know that the door would be unlocked?'

'Did I know? Of course I didn't bloody know. I couldn't have foreseen that, any more than I could have foreseen that he'd be dead. I just knew that we couldn't hang around and wait for the warrant.' Mulligan exhaled, a long drawn-out breath of self-reproach. 'If I'm honest, Scottie, I thought that we would find him alive. I thought we were going to be able to ask him whose body it was that he left in the car.' He put up a hand and rubbed at his forehead. 'And instead we're just back where we started.' He pointed down at the bent-over corpse. 'Scratching our heads over a body, and trying to work out for a second time who murdered Leo Pearson.'

18

Toby Dugdale folded his arms across his chest, and turned his eyes wearily downwards to stare into his first coffee of the day.

From the other side of the small table in Julia Spencer's office, Rose considered him with something close to sympathy. His face looked drawn this morning, his thick, blond hair dishevelled, and she would have bet a pound to a penny that he was still wearing yesterday's pale grey shirt with its matching slate-coloured tie. 'I have aspirins in my bag, if you think it would help.'

He lifted a bleary eye to look at her. 'I should know better than to start out on vodka and move on to Jack Daniels.'

'Ah, the demon drink.' She sounded understanding. 'Was it a celebration, or were you drowning your sorrows?'

'I think I was just trying to numb the pain.' He laughed wearily under his breath. 'Before you ask, it didn't work, and things got a whole lot worse when I came into the office this morning. I couldn't find my security pass, and they wouldn't let me into the building.' He laughed.' It's crazy, isn't it? I've lost count of how many years I've worked here, they all know me on the security desk, and yet they insisted on calling Julia to come down to the front door to sign me into the visitor's book. She was furious.'

'Well, I wouldn't be too surprised about that. Clive Barden is giving her a hard time over the whole Pearson the Bookmaker affair. Julia's done a lot to help you progress your career, and if she's cross with you now, then you only have yourself to blame. What you do at the bank doesn't just reflect on you, it reflects on your manager. You've been here long enough to know how it works. Your screw-ups are Julia's screw-ups. You might do well to think about that while you're working here.' Rose opened up her soft leather notebook and scribbled the date at the top of an empty page. 'For what it's worth, you got me into trouble with Clive too. Just where the hell did you disappear to yesterday afternoon?'

He cast his eyes back down into the depths of his coffee. 'I went to visit Verity. I just couldn't understand why she wasn't grieving for Leo. And before you say anything, I know I shouldn't have done it.'

'You don't need to explain yourself to me any more, Toby. I've given up trying to fathom how your mind works.' Rose gave a dismissive shake of the head. 'How was she?' She tried to make the question sound unimportant.

'Pretty angry. The police have accused her of having an affair with a customer at Leo's shop. But I know that couldn't be true.'

'You know?'

'Yes.' He took a sip of his coffee. 'She was talking about a man called Neil Redfern. I told Verity that I'd never heard of him, but I had. I know all about him, and I know that they weren't having an affair. Because if they were, Leo would have known about it.' He looked up at Rose. 'You see, I know that Leo was using Neil Redfern. The man had a chronic gambling habit, and Leo gave him cash from the business account to place bets that would make Pearson the Bookmaker look like a profitable business. I suppose you could say that it was an arrangement to mutual benefit.'

Rose blinked, and wondered if she had misheard. And then she looked up at him and asked 'is this how you knew for certain that Leo Pearson's business accounts weren't worth the paper they were printed on? Because you already knew how he'd been falsifying the accounts?' She watched his face closely as she spoke. 'Forgive me, Toby, but I have to ask – why are you telling me this now?'

'Because of something Verity said. She thinks that Neil Redfern might have been involved in Leo's death somehow. And I think that someone ought to tell the police. Neil Redfern had a motive to murder Leo, didn't he? Perhaps he was angry that Leo was using him like that, making his addiction worse. Perhaps they had an argument about it. Don't you think that the police should be investigating that as a line of enquiry?'

Rose dropped her pen onto the notebook and took a good, long look at Toby Dugdale. There was no denying that he'd already lied to her on more than one occasion, and she couldn't help wondering whether this was just another bluff to cover up the truth. 'Does Verity Pearson know about these attempts at false accounting?'

'No, I don't think so. Leo always made out to me that she didn't know, and that we had to keep it from her. He used to say that what she didn't know wouldn't hurt her.'

'I see. So it was just a case of "keep the little woman in the dark"?' There was an unexpected anger in her voice that came as a surprise to even Rose herself. 'Well, I'm pleased you've decided to tell me about this now, Toby. Because when you decided to go missing from the office yesterday afternoon, it left me with some time on my hands, and I decided to spend it looking at the Pearson accounts more closely. And I managed to identify that scam pretty much all by myself, just by looking at the numbers in the books.' She rested her elbows on the edge of the table. 'The thing is, I managed to account for two thirds of the cash that was withdrawn, but not all of it. In fact, it looked to me as though one withdrawal in every three or four was disappearing up in smoke. I don't suppose you would happen to know what happened to that cash? The cash that wasn't handed over to Neil Redfern to gamble with?'

There was an inflection in her voice that suggested she already knew the answer to the question, and it only took an unmistakable flush of remorseful colour into Toby Dugdale's cheeks to let her know that she was right.

George Mulligan reclined against the side of the black Mercedes and pulled a crumpled packet from his pocket. He stretched out his hand to Benny Bradman. 'Mint?'

Benny offered a rueful smile in reply. 'It's goin' to take more than a mint to banish that memory, George.' He thrust his hands deep into the pockets of his overcoat and shivered. 'Poor old Leo, eh?' He threw a casual glance back over his shoulder towards the soulless low-rise building they had both just exited. 'I've never been in a mortuary before. I can't say it's an experience I would be keen to repeat.'

Mulligan popped a mint into his mouth and then rolled the crumped packet around between his fingers. 'I know what you mean. But you know I appreciate what you've done for us this morning.' He shoved the packet back into his pocket. 'We recognised Leo Pearson from the photograph supplied to us by his wife, but we still needed a formal identification.'

'How the hell are you goin' to break this piece of news to Verity Pearson? You've already told her once this week that her old man was dead.'

'I haven't quite worked that one out yet.' Mulligan sounded unsure. 'But I'll have to come up with something. I take it you're still going ahead and buying the business?'

'Is there anythin' in this latest turn of events to stop me?'

'Not legally. Nothing that I can think of, anyway. But

Leo Pearson did pull the wool over your eyes about the value of the business. As things stand, you're paying over the odds.'

'I know that, George. But what the hell do I do? Do I back out, and lose a business that I want to own? Or do I try to force the price down at the last minute, and make things worse for a widow who has lost her husband twice in one week?' He forced a bewildered grin. 'Which of those two options would you go for?'

'Me? I'd force the price down. What Leo Pearson did was false accounting. He didn't just overstate the value of the business, he actually took steps to artificially inflate the takings. And then he tried to defraud you out of thousands of pounds by basing the sale price of the business on a fraudulent set of accounts.' Mulligan crunched on his mint. 'I'm only sorry that the devious bastard isn't still alive so that we could have done him for that on top of everything else.'

'Is there any danger that Verity Pearson could be prosecuted for it? She is the other director of the company.'

'I doubt it. I can't see that anyone would consider it in the public interest to chase her for something like that. Even if she did know about it, with Leo Pearson and Neil Redfern both dead I don't know how we'd prove it. Anyway,' Mulligan gave a shake of the head, 'I wouldn't waste your sympathy on Verity Pearson. She agreed to be a director of the business. If she chose to stick her head in the sand and leave everything to Leo, then she really only has herself to blame. No, if you want to show some sympathy I would save it for someone who deserves it.'

'Such as?'

'We don't have any evidence yet, but we're assuming that the remains we found in Leo Pearson's car belonged to Neil Redfern. We're waiting for his dental records to come in this morning, but Scottie's gone over to see his sister and prime her to expect bad news.'

Benny drew in a breath, and then blew it out again slowly. 'Jesus, George, what a bloody mess.' He looked down at his shoes. 'What the hell does it all mean?'

'We don't know for certain. It's possible that Leo Pearson murdered Neil Redfern and tried to pass the body off as his own. And it looks as though he's been hiding out in Redfern's flat since Monday. But that doesn't explain who murdered Leo Pearson. And it doesn't tell us whether Verity Pearson knew what was going on. She isn't just a widow. If those insurance policies with the ENB pay out, she'll be a very wealthy widow.'

'So you think they were in on it together?'

'Well if they weren't, how else would Leo have been able to access the money?'

Benny shrugged. 'I don't know, George. But I can't say it makes me feel any better. You've got no evidence at this stage that Verity Pearson had anythin' to do with it. And I'm standin' on a precipice here, tryin' to decide whether to reduce my offer on the business, or chuck it in altogether. Either way it's goin' to leave her without any real means of support, and heavily in debt.'

'Unless her claims on the insurance policies pay out. Leo Pearson might not have been dead on Tuesday, but he really is dead now. What I need to do is find out who killed him.' Mulligan nodded to himself. 'Find out who killed him, and find out why they wanted him dead. I just wish there wasn't more than one runner in the field.'

'So yesterday you thought my brother was a criminal, and that he colluded with Verity Pearson to murder her husband. And today you've come to tell me that he might be a corpse?' Evie Green turned her face towards the window of her lounge, and stared out through the pristine white net curtains to the vague outline of the garden gate and Mulberry Avenue beyond.

The rebuke was hardly unexpected. DS Scott lowered his eyes with a contrite bow of the head. He knew the gesture would go unnoticed, that her stubborn gaze was fixed on some indeterminate point beyond the window, in a deliberate attempt to avoid eye contact. But that was no reason not to make at least some small display of remorse. 'We don't always get it right, Evie. But I want you to know that I'm glad. I wanted Neil to be innocent. I wanted it for your sake. Because you believed in him.' He stopped short of saying he wanted it for his own sake too.

'You're glad that my brother might be dead?'

He shook his head. 'Of course not. I'm sorry that we didn't have any other way to prove his innocence. And given a choice, don't you think I'd rather that any man was alive and guilty than innocent and dead?' He didn't expect an answer. 'Look Evie, we believe that Neil was caught up in a scam with Leo Pearson.'

'I know. I've heard about it from Benny Bradman.'

'From Bradman?' The information threw him. 'You mean you've been speaking to him?'

'He asked to see me yesterday, to talk about Neil. He told me that Leo Pearson had inflated the value of his business, and that he thought Leo had used Neil, that he'd given him money to gamble back over the counter to make the takings look good.' She drew her eyes away from the window and turned them down towards her hands. 'Is that why you think he might be dead? Because Leo Pearson wanted to cover his tracks? Is that why you think Neil might be the one who died in that fire on Monday night?'

It was a difficult question to answer. 'It might be a part of it.' He wasn't sure how much he should reveal. 'Look, we know now that Leo Pearson didn't die in that fire. But someone did. And your brother is missing. I want you to know that we're doing everything we can to identify the remains we found in that car. We've requested your brother's dental records, and we've put in a request to fast-track the identification when they arrive. I'm hoping we're going to have an answer today.'

Evie Green sat motionless on the sofa. And then a deep crimson flush suffused into her porcelain cheeks, and she lifted her eyes to the policeman's face and fixed him with a penetrating stare. 'How do you know that the body in the car didn't belong to Leo Pearson?'

'I'm sorry Evie, that's not something I can share with you.'

'Not something you can share with me?' She uttered an astonished laugh. 'You think my brother is dead, and you think that Leo Pearson might have been responsible, but you can't tell me how you know that the body might be Neil, and not Leo Pearson?' She closed her eyes and shook her head, and then she froze, and the eyes flashed open. 'Oh my God, he's still alive, isn't he? Leo Pearson?'

Scott looked sharply away, muted by a question that he knew he couldn't answer. And then he turned back to her with a look which he hoped implored her understanding. 'I can't tell you any more at this stage.'

'You don't have to.' Her eyes with blazing with fury now. 'You know that unspeakable bastard is still alive. And you know he killed my brother.'

19

'I'm sorry to bother you again, Clive, but I've heard from Mr Mulligan.' Rose kept her voice as low as she could. She was sitting at a small table in the ENB's staff restaurant, and the risk of prying ears was ever-present. 'He called ten minutes ago to let me know that the body in the car wasn't Leo Pearson's. That's official.'

There was pause, and then Clive Barden whistled down the phone line, and clicked his teeth in disapprobation. 'We were right to be cautious, Rose. We knew, did we not, that Verity Pearson's insurance claim was a bogus one?'

'Did we?' Rose jammed her phone into the crook of her neck, freeing her hands to add sugar to a cardboard cup of tea. 'I would agree that we were approaching the situation cautiously. And that we were right to have our suspicions. But we don't have any grounds at this stage to say that the insurance claim was a bogus one.'

'But Verity Pearson attempted to make a claim against those policies two days ago. When her husband was quite clearly still alive.'

'I know. But we haven't had anything yet to confirm that she knew he was still alive when she tried to make the claim.'

'Still, if the body in the car wasn't Leo Pearson ...'

'Clive, I need to stop you there. You haven't heard the full story. The body in the car wasn't Leo Pearson, but Leo Pearson is dead. I don't know the circumstances. At this stage, all I've been told is that his body was found yesterday evening, and Mr Mulligan believes that he was murdered either late in the afternoon or early in the evening.'

At the other end of the line, Clive Barden fell silent, and then he said 'I have to admit, Rose, that this case is venturing far beyond anything else I have experienced. To consider this a simple case of insurance fraud, the possibility that Verity Pearson may have been complicit in her husband's death to benefit financially from it - that is not beyond either my imagination or my experience. But to discover that the assumed deceased has actually been alive for several days, only for his body to turn up unexpectedly ... whatever can one make of it?'

'I don't know, Clive. And for what it's worth, I don't think that Mr Mulligan knows what to make of it, either. Whether this is an insurance fraud or not, he's dealing with a double murder.' She drew in a breath. 'He's on his way now to break the news to Verity Pearson, and he's asked us to notify him immediately if she makes any attempt to contact the bank today, regarding either the insurance policies or the sale of the business. Now that her husband's body has been found, she still has the basis for a valid insurance claim.'

'It would appear that the Inspector still harbours a suspicion that she was complicit in these crimes, one way or another. We can only hope that she acted alone, and that Toby Dugdale wasn't somehow involved.'

'Ah.' Rose let out a sigh. 'Mr Mulligan has asked if he can come into the Kirkby office this afternoon to talk to Toby about the case. He has some questions for him in his capacity as Leo's business account manager.'

'Of course. You must make sure that you are in attendance, Rose, and that you fully record the details of the conversation. I don't want Toby Dugdale on his own with Inspector Mulligan. We need to understand if there will be any reputational risk for the bank. I would hate for the Inspector to think that the ENB fell short in some way by permitting Toby to act with any impropriety.'

'I'm afraid it's probably a bit late for that.' Rose licked a finger and leafed back through the soft leather notebook, searching for the relevant page. 'Toby has admitted to me that he knew everything about Leo Pearson's scam to inflate the value of the business. He knew that Leo Pearson was making use of a gambling addict to place false bets to bolster the shop's takings. And he was doing that using money borrowed from the bank.'

'You mean that he knew a financial crime was taking place, and he just turned a blind eye? He didn't file a report?' Clive whistled angrily through his teeth. 'Why on earth has he admitted to that now?'

'I'm not sure I understand that myself. He's also admitted that some of the cash withdrawn from Leo Pearson's business account made its way to him. He didn't just breach the lending rules out of some romanticised notion of helping a beloved cousin. He was lining his own pockets with some of the proceeds as a pay-off for arranging the additional borrowing.'

'Just like any other petty criminal.' Clive snorted his disapproval down the phone line. 'Toby Dugdale has proved to be an habitual liar, and he cannot be trusted. Once the Inspector has finished with him, we must act swiftly to secure his departure from the bank.' He softened his tone. 'What did we do to deserve such disloyalty, Rose? Toby Dugdale has been an employee of this bank for sixteen years, and never a bad word about him.'

'I don't know, Clive. Perhaps he did it for the thrill.'

'Did it for the thrill? Then perhaps we must hope, Rose, that the thrill stopped at fraud, and that it didn't extend to murder.'

'I don't understand.' Verity Pearson frowned at the

policemen. 'You told me on Tuesday morning that my husband was dead. And now you've come here again to tell me that you were mistaken?'

'We came here on Tuesday to tell you that you're husband's vehicle had been found with the remains of a body in it. Based on your confirmation that the vehicle belonged to your husband, and your identification of several items found in the vehicle, we have proceeded with our investigation on the assumption that the remains were those of your husband.' DI Mulligan kept his voice as level as he could, but his anger was beginning to grow. It had been a reasonable assumption to make at the start of the case, and one that Verity Pearson had been keen to encourage. 'We are certain now that the remains in the car did not belong to your husband after all.' He turned to look at DS Scott, perched uncomfortably beside him on the edge of the lilac sofa, in the hope of some moral support. But the sergeant, tight-lipped and humourless, was staring at Verity Pearson in the way that a tiger might look at its prey.

'So you have positively identified them now? The remains in the car? You know who they belonged to?'

'Oh yes, we know.' There was an incongruous inflection in DS Scott's gentle Welsh lilt, an uncharacteristic hostility towards the woman he had once believed to be a victim.

Mulligan put up a hand and shot his colleague a warning glance. 'We believe that we know who they belonged to, and we'll obtain confirmation of that later today. But for now, I'm afraid I have to inform you that the body of your husband, Leo Pearson, has been found.' The policeman's words hung in the air, and then dissipated into a hollow and unnerving silence.

For one fleeting moment it looked as though Verity Pearson might actually pass out. And then she took in a deep, sustaining breath, and used it to blow out a question. 'How do you know it was Leo? I mean, you've already told me once this week that he was dead. How can I believe you a second time?'

'Because we've already secured a formal identification of his body. Benny Bradman offered to step in on your behalf, Verity. He thought it would be less distressing for you, under the circumstances.' It wasn't necessarily the truth, but it was as good an explanation as any.

Verity looked down at her hands. 'It seems too cruel, to have to face this a second time in the space of just a few days. But I suppose if Benny has actually seen the body ...' She hesitated, and swallowed back what might have been a sob.

'We're very sorry for your loss, Verity.' George Mulligan kept his eyes on her face, watching as a solitary mascara-stained tear made its way down her left cheek. 'Is there anything you would like to ask us?'

'Ask you?' The question appeared to confuse her. And then the penny dropped, and she lifted her head. 'Of course. What happened to him, Inspector? What happened to my husband?'

'I'm afraid he was murdered. By a blow to the back of the head. We believe that it happened yesterday, between five and seven o'clock in the evening.'

'And where did you find him?' Her voice was a whisper now.

'We found him in Neil Redfern's flat.' It was DS Scott who answered. 'It looks as though he'd been living there for some days. We're guessing that he'd been there since disappearing on Monday evening.'

'Was Neil Redfern with him?'

'Neil Redfern is still missing.' Scott hissed out the words through clenched teeth. 'And we believe that his was the body left in your husband's car before it was set alight.'

Verity's green eyes narrowed slowly. 'Do you have any evidence of that?'

'No, but we will by the end of the day.'

She held Scott's gaze. 'What on earth could he have been doing in Leo's car? Do you think he stole it?'

Mulligan blinked his disbelief, and then tilted his head to look at her closely. 'No, we don't think he stole it. Any more than we believe he set fire to it himself. We believe he was murdered, and that his body was left in the car before it was set alight, to make everyone think that your husband was dead.'

'Why on earth would anyone do that? You surely don't think that Leo murdered him?' She turned her eyes across the room. 'Oh my God, you do. You think that Leo murdered him?' She looked up to the ceiling, and she gave a disbelieving shake of the head. 'Why on earth would Leo do that? Is this back to your nonsensical theory about my having an affair? You think that Leo murdered Neil Redfern because he thought we were having an affair?'

Mulligan bit on his lip, and considered his response. Then he said 'we have a very different theory as to why your husband might have murdered Neil Redfern.' He chose his words carefully. 'When did you last speak to him, Verity?'

'You already know the answer to that question, Inspector Mulligan. I spoke to my husband on Monday afternoon. I tried, as I've already told you, to contact him by phone on Monday evening, but he didn't answer my call. And I haven't had any communication with him since.' She gave a desultory sniff. 'Don't you think that I would have contacted you immediately if I'd heard from him? I mean, considering that you had already led me to believe that he was dead?'

It was a question for which he didn't have an answer. He placed his hands on his knees, and began to push himself to his feet. 'I think it would be best if we left you now, and gave you time to reflect on this latest turn of events. I know this must be a very distressing time for you, but I would ask you to bear in mind that we are now dealing with a double murder. Until we have established who is responsible, I would ask for your full cooperation.' He turned to glance down at Scott. 'I think we're done here, Sergeant, unless there is anything else you would like to ask of Mrs Pearson?'

'No, I don't think so.' Scott was already rising to his feet.

'We'll be in touch with you as soon as we have any further information. And you have my absolute assurance that I will find the person responsible for your husband's death, and bring them to justice.' Mulligan fixed her with a meaningful stare. 'Whoever that person turns out to be.'

Verity Pearson returned his gaze with a wan smile, her composure beginning to recover. 'I'm sure I can rely on you to do that, Inspector Mulligan. But in the meantime, and before you leave, there is one final question I would like to ask you, if I may?' She licked her lips thoughtfully, and observed him through widened eyes. 'Now that you are absolutely certain that my husband is deceased, how long will it be before I can expect to obtain a copy of the death certificate?'

'Blimey, Rose, what the hell are we doin' in this place?' Benny cast a glance around the dismal interior of the Abbey Tearooms. 'Even Mac don't look impressed.' He pointed down under the table and the terrier, curled up against his feet, turned his head on cue to look up at Rose with disapproving eyes.

'It's close to the office, and it's empty. I don't want us to be overheard.'

'I'm not surprised it's empty. Have you seen the colour of that table cloth?'

Rose nudged his arm. 'Not so loud. They might hear you.' She forced a smile as a sullen waitress deposited two large mugs of coffee onto the table without a word. 'Thanks.' The girl turned without acknowledging her, and retreated silently towards the kitchen. 'OK, I'll admit that the service isn't up to much, either. Just try to think of it as any port in a storm.'

Benny stretched out a hand and wrapped it around one of the mugs. 'Well, I suppose on the bright side no one will hear you scream when I tell you that I've instructed my solicitor to lower my offer to Verity Pearson.' He lifted the mug and sipped on the coffee with a grimace. 'I've knocked thirty thousand off.'

'You do know that will leave Verity Pearson significantly deeper in debt?'

'I've decided not to worry about that. Verity will either turn down the offer flat, in which case she'll have to go on runnin' the business until she finds another buyer. Or she'll accept it, and make up the losses out of her insurance money.'

'Always assuming that the claims are upheld by the bank.'

'Leo Pearson's dead, Rose. I can't see that they have a choice.'

'They'll have a choice if it turns out that she was involved in his death.' Rose leaned a little closer to him and lowered her voice. 'Did you really identify the body for Mr Mulligan?'

'I did. And a very unpleasant experience it was too.' He balked at the memory. 'I can't see any way that Verity Pearson was responsible for doin' that to her old man, whatever she thought of him. It would have taken anger, real venom to smash somethin' down on his head. She's far too delicate for that.'

'She didn't have to do the job herself. Don't they always say that an attractive woman doesn't have to do her own dirty work?'

Benny risked a grin in her direction. 'Is that the reason you've had me runnin' around diggin' into Leo Pearson's business, then? So you didn't have to do it for yourself?'

'I suppose it might be.' She sounded coy. 'Anyway, it

hasn't really done us any good, has it?' She tried not to sound disappointed. 'Mr Mulligan's coming in to see me this afternoon, he wants to interview Toby Dugdale about the Pearsons' accounts. I don't know where that's going to lead.' She looked away for a moment, thinking, and then turned back to him and asked 'do you think Verity Pearson will accept your new offer for the business?'

'Are we back to Verity Pearson again? You keep bringin' that name up, Rose. What's on your mind?'

'I know it sounds silly, but I'm worried about what's going to happen to her now. I know that she's lost her husband, and I know that both Clive and Mr Mulligan have suspicions about her involvement in his death. But …'

'But?'

'When I met her the other day, the first time she came into the bank to speak to me, I thought I saw something in her eyes that I couldn't quite place. But now I think it was fear.' Rose stared down into her coffee. 'Not the fear of being found out. But the fear of not understanding. Of not understanding what sort of a mess she was in.'

'Rose, you're not makin' sense.'

'I know.' She gave a self-deprecating laugh and lifted her eyes to Benny's face. 'I think what I'm trying to say is that she seemed afraid of her situation. Of being a director of the company without knowing what it meant. As if Leo had probably told her it was a tax-efficient thing to do, without pointing out to her that if anything happened to him she would be liable for the company's debts.'

'She's got the insurance policies.'

Rose shook her head. 'If there is any suggestion at all that Verity was involved in Leo's death, even if no charges are brought, the bank will do everything they can to avoid payment.'

'Then she'll have to sell that fancy pile of bricks in Kirkby Park, won't she? She won't be able to go on livin' there without Leo to pick up the bills. She might as well free up the equity and use it to pay off her debts.'

'But she has other debts to cover too. And the equity won't cover it all.'

'Blimey, Rose, Verity Pearson is a grown woman. And she's done you no favours. Where's all this comin' from?'

'I think it was something that Toby said to me this morning. Something about Leo Pearson, and the scam he was pulling with Neil Redfern to bolster the value of the business. Leo hadn't wanted her to know what he was doing. He told Toby that what she didn't know wouldn't hurt her.' She shook her head. 'You know, I don't know how many times in my life I've heard those words - "what she doesn't know won't hurt her". But it isn't always true, is it? In this case there seem to be a lot of things that Verity Pearson didn't know, and most of them could hurt her very badly indeed.'

'Such as?'

'Well, Leo didn't want her to know that he'd falsely inflated the value of the business, but now that you've found out about it, you've reduced your offer and left her thirty thousand pounds worse off. How is that not going to hurt her?'

Benny gave an exasperated shake of the head. 'Are you tryin' to guilt trip me into puttin' the original offer back on the table?'

'No, of course not. You have to do what you think is right. But someone needs to offer Verity Pearson some help. Someone who understands the situation she is in.' Rose stretched out a hand and placed it down on Benny's arm. 'Someone she knows, and can trust.'

'Oh no.' Benny pulled back his arm. 'If you're lookin' at me, you can forget it. I've followed that instruction once already, "get close to Verity Pearson, Benny, and see what you can find out". And look where that got me. I ain't goin' there again, Rose.'

'I just think that she needs a little bit of help.'

'Well if you think that Verity Pearson needs a little bit

of help, maybe you should think about invitin' her into the bank and offerin' that help to her yourself.'

20

George Mulligan gently placed the receiver down on the telephone cradle on his desk, and drew back his hand to pick up a pen. He looked at the sheet of notes in front of him, and then slowly – almost regretfully - added another line to bottom of his carefully curated list.

Body in Leo Pearson's car formally identified as Neil Redfern.

He dropped the pen onto the page. Yesterday he'd been dealing with a suspicious death, a potential insurance fraud, and a missing person who may or may not have been of interest. Today, whether fraud had been attempted or not, he was looking at a dose of double murder and an embarrassment of questions to go with it.

And that, he supposed, was what happened to a policeman when his instincts began to lose their edge.

He wasn't sure which it was that hurt the most – the fact that if he'd followed his instincts sooner, he might have found Leo Pearson alive, or the fact that Scottie had felt the need to point it out to him. That was evidence enough, if evidence were needed, that the sergeant was losing his judgment. Mulligan knew that the case had really wormed its way under his colleague's skin, or at least Neil Redfern's sister had, but he hadn't expected it to come between them.

He cast the thought aside, and lifted a hand to run a

finger down the list. There was no doubt in his mind that Neil Redfern had been murdered by Leo Pearson. Pearson might have made a good job of lying low in that shabby flat on the Barnfield Estate, but he'd made the mistake of leaving the tools of his murderous act in the tiny spare bedroom for everyone to see. Clothing that smelled strongly of petrol fumes, a folding bike that could easily have been used to cycle back from Cayton Bay to the Barnfield – it wasn't going to be difficult to get forensic confirmation that Leo Pearson wore those clothes or rode that bicycle, even if they couldn't link him directly to the murder scene. Now that the body in the car had been identified, working out who murdered Neil Redfern, and how, had been a fairly simple affair.

But working out why it had been necessary for Leo Pearson to die? Well, that was a different matter.

He put out a hand to rifle through the contents of the in-tray on his desk, sifting through the pile of papers until his fingers alighted on a photograph, and he pulled it out of the pile and up to his face. The picture was of a trophy, a long shard of glass set into a heavy marble base. A small brass plate attached to the base was engraved with Neil Redfern's name and the words "Warwick University 1999". As murder weapons went, Mulligan had to admit it was original, and it had certainly been up to the job. The corner of the trophy's base had cracked open Leo Pearson's skull like a hammer to a nut.

The policeman shuddered at the thought. He had asked Jimmy Miller if the blow could have been delivered by a woman, or whether it would have required the strength of a man. The question had been met with a withering look, and the observation that with a piece of glass and marble of that shape and weight, providing the victim had been sitting down below the trajectory of the blow, a child of nine or ten could have delivered the fatal strike without barely losing a breath. Jimmy Miller had laughed at the idea, and goaded him with another consideration.

Always supposing that a child of nine or ten had known that Leo Pearson was hiding out in Neil Redfern's flat.

A child of nine or ten, or perhaps another unlikely killer? Had Verity Pearson known that her husband was in that flat? Had she known all along that he was hiding out there? Or had someone else stumbled across the elusive Mr Pearson, calling at the flat in the hope of finding Neil Redfern, and finding Redfern's killer in his place?

And always supposing that the child of nine or ten — or some other unlikely killer - had a motive to murder the victim.

He swivelled to and fro in his seat, and then placed the photograph back down on the desk and tapped gently on it with his finger. Evie Green had a motive to murder Leo Pearson. He had manipulated her brother for his own nefarious ends, aggravated his gambling addiction, murdered him, tried to dispose of the body, and then made use of his flat as a hide-out. What if Evie Green had stumbled unexpectedly upon Leo Pearson? What if she had gone to the flat in one last desperate attempt to find her brother, found Leo Pearson there in his place, and reached out for that glass shard not as a tool for a premeditated act of violence, but an impromptu murder weapon for an act of impassioned revenge?

Mulligan bowed his head. It was a possibility that didn't bear thinking about, but someone would have to test out the theory. Someone would have to ask Evie Green if she had an alibi for the time of Leo Pearson's death.

And that someone would have to be Scottie.

Toby Dugdale sank his hands awkwardly into the pockets of his overcoat, and stared out through the lace-shrouded windows of Verity Pearson's lounge. 'I see you've put the house on the market.' His eyes were fixed on a large wooden board in the garden, a hastily-erected "For Sale" notice that leaned ominously towards a neighbouring holly bush. 'When did that happen?'

'I spoke to the estate agent yesterday. He came about an hour ago to put up the sign.' Verity sounded brittle. 'They don't think the house will take long to sell. We've agreed a price just below market value to hurry things along.' She coughed quietly, a subtle hint. 'Shouldn't you be at work?'

'I'm on my lunch break.' He turned around to look at her. She was standing beside the fireplace, dressed for an outdoor excursion, a soft blue shawl swathed around the shoulders of her green woollen coat, the burgundy curls crimped to perfection and cascading around her face. He could see no sign of grief. 'I lost my ENB security pass yesterday, I'm trying to retrace my steps to see if I can find it. I thought I might have dropped it here, when I came to see you.'

'Well if you did, I haven't seen it. I don't remember you coming into this room. You crossed the hall from the front door to the kitchen, stayed a while in the kitchen, and then crossed the hall back to the door again when you left. I think I would have noticed if you'd dropped it.' She nodded to herself. 'Where did you go when you left here? Did you go back to the office?'

'No.' He hesitated, and then said 'I drove home and dropped off my car, and walked down to the Jug and Ferret for a couple of drinks. I've called the pub. They say nothing has been handed in.'

'And you've checked your car?'

'Yes, of course. It was the first thing that I did.'

'Well,' she launched herself away from the fireplace and began to move towards the door, 'it's not here, Toby. I think I would have noticed if it was.' She placed a hand on the door handle, and turned back to look at him. 'I don't mean to be rude, but I have an appointment at the coroner's office in thirty minutes. I really need to make a move.'

'The coroner's office? Has there been some news?

Have you heard something from the police?'

Her eyes took on a guarded look. 'I had a visit from Detective Inspector Mulligan this morning, and they have confirmed that Leo is dead. The coroner opened the inquest this morning, so that an interim death certificate could be issued. I don't really understand how these things work, but I'm grateful for their help. I believe the inquest is now adjourned until the police gather all the evidence they need to confirm the facts.'

'I don't believe you.' He studied her face, searching for a lie. 'I don't believe that Leo is dead. I don't believe that it was Leo's body they found in that car.'

Verity blinked, and then she gave a sorrowful shake of the burgundy curls. 'Don't do this to yourself, Toby. I know how much you cared for Leo, but you have to face the truth. Leo is dead.'

'You're lying.' His words cut across hers like a knife. 'You're hiding something. I know you are.'

She threw back her head and snorted a quiet yet contemptuous laugh. '*I'm* hiding something?' Her green eyes flashed in a glare of condemnation. '*How dare you?*' The words hissed out towards him. 'How dare you accuse me of hiding something?' She pushed at the door, slamming it into the frame. 'Are you aware that Benny Bradman has reduced his offer for the business?' She didn't wait for him to answer. 'And do you know why he's reduced it? Because that lying piece of filth that I was married to for thirty years falsified the company's accounts behind my back.' She stepped forward towards him, enveloping him in a cloud of musky perfume. 'Never mind that I was a company director, too. Never mind that I could face a charge of false accounting. And *you*,' she pushed at his chest with an angry hand, 'you knew that he was doing it, and you said *nothing*.'

Toby stumbled backwards. 'Verity, I …'

'Don't.' Her jaw stiffened, and she put up a hand. 'Don't even think about snivelling your excuses. I've spoken to the accountant. And he's put me well and truly in the picture.' She drew in a deep breath. 'I've instructed the solicitor to accept Benny's offer. I'm going to the coroner's office to collect the interim death certificate, and then I'm going to the bank to present it.'

'Verity, Leo loves you …'

'For God's sake stop talking about him in the present tense.' She spoke through gritted teeth. 'Leo is *dead*, Toby. And he didn't love me. Leo never did anything for me that wasn't intended to create a benefit for himself. He used me as a director of his precious business so that he could cheat the tax man by paying me a salary for work I didn't do. He gave me a generous clothing allowance, but only so that I always looked good on his arm. He'd book me a spa break, or a holiday, and tell me that the break would do me good, but he was only getting me out of the way so that he could carry on with some little tart behind my back.' She lowered her voice to a whisper. 'Leo used me, just like Leo used you. He didn't care if you were breaking the rules at the bank. He didn't care if you lost your precious job. And I think that deep down in your heart you already know that.' The whisper became a hiss. 'And I think that makes you angry.'

Toby swallowed hard. 'You know that the bank suspects you of committing an insurance fraud?'

She let out an incredulous screech. 'They suspect me of insurance fraud? What am I supposed to have done? Murdered my husband for the insurance money?' She hesitated, and then turned disbelieving eyes up towards his face. 'My God, you mean it. You actually think that I killed Leo?'

'I didn't say that.' He shook his head. 'Verity, are you telling me that you really believe that Leo is dead? That his was the body they found in the car?'

'The body in the car?' A curious expression flitted across Verity's face. 'I have no idea, Toby, what it is that you're attempting to suggest. Because if it wasn't Leo's body in the car, whose body do *you* think it was?'

DS Scott paused outside the door of Neil Redfern's flat, and turned his head to glance at Evie Green. She was standing at the top of a flight of concrete stairs, her hand still resting gently on the sticky iron handrail, her eyes unfocused, her lips moving silently in what might have been a prayer.

'Why is *he* here?' She nodded towards a lanky, sallow youth standing beside the door.

Scott followed her gaze, and acknowledged his uniformed colleague with a reassuring wink. 'PC Goodwin is here to keep the place secure while we carry out a thorough search. This is a crime scene now, Evie.' He pushed on the door and stepped through into the hall.

'But the crime didn't happen here, did it?' She shivered as she followed him through the doorway and across the hall. 'It happened at Cayton Bay.' She stopped at the threshold of the small, brightly-lit lounge. 'You've turned all the lights on. I'm not used to seeing it like this. Neil always had the lights turned down low. He was worried about the electricity bills.' She stepped slowly forwards towards the back of the sofa, and rested her hands on the edge. 'What will happen to this place if Neil is dead? Who will pay his bills?'

'Don't worry about that now. Let's just concentrate on what we have to do while we're here.' He tried to sound encouraging. 'Do you notice anything different in here, apart from all the lights being on?'

Evie glanced around the room. 'The curtains are drawn back, and the windows are open. Neil always kept the windows closed to keep the heat in.' She sniffed gently. 'And it smells different. It used to smell of Neil's aftershave in here, some horrible cheap stuff that he used to buy in the market. He used to spray it around like air freshener, to mask the stale smell of the carpet.'

'And now?'

'It's sweet. It smells … I don't know. Sweet, like an expensive cologne.' She turned to Scott. 'Why is that?'

He gave a noncommittal shrug. 'What else do you see?'

'Well, it looks cleaner than normal.' She frowned and shook her head. 'What do you expect me to see?'

'Is there anything missing?'

She paused, and then pointed to the mantelpiece. 'There should be a glass trophy on that mantel. It was a long, sharp thing with a heavy base. Neil won it in a tennis tournament when he was at university.' She smiled at the memory. 'One of those stupid things that you hang on to from the past. I think he kept it because he met his wife during that tournament.' She turned her eyes from the mantel to the small table against the wall, and then round towards the kitchen. 'Where is it? Has it been moved?'

'It's in a safe place, Evie. It's been moved for safe-keeping.'

'Moved? Moved where?' She sounded annoyed rather than curious. 'Why would anyone do that?' Her anger was beginning to build. 'Why would anyone move my brother's things?' She turned her head to look down at the sofa, her hands still placed on the edge of the backrest. 'What the hell is this all about?'

Scott stepped forward away from the wall, and put his hands very gently on her shoulders. 'I have something I need to tell you, Evie, but I want you to stay calm if you can. Very, very calm.' His voice was low, and he moved his head closer to hers. 'You asked me this morning if Leo Pearson was still alive, and I couldn't answer you. But I can tell you now that he isn't. Leo Pearson is dead.' He felt the muscles in her shoulders begin to stiffen under his hands. 'Leo Pearson's body was found yesterday evening, by myself and Inspector Mulligan. We found him here, in your brother's flat.' Now her body felt rigid. 'Someone murdered Leo Pearson, here in Neil's flat. He died as the result of a blow to the head. And the killer used the glass shard trophy to do it.'

Evie was breathing rapidly now, short sharp bursts of breath that hissed and flowed between anxious lips. 'Did Leo Pearson kill my brother?'

'We don't know. We believe it's possible, but we have no evidence. We believe that Leo Pearson had a motive to kill Neil, but I can't discuss that with you yet.'

'Was it because of the money Leo Pearson gave him? The money to place those bets?'

'I've already told you that I can't discuss that with you. All I can tell you is that he was murdered here. In your brother's flat.'

'What was he doing here?

'We think he was hiding out. We think that he was with Neil on Monday evening, and that after Neil ... after Neil's body was left in the car, he came back here to lie low.'

'Why would he do that?'

'I'll answer that question when I can.' She still hadn't asked the question he was waiting for. There should be at least one more question, maybe two.

Slowly, she turned her head to look at him with hollow, grieving eyes. 'Could you take me home now, please?'

The question made his heart sink. 'Of course.' He turned her gently by the shoulders, and steered her towards the door. It wasn't the question he'd been hoping for.

He could only hope that she'd ask it on the drive back to Mulberry Avenue.

21

Rose Bennett closed the door of Julia Spencer's office behind her, and sank onto a chair beside the table in the corner. 'Toby isn't back from his lunch break yet. I've asked his manager to send him in here when he returns.'

George Mulligan, already seated at the table, gave a distracted nod, and then pointed to a basket in the corner of the office. 'Is that Lu's dog?'

Her mouth curved into a gentle smile. 'I picked him up from Benny half an hour ago. I've got far too much to do this afternoon to take him back to Market Melbourne. And no one seems to mind him being in the office.' The smile became wistful. 'To be honest, he mostly sleeps these days. He's getting so old he doesn't seem to have the energy for anything else.'

'I know how he feels.' Mulligan pulled up his jacket sleeves, and rested his elbows on the table. 'And what about Toby Dugdale? Have you noticed any changes in his behaviour over the last few days?'

'He's certainly feeling a bit sorry for himself today. He turned up this morning with the mother of all hangovers. He hasn't really said why he came by it, but I know he went to see Verity Pearson again yesterday afternoon.' Rose leaned back in her seat. 'Did you by any chance suggest to Verity Pearson that you thought she was having an affair with Neil Redfern?'

Mulligan let out an astonished laugh. 'Did she actually admit that to Toby Dugdale?'

'It would seem so. But Toby said he knows that it

couldn't be true, because he would have known about it. He's admitted to knowing all about Leo Pearson inflating the value of his business by giving Neil Redfern cash to gamble with. He reckons that Leo wouldn't have done that if there had been any question of Neil having an affair with his wife.'

The policeman considered the suggestion. 'I suppose that's possible. Did he say anything else about it?'

'He thinks that someone ought to tell the police to investigate Neil Redfern further. I have no idea where that suggestion is coming from, only that he thinks that Neil had a motive for murdering Leo Pearson. He has a theory, that when Benny put in an offer for Pearson the Bookmaker, there was no longer any need for Leo Pearson to go on inflating the value of the business. He thinks that Neil Redfern could have been angry about Leo not giving him any more cash to gamble with, angry enough to murder him.'

'And what do you think, Rose?'

'I don't know. I suppose it's possible that Leo made Neil Redfern's gambling addiction worse by feeding it with ready cash. And that when the cash stopped, it could have caused some sort of withdrawal symptom.' She shook her head. 'But somehow I can't quite see it. It all sounds a bit too far-fetched.'

'And what about Verity Pearson? Has Toby said anything more about her? Does he think she knew about the false accounting?'

'No, he doesn't. Leo seems to have kept his wife in the dark about a lot of things. I'm beginning to think that she doesn't really understand her own financial situation. Some women don't, they just trust their husbands to deal with the finances.' Rose frowned. 'I've asked Benny to help her, but he won't.'

Mulligan grinned at the suggestion. 'Well you can't be surprised about that. The way I heard it, the last time he followed your instructions regarding Verity Pearson, he ended up in the dog house.'

'Oh, don't worry about that. He'll get used to it.' Rose laughed, and then shifted in her seat and tilted her head towards Mulligan, her expression more serious now. 'Can I ask exactly what it is that you propose to discuss with Toby?'

He met the question with a wry smile. 'Are you on guard duty for Clive Barden this afternoon?'

Her cheeks dimpled. 'You know how it is, Mr Mulligan. I give you all the help that I can, and more. But I still have to remember who pays for my time. And you can't blame Clive for wanting to keep tabs on Toby Dugdale. He hasn't exactly been a model employee, and that means a risk for the bank.'

The policeman thought for a moment. And then he said 'well, originally I wanted to speak to Toby in his capacity as Leo Pearson's account manager. I think he knows a lot more about this case than perhaps he has been letting on. But there's been a development this morning, something I can't tell you about just yet. All I can say is that it's more important than ever that I speak to Toby.'

'I see. And are you able to share any more details with me about Leo Pearson's death?'

'Not yet. Are you worried about the insurance policies?'

'No. I'm worried about Toby. Do you think that he was involved in Leo Pearson's murder?'

'Come on, Rose. You know better than to ask me that.'

'I know, but he's a bank employee. I have to watch out for him, just as I have to watch out for the bank's interests. That's what Clive is paying me for. And he isn't going to take too kindly to the idea of a bank employee being a murderer.'

'No?' Mulligan raised a sardonic eyebrow. 'I should have thought he'd be getting used to it by now.'

A hesitant knock on the door absolved Rose of the need to reply. 'That's probably Toby now.' She locked eyes with the policeman, a meaningful exchange of stoical glances.

And then Mulligan smiled. 'Well, we'd better get it over with. Let's have him in here, Rose. Let's see what story he has to tell us.'

Benny Bradman looked up from his desk, startled by an unexpected intrusion. 'Verity, what a nice surprise.' He tried to make the greeting sound convincing. 'Come and take a seat.' He gestured to the visitor's chair at the other side of the desk. 'I hope there's no hard feelin's about me lowerin' my offer for this place? It was just a matter of business.'

Verity hovered in the doorway of what used to be her husband's office, and then put up a hand to the collar of her green woollen coat, and began to undo the buttons. 'Of course not, Benny. I'm just relieved that you didn't back out of the purchase altogether.' She moved towards the chair and lowered herself onto it. 'I can only apologise for my late husband's dishonesty. The accountant tells me that Leo was a little creative with the accounts, and that I should be grateful that no charges will be brought.' She gave an affected shake of the head. 'False accounting, indeed. As if I would stoop to something so dishonest.'

'Well, it's all water under the bridge now.'

'And another good reason for me to get the place off my hands.' She rested an elbow on the edge of the desk and lowered her chin on to her upturned hand. 'It's one thing less to worry about. As if things weren't bad enough already. I've had the most dreadful morning.' She turned doleful eyes in his direction. 'But of course, you already know about that.' She stretched out her free hand towards him. 'Inspector Mulligan told me that you identified Leo's body. I can't thank you enough for saving me from that ordeal.'

Benny looked at the hand, and then rolled his chair

slowly backwards away from her. 'I was sorry to hear about Leo. It's not like George Mulligan to get something so wrong.'

A bitter note crept into Verity's voice. 'What an idiot that man must be. He told me on Tuesday that Leo was dead, and then this morning he rolled up to the house to tell me that he'd made a mistake. But that Leo really is dead now.' She gave a shake of the burgundy curls. 'It's just too cruel, Benny. I've had to accept my husband's death this week, not once, but twice. Can you imagine that?'

He mumbled what he hoped was a sympathetic noise. 'Do they have any idea what happened to him?'

'He was murdered. Murdered in Neil Redfern's flat. But it just doesn't make any sense.' She frowned. 'The police think that Leo murdered Neil Redfern, but they don't have any firm evidence yet to prove it. How do I know that Neil Redfern isn't still alive? How do I know that he didn't murder Leo, rather than the other way around? Still,' she paused for the shortest of breaths, 'I suppose it really doesn't matter now. The police have confirmed that Leo is dead. Asking all these questions isn't going to bring him back. I have to think about moving forward.'

'And how's that all goin' for you, Verity? Still plannin' to head out to Portugal when Leo's affairs have been settled?'

'Well, the house is on the market now, and I don't expect it will take too long to sell. I have to call in to the bank later this afternoon, to drop off the interim death certificate, and find out how long it will take to process Leo's insurance policies. But then yes, once that's been confirmed, I'll be booking a flight and a hotel. There isn't really anything for me to stay here for now.' She tilted her head further until a single burgundy ringlet dislodged from the rest and cascaded seductively over her cheek. 'I suppose what I really mean is, there isn't any*one* for me to stay for.'

Benny felt suddenly warm, and he put a hand up to his collar and ran a finger around its edge. 'It'll probably take you a while to get used to Leo not bein' there.'

'Do you think?' She considered the suggestion, and then her face brightened. 'It was so nice to have your company the other evening, Benny. Perhaps we could do it again? I thought it might be nice to celebrate the transfer of the business. Dinner at Umberto's, perhaps?'

Dinner at Umberto's, and the body barely cold? He gave an involuntary shiver, and then forced an apologetic smile. 'Well, that's a nice idea Verity. And a very kind thought. But I'm afraid I'm on dog-sittin' duties again this evenin', and even if his paws are clean, Mac just doesn't have the right credentials for a fancy place like Umberto's.'

'Then perhaps we could find an alternative venue? I'd be happy to cook for you again this evening. And it's no trouble if you want to bring the animal with you. I can't say I've ever been much of a dog-lover, but you do know, Benny, that I'd be only too happy to make an exception for you.'

'Can I ask what will happen to me now?' Toby Dugdale's face was pale, and beads of perspiration were beginning to show along his brow. 'I've admitted that I knew Leo Pearson was using Neil Redfern to launder money over the counter at Pearson the Bookmaker. And I've admitted to knowing about the accounts being falsified. I'm not sure what else I can tell you.'

From the other side of the table, George Mulligan regarded the young man with an almost avuncular gaze. 'I understand that the buyer of the business has revised his offer, but that he doesn't plan to take any further action over the deception. There would be no point in prosecuting you just for the sake of it.' He turned a questioning eye towards Rose Bennett, seated between them. 'Has there been any confirmation yet that the sale has gone through?'

'We're expecting the purchase funds to be deposited electronically into Pearson the Bookmaker's bank account in the next hour or so.'

'And will Verity Pearson have access then to the sale proceeds?'

'No, I'm afraid it doesn't work quite like that. The bank has a right of offset for the commercial mortgages and the business overdraft. That means that they can ring-fence the money to pay off any outstanding balance on those accounts.'

'So she doesn't benefit financially from the sale.' Mulligan swung his attention back towards Toby. 'Leo Pearson was your cousin, Toby. Is that right?'

'He was.'

'And is that why you went to visit Verity Pearson yesterday? Because she was family, and you wanted to help her?'

'Not exactly. I wanted to talk to her about Leo. I didn't believe she was grieving. And while I was there, she talked to me about Neil Redfern, and your theory that she was having an affair with him. I knew that couldn't be true. But I also knew that Neil Redfern might have a reason to want Leo dead. I thought there might have been an argument between them, over the money that Leo had been giving Neil to gamble.'

'And why would they argue about that?'

'Because as soon as Benny Bradman put in an offer for the business, there was no need to go on making it look more profitable than it was. Leo just stopped giving Neil the money to gamble, and it really caused him a problem. He still needed the fix, but he didn't have the additional money to gamble with.'

'Did you know for a fact that Neil Redfern had threatened Leo Pearson in any way? Or is that just a supposition?'

Toby blinked. 'I think I just supposed it.' He turned to look at Rose with hesitant eyes. 'I mentioned to Rose this morning that I thought the police should go to Neil Redfern's flat and question him.' The confidence was fading from his voice.

The policeman drew in a breath. 'Tell me, Toby, what did you do after you'd been to visit Verity? Did you come back to the office?'

Toby blushed. 'No. I was quite shaken after I'd seen her. I wanted to calm down and think things through, so I went for a walk around Kirkby Park to clear my head.'

'Did anyone see you? Did you talk to anyone?'

'No.'

'And after that, what did you do?'

'I drove home and dropped off my car, and then I walked back into town to the Jug and Ferret for a drink.'

'And did anyone see you in there?'

'Yes, Stacy Singleton. She works here, at the bank.'

Mulligan gave nod of recognition. 'I remember Stacy. I've met her before. She's a nice girl.' He tilted his head towards Rose. 'And a very sensible one, if I remember rightly.' He turned back to Toby. 'Did you speak to her?'

'Yes. We talked about … well, I told her that I was worried, that I knew I'd done something wrong, and that I didn't know what to do about it. She suggested that I speak to Rose, which is what I did this morning.'

'So you were worried about the false accounting, Toby, and you decided to come clean? Was that all?'

A look of bewilderment passed across Toby's face. 'Wasn't I right to be worried?'

'Well, I'm pleased that you've told us about it. But I can't help wondering whether you've told us everything you know. I mean, you were close to Leo Pearson, weren't you? You knew all about his financial difficulties, you were prepared to go out on a limb and risk your own job to advance extra cash to him. You even broke the law, and failed to disclose his false accounting, in order to protect him.' Mulligan leaned forward across the table. 'In fact, I can't help wondering whether you knew anything about another little scam that Leo Pearson might have had hidden up his sleeve?'

Toby fidgeted in his seat. 'I don't know what you're driving at.'

'No? Well, you said yourself that Verity stood to benefit from her husband's death. She might not make anything out of the sale of the business, but there's the house in Kirkby Park.'

'She won't be able to stay there now that Leo is gone and the business is sold. She won't be able to afford the repayments on the mortgage.'

'But she won't have to, will she? Isn't there an insurance policy assigned to that mortgage? If that pays out, there won't be an outstanding mortgage to repay.' Mulligan risked a sly glance at Rose Bennett. 'And then there are the other two insurance policies. If they pay out too, then Verity will be able to settle her outstanding debts and still walk away a very wealthy woman.'

'I don't know what you want me to say, Inspector.'

'So you never heard Leo or Verity Pearson say that the proceeds from those insurance policies could be the answer to all their financial problems?'

Consternation settled across Toby's handsome features, and he glanced from Mulligan to Rose, and back again. 'Are you suggesting that Leo took his own life, so that Verity could benefit from the insurance policies?'

'No. I'm suggesting that Leo took someone else's life, so that they both could benefit from the insurance policies.'

Toby shook his head. 'Now I'm really confused.'

'Well, we know now that the body found in Leo Pearson's car on Tuesday morning didn't belong to Leo Pearson.'

'It didn't?'

'No, it didn't. I had confirmation at lunchtime that it

was Neil Redfern who died in that fire on Monday night, not Leo Pearson.' He waited for his words to sink in. 'And we believe that Leo murdered Neil Redfern to provide a convenient body that his wife could pass off to the authorities as that of her husband. So that they could claim on the insurance policies, pay off their debts, and start that new life in Portugal that they've been crowing about so much.'

Toby let out a laugh. 'That's ridiculous. If Leo did that, then he'd still be alive. And if he's still alive, where on earth has he been since Monday evening?'

'Well, that's an easy one to answer, Toby. He's been hiding out in Neil Redfern's flat. We know that for a fact, because that's where we found him yesterday evening. In the same place that we found this.' Mulligan dug his hand into the inside pocket of his jacket and pulled out a small, laminated card.

And then he slowly and deliberately pushed Toby Dugdale's bank security pass across the table towards him.

22

DS Scott pulled the Audi carefully up and over the curb and trundled the car slowly across the scrubland. An insidious drizzle was persisting against the windscreen, and he flicked on the windscreen wipers. Even through the misted glass there was nothing much to see. The plain white tent that had once protected the crime scene had been removed, and the spot was marked now by a lone piece of blue and white police tape that fluttered valiantly from the end of an abandoned stake. He brought the car to a halt about fifty feet from the tape, and then turned to look at Evie Green. 'Would you like me to come with you?'

Evie turned her head a fraction in DS Scott's direction, but her eyes were still fixed on the modest bunch of white carnations that were resting in her lap. 'No.' Her voice was low. 'I'd like to do this alone.' She unclipped her seat belt, and then hesitated. 'This is definitely where Neil died?'

'This is where Leo Pearson's car was found. There was a tent protecting the site. I didn't know that it had been removed.'

'But this is where he died?'

He lowered his head. 'I'm sorry, Evie. We can't be sure.' What the hell was he supposed to say to her? That Neil could have been murdered before Leo put his body in the car? Or worse, that Neil might still have been alive when Leo Pearson lit the match? 'All I know for certain is that this is where his body was found.' He knew it wasn't the answer she wanted, but it would have to do.

'Will anyone be prosecuted for Neil's death?'

'Prosecuted?' The question threw him. 'We have no hard evidence that Leo Pearson murdered Neil. We're basing that assumption on the fact that your brother's body was found in Leo's car, with Leo's jewellery. And that Leo subsequently secreted himself in your brother's flat. But even if we had more than an assumption, Leo Pearson is dead. And we can't bring charges against a suspect who is deceased.'

'So if your assumption is correct, there will be no justice for my brother.' It was a statement, not a question. She turned away from him to open the Audi's passenger door.

He watched in silence as she pushed herself out into the cold, damp air, the fingers of her right hand still clutching tightly to the carnations. An unforgiving breeze had risen off the sea, and she hesitated as the car door slammed behind her and a strong gust of salty air threatened to wrest the flowers from her grasp. She steadied herself against the side of the car, bracing herself for the heart-breaking walk, holding the small bouquet close to her body, and then launched herself bravely towards the fluttering blue and white tape.

Don't let your heart rule your head.

Ian Scott cursed George Mulligan silently under his breath for planting a seed of mistrust.

Don't let your feelings cloud your judgment.

She was almost at the spot now, her pace slowing, her courage decreasing. It was the second time in a week that he had watched a woman approach that spot. Just days before he had watched the glamorous Verity Pearson play the part of a grieving widow, elegantly attired for the performance in her dark green woollen coat, the soft blue shawl draped artlessly around her shoulders. And now he was watching Evie grieve her brother. But this time there was no pretence.

Consider everything, reject nothing.

There was no denial that Evie Green's brother was a victim. But his killer, the late and unlamented Leo Pearson was a victim too. And as for Evie ... her grief was real, her sorrow unconcealed, her quest for justice unabated. But how far would that quest for justice take her?

How far had that quest for justice already taken her?

He rested his head against the cold glass of the Audi's window. She still hadn't asked him who murdered Leo Pearson, let alone what Leo Pearson was doing in her brother's flat. The fact that he couldn't answer either question was simply immaterial. Worse still, she didn't have an alibi for the time of Leo's death. How could he look George Mulligan in the eye, and say "she was home alone, and watching TV"?

He lifted his head and stared out through the windscreen. She was making her way back to the car now, her head down, her porcelain cheeks made red from the sting of salty air, her shoulders braced forward against the relentless icy wind that blew across the cliff top. And he couldn't help wondering how he would cope if she turned out to be Leo Pearson's killer.

It was an agony that he wouldn't have to face. She was still a dozen metres from the car when his mobile phone vibrated with the sound of an incoming text. He yanked the phone out of his pocket and pulled it up to his face, and squinted at the words on the screen.

The sob that strangled in his throat took him utterly by surprise, and he threw his head back against the cold, hard fabric of the car's seat, and bit at his lip to stifle any risk of a sound. He never had – nor ever would again – be so relieved to be called away from a troubling line of enquiry. Nor would he ever complain again if DI George Mulligan tersely called him back to heel.

Rose placed the glass of water gently down on the table,

and slid it towards Toby Dugdale.

He lifted it without looking at her, and sipped once, twice, three times. 'I've already told you. He was alive when I left him.'

'I think we should begin at the beginning, don't you?' Mulligan cast a sombre glance at Rose as she returned to her seat at the table, and then turned his attention back to Toby's face. 'You went to visit Verity Pearson, to see if there had been any news about Leo. And then because she suggested Neil Redfern might have had something to do with Leo's death, you decided to go to Redfern's flat and confront him? Because you believed there might have been some argument between him and Leo which led to Leo's death?'

'Yes. It was Verity who put the idea into my head.'

'But when you got there, it wasn't Neil Redfern in the flat?'

Toby's eyes were still turned down towards the glass in front of him. 'I hammered on the door, but no one answered. I bent down and opened the letterbox, and I could see a shaft of light on the floor at the end of the hall, as if there was a light on in one of the rooms. So I hammered on the door again, and called through the letterbox.' He swallowed hard. 'After a couple of minutes, I heard someone moving around behind the door, and then I heard Leo's voice. He said "is that you, Toby?" really quietly. I thought I'd imagined it.' He blinked back what might have been a tear. 'When he opened the door, I was so pleased to see him.'

Rose placed a hand on Toby's arm. 'It's OK, Toby. Take your time. I'm sure Mr Mulligan just wants you to remember what you can.'

He flicked a grateful glance in her direction. 'We argued, Rose. I mean, I was pleased to see him, and then … I just felt angry. So angry that he'd been lying. That he wasn't dead. It was the last thing I expected, to find him there in Neil Redfern's flat.'

'And what was he doing there?' She spoke softly.

'He said he was hiding. That he wanted people to think that he was dead, so that Verity could claim on his insurance policies. I asked him about the fire on Monday night, and who had died. And he said it was Neil Redfern. He said that Neil had been trying to blackmail him. That he'd threatened to tell the police about the false accounting unless Leo came across with more money.' He turned uneasy eyes towards George Mulligan. 'I didn't ask him how he did it. How Neil Redfern died. I didn't want to know.'

'And what about Verity Pearson?'

'Leo said that she didn't know. He said "you know what she's like with this sort of thing, Toby. She's useless when it comes to business. If I'd told her about this, she'd have screwed it up for us. She'd have given herself away." It was how he always talked about her. It wasn't that he didn't love her. He just thought she was an airhead. He said it would be more authentic if she really believed that he was dead, and then there would be no risk of her slipping up.'

'And he didn't think it would come as a terrible shock to her later, to discover that he was still alive?'

'He said he'd find a way to do it. He said she'd soon forgive him, when she realised that he was still alive, and that it was the end of all their financial problems.'

'Did you believe him, Toby? When he said that Verity had no idea what he'd done?'

'I wasn't sure. That's why I went to see her again at lunchtime. I tried to find out how much she knew. I tried to trip her up, by talking about Leo as if he was still alive.' He shook his head. 'She was furious with me. She was adamant that Leo was dead, that his was the body in the car.'

Mulligan blinked, a surprised flick of the eyelids, and glanced away sharply. Then he turned back to Toby and asked 'so what else happened with Leo?'

'He asked me how Verity was getting on with the insurance claims, and I told him that it wasn't going very well. That he'd slipped up, that his plan wasn't watertight, because the police knew the fire had been started deliberately.' He gave a disparaging laugh. 'He offered me twenty thousand pounds from the insurance proceeds to help Verity collect on the policies.' He shook his head. 'He actually thought that after all those lies, I would keep my mouth shut and not tell the police he was still alive.'

'But you did keep your mouth shut, Toby.' Rose sounded perplexed. 'You could have told them last night. Or this morning. And why on earth did you tell me this morning that you thought Neil Redfern could have been involved in Leo's death? You actually suggested that I should tell the police to investigate Neil Redfern, and all the time you knew that Neil was dead and Leo was in his flat?'

Toby winced. 'I'm so sorry, Rose. When it came to it, I just couldn't betray him. I just couldn't come out and tell you that he was still alive. I didn't want to be the one to give him away.' He turned an earnest face towards her. 'But I didn't want him to get away with it. I thought that if I hinted about Neil Redfern, the police would go to Redfern's flat to talk to him and they'd find Leo still alive.'

George Mulligan hissed under his breath. 'Well, we didn't need you to give us any hints, Toby. We'd already worked out that we needed to go to Neil Redfern's flat. Only we went there last night, not this morning. We went there because I had already worked out that it wasn't Leo Pearson who died in the fire, and I had a pretty good idea where we'd find him.' He bent towards Toby and lowered his voice. 'And when we got there, we found him alright. And he was *dead*.'

'He was alive when I left him.'

'He'd been battered on the back of the head with a heavy ornament, Toby. Someone had lifted that ornament off the mantelpiece, and brought it down on the back of his head with such force that it cracked his skull.'

'I didn't do it.' Toby turned determined eyes towards Rose. 'I didn't do it, Rose. I swear.'

Rose studied his face. 'It's OK Toby.' She gave his arm a gentle squeeze, and then said 'you've heard what Toby has to say, Mr Mulligan. And for what it's worth – and I can't quite believe I'm saying this – for once, I actually believe him. The important question now, I suppose, is "what happens next?"'

'So it's official, then? We actually work for you now, Mr Bradman?' There were still the remnants of mistrust in Beverley's quiet voice.

Benny grinned, and handed her a glass of champagne. 'How come all the other girls call me Benny, and you still call me Mr Bradman?'

She dared a smiled. 'I suppose it's habit. I never called Mr Pearson "Leo". He wouldn't have been happy if I had.'

'Well, I ain't Leo Pearson.' He clinked her glass with his own. 'Here's to a new future for the business, Beverley. And I hope we're goin' to have some good times puttin' this place back on its feet.' He took a sip. 'Now why don't you pour out a few more glasses, and hand them round to the punters. This is hardly an official celebration, but I don't want the event to go completely unmarked. When this bottle is finished, there are a couple more in the office.'

Beverley blushed. 'Anything you say, Mr Bradman.' She giggled. 'Sorry, anything you say, *Benny*.' She lifted the bottle from the shop's counter and began filling the glasses that Benny had lined up neatly in a row behind the screen.

He turned away from her to glance around the shop. It was going to be a challenge, but he still believed the place had possibilities. At least, he hoped it did, given the hoops he'd had to jump through to get his name above the door.

He gazed down into his glass and lost himself in a momentary daydream, until a now-familiar voice brought him back into the room.

'I've never seen those girls look so happy.'

Benny started, his musings broken, and he looked up to see Harry Tennant grinning toothily at him across the counter. He winked at the old man, and put out a hand to open up the glass screen that stood between them. 'I hope you'll join me for a drink, Harry? I always think an occasion like this is worth the markin'.' He picked up a glass from the counter and offered it to Harry with a smile.

'Champagne, is it? I can't say it's my preferred tipple, but I'm not one to refuse a toast.' Harry took the glass and lifted it to his lips. 'Here's good health to you.' He swigged noisily, and then leaned an elbow on the counter and regarded Benny with a curious eye. 'Planning to make many changes?'

'Only improvements, Harry. All the girls are stayin' with me. Some new signs will go up on Monday, with my name on them instead of Pearson's. Other than that, there'll be a lick of paint, and a few bits of new furniture.'

'Those girls all thought they were out of work. I hope you're not one of these "smoke and mirrors" merchants, telling them they still have a job and then making them redundant when they're not looking.'

Benny took the accusation in good part, and dismissed it with a shake of the head. 'Beverley will still be the day-to-day manager, and the other girls will still be workin' the tills. You'll see me now and again, like you used to see Leo Pearson. The rest of the time, Michael will be here. He runs my shop in Market Melbourne, but we'll share the runnin' of this place for a while. You'll like Michael, when you get to know him. He has his moments, but his heart's in the right place.'

'Well, that's good to know. Leo Pearson was a sour-faced beggar, and no mistake. He made those girls' lives a misery. It'll be good when everything settles down again.

It's been a rum do, all that business of Leo going missing.' He glanced thoughtfully into his near-empty glass. 'They've been turning poor Neil Redfern's flat upside down this morning. Police all over the place. God knows what he's been up to.' He drained off the remnants of his drink. 'He's a decent enough bloke, always has a few words for an old codger like me. But he's been keeping his head down these past few days.' He gave a salacious grin, and leaned a little further over the counter, lowering his voice. 'Between you and me, I think it has something to do with Leo Pearson's disappearance. There was something going on there, you know. There had to be.'

Benny bent forward to meet him, mid-counter. 'Somethin' going on between Leo and Neil?'

'No, keep up.' Harry coughed out a laugh. 'Between Neil and that fancy wife of Leo's. Definitely something going on. There had to be.'

'What makes you say that that, then?'

Harry eyed the empty innards of his glass, and tilted it optimistically towards Benny. 'I've never seen Verity Pearson before today. But that was her, wasn't it? That fancy piece in the dark green coat, the one with all the dark red curly hair?'

Benny took the hint and stretched out a hand to retrieve a bottle from the other end of the counter. 'Yes, that was Verity. She came to let me know that the sale was goin' through.'

'She's a good looking, piece. I'll say that for her.' Harry mused as Benny refilled his glass. 'She used to avoid this place, you know. The word was that she didn't want anything to do with it.' He gave a throaty chuckle. 'She obviously didn't mind having something to do with Neil Redfern, though. That must have put Leo Pearson's nose out of joint.'

Benny dropped his voice to a conspiratorial whisper. 'You've lost me now, Harry. What makes you think there was somethin' going on between Verity Pearson and Neil

Redfern?'

The old man grinned. 'I live in the flat next door to Neil, Benny. Those walls are paper thin. I might never have seen Verity Pearson before today, but I've certainly heard her.'

23

Verity slipped off her dark green woollen coat and draped it over a chair, and then sank into an adjacent seat. 'Can I smell lavender?'

Rose gave a vague smile as she opened up her soft leather notebook. 'Stacy often uses this room to conduct her bereavement interviews.' They were in a small private room on the ground floor of the ENB's Kirkby office. 'I think she had one of those this morning. She often drops a lavender-scented tissue into the waste paper basket. It's a little foible of hers. She finds it calming, not just for the bereaved but for herself, too.' She cast a swift appraising glance at Verity Pearson. 'I'm afraid Stacy won't be joining us for this discussion, she's busy with another client. I volunteered to stand in for her. I hope that's alright with you?'

'Of course.' Verity's tone was condescending. 'I'm sure you'll be just as well-equipped to assist me. I've come to deliver this.' She reached into the bag on the chair beside her. 'It's an interim death certificate. I picked it up from the coroner's office on my way here.' She pushed the document across the table towards Rose. 'Now that I've provided all the necessary paperwork to the bank, I'm hoping that you'll be able to tell me how quickly my claims against the insurance policies will be processed.'

Rose cast a perfunctory glance at the document and then slid it gently to one side. 'Each of the policies in question was issued by a different department at the bank. I can't confirm today with any degree of accuracy exactly when you will receive a payment against each of them. Each department has their own process to follow, and their own investigation procedure.'

'Investigation procedure?' A hint of anxiety crept into Verity's voice. 'But I've given you the interim death certificate. You have proof now that my husband is dead.'

'You'll have to forgive me, Mrs Pearson. I'm afraid I'm only the messenger. I will do what I can to get an answer for you before I leave this evening.' Rose studied the other woman's face. It was impeccably drawn, the green eyes precisely outlined, the rosebud pout neatly edged with a fine pink pencil and embellished with a generous smear of lip gloss. But behind the mask Rose thought she could detect the merest hint of anxiety, a faint twitching of the eyelids, a barely imperceptible trembling of the lips. 'I understand that the sale of Pearson the Bookmaker has gone through now. That must be one less thing for you to worry about.'

'Must it?' Verity sounded unconvinced. 'It's quite ironic, isn't it? I wanted so much for Leo to sell the place, but now that it's gone I'm still not free of it. My accountant has confirmed that the sale proceeds weren't enough to cover Leo's outstanding business debts to the bank. And as you pointed out to me the other day, I signed a guarantee for those debts. But I'm not going to be able to repay the balance until the insurance policies have paid out.' Her eyes looked suddenly moist. 'This is all very embarrassing for me, Rose.' She checked herself. 'May I call you Rose?'

'Of course.'

She cleared her throat, and then rolled her eyes in a curious gesture of what might have been self-reproach. 'The thing is, I can see now that Leo's death has left me in a very difficult position financially, and not just because of the outstanding business debts. You see, Rose, I was totally dependent on Leo. He paid our bills, and funded our lifestyle. He even gave me a personal allowance for my day to day expenses. At least, he did when he was alive. But now that he's gone, and the business has been sold, I have no means of paying the mortgage, and no way of paying my bills.' She let out a deep, heartfelt breath of resignation. 'Apart from the final salary I have drawn from the business, I have no means of financial support until the claims on Leo's insurance policies are processed. And that's why I need to know how quickly the money will come through. I simply can't afford to go on waiting.'

'I see.' Rose lifted a hand to the table and picked up the interim death certificate. 'I can see how difficult this must be for you, especially in the light of your husband's death. And I wish there was something more I could do to help, but I'm afraid my hands are tied by the bank's procedures.' She skimmed her eyes across the document, and then flicked them back up to Verity Pearson's face. 'This certificate says that your husband died yesterday, and not on Monday, as we were previously advised?'

'I'm afraid the police are not as efficient as one might think. They were convinced that the body discovered in Leo's car was my husband's. But it appears that they made a mistake.' Verity gave a desultory sniff. 'I'm afraid I've had to endure the news of my husband's death not once but twice this week. They found Leo's body yesterday evening, in a flat on the Barnfield Estate.'

'I'm sorry to hear that.' Rose tried to sound surprised. 'Do they know yet what happened to him?'

Verity's face contorted, and she reached into her handbag for a second time to pull out a crisp white handkerchief. 'He was murdered.' She dabbed at her nose, and then hesitated, and flicked the cool, green eyes up to Rose Bennett's face. 'You must have heard, surely? Detective Inspector Mulligan, the senior investigating officer, called me barely half an hour ago to confirm that Toby Dugdale had been arrested. They believe that he was responsible for Leo's death.' She swallowed hard, and the green eyes became suspicious. 'I thought you'd been working quite closely with Toby? I find it hard to believe that the news hasn't reached you.'

Rose chose her words with care. 'I am aware of the latest development in the case. I haven't really had a great deal to do with Toby, other than in relation to your husband's business affairs. I know that he can be economical with the truth some times, but I didn't have him down as a murderer.'

'I will admit that I find it hard to believe myself.' Verity glanced away. 'I only spoke to him at lunchtime. He came to see me at home.' She turned back to Rose. 'Can you believe that he actually kept referring to Leo in the present tense, as if Leo was still alive? I found it quite distressing.' She sniffed again into the handkerchief. 'I can only think that he was trying to cover his tracks. Trying to make out that Leo was still alive, when all the time he knew that he'd murdered him.'

'In the version of the story that Toby related to me, Leo was still alive when he left him.'

'He told you that Leo was still alive?' Verity Pearson's eyes flashed with a sudden anger. 'Then why on earth didn't he say that to me? Why didn't he just come out and tell me that Leo was still alive?' She bit her lip, and stifled a makeshift sob. 'Oh this is just too cruel. Isn't it bad enough that Leo *was* alive? That he was hiding out in that flat, and I knew nothing about it? I just don't understand why he would do that to me, never mind why Toby would murder him.' She lowered her head. 'What on earth have I done to deserve this?'

'I'm afraid I can't answer that question.' Rose rested her forearms on the table. 'But I can hazard a guess as to why your husband didn't tell you that he was still alive.' She watched Verity Pearson's face closely. 'I think it's possible that your husband wanted everyone to think that he was dead, so that you could collect on his insurance policies. I think that he murdered Neil Redfern simply to provide himself with a handy corpse that he could pass of as his own. He made an amateurish attempt to dispose of the body at Cayton Bay by leaving it in his car and setting fire to it, and then he hid himself away in Neil Redfern's flat, leaving you to deal with the mess. I think he was waiting there until you had collected on the insurance policies. And then once the ownership of Pearson the Bookmaker was safely transferred to the new owner, your house in Kirkby Park was up for sale, and all of your outstanding debts had been settled using the proceeds from the insurance claims, it would be time for the two of you to begin that new life in Portugal that both of you were so keen to move on to.'

Verity Pearson sucked in her cheeks. 'That is an extraordinary allegation, Rose. But it still doesn't explain why my husband didn't let me know that he was still alive.'

'I'm sorry, I thought that was implied in my explanation.' Rose gave an enigmatic smile. 'Your husband didn't let you know that he was still alive, and living in Neil Redfern's flat, because he didn't need to.' She leaned across the table towards Verity Pearson, and her voice became a whisper. 'He didn't need to tell you that he was still alive, because you already knew that he wasn't really dead.'

DS Scott closed the door of George Mulligan's office, and turned to face his superior officer. 'What's happened?'

'Toby Dugdale's security pass turned up in Neil Redfern's flat.' Mulligan leaned back in his seat. 'So I went over to the ENB and had a word with Rose Bennett. She agreed to sit in while I spoke to him informally, and he's come up with a doozy of a story. He doesn't deny that he went to Neil Redfern's flat. He says he went there looking for Neil Redfern, and found Leo Pearson instead, still alive and kicking. He claims that they argued, but he's adamant that Leo Pearson was still alive when he left him.'

Scott's face ran a gamut of emotions as he took in the news, and then his face lit up with relief. 'So Evie's definitely off the hook?'

Mulligan rolled his eyes. 'I didn't call you back here to discuss your love life.' The words sounded harsh, and he put up a hand. 'Sorry, Scottie, I didn't mean to chew you out. Of course I'm pleased if it means we don't have to investigate Evie Green any further. But we've got to get to the bottom of this case.'

The sergeant took the hint with a nod. 'Do you believe Toby Dugdale?'

'I don't know what the hell to believe.' Mulligan puffed out his cheeks. 'We've got nothing concrete to tie him to either of those murders. He's admitted to assisting Leo Pearson with the false accounting, but we have no evidence that he was involved in the murder of Neil Redfern. He claims that Leo Pearson confessed to him that he committed the murder to create a handy corpse for his insurance fraud. And as for Leo Pearson's murder, there are no useable fingerprints on that glass shard, everything was too badly smudged.' He shook his head. 'We just don't have any grounds to charge him.'

'What about Verity Pearson?'

'What about her?' Mulligan turned his head to glance at the clock on the wall. 'She'll be at the bank by now, I should think. Rose was expecting her to come in and deliver the interim death certificate.' He turned back to Ian Scott. 'There's something at the back of my mind, but I can't quite pin it down. Something about the body in the car.' He put up a hand and rubbed at his temple. 'We told Verity Pearson this morning that it wasn't her husband's body in the car. But when I spoke to Toby Dugdale, he said he'd spoken to her at lunchtime, and she was adamant that it *was* Leo who died in the vehicle fire.'

'If that's true, then she lied to him. But why on earth would she do that?'

'I don't know.' Mulligan lowered his head into his

hands. 'Hell, Scottie, one of them is lying. But which one is it?' He let out a growl of frustration, and then started as the ring of his mobile phone announced the arrival of an incoming call. He scooped up the phone with an impatient hand, and glanced at the screen before rejecting the call with a jab of his thumb, and dropping it back onto the desk. 'Benny Bradman.' He muttered the name with a sigh. 'It'll have to wait.'

DS Scott leaned back against the door frame. 'What are you going to do with Toby Dugdale?'

'What the hell can I do? I've still got him here in an interview room, but I'm going to have to let him go.' Mulligan flicked idly with his fingers at the mobile phone in front of him, sending it spinning slowly across the desk. 'For what it's worth, Rose doesn't believe that Toby is guilty. And she has a bloody infuriating way of being right when we've got it wrong.' He blew out another sigh. 'If we get this wrong, whoever murdered Leo Pearson will get away with it, and Verity Pearson will walk away with a fortune.' The spinning phone came to rest against the in-tray on his desk, and Mulligan swore under his breath when it let out a loud and demanding bleep. He snatched it up with an impatient hand. 'What the hell is it now?'

'Benny Bradman again?'

Mulligan blinked at the text in front of him, and then he lifted his eyes to DS Scott's face. 'Get your jacket, Scottie. I need you to go over to Scarborough.' He pushed himself to his feet. 'Benny's got Harry Tennant with him. I want you to take a statement.' He lifted his own jacket from the back of his chair. 'I damn well knew that Verity Pearson was lying.'

Bewildered, Ian Scott stepped aside as Mulligan made for the door. 'What's happened?' He followed the Inspector into the outer office, grabbing at his jacket as he passed his own desk, pulling it quickly from the back of his chair.

'What's happened is serendipity.' Mulligan chuntered

under his breath as he strode into the corridor that led to a nearby interview room. 'Benny Bradman's just come up with another piece of the jigsaw, and I've just realised that there was one very important question that I should have asked Toby Dugdale.' He glanced over his shoulder. 'And I need to ask him that question now, even though I think I already know the answer.'

Verity Pearson's green eyes narrowed to an icy stare. 'Just what exactly are you accusing me of?'

'Try not to think of it as an accusation. More of a suggestion.' Rose settled back in her seat. 'I'm suggesting that you knew your husband was planning to defraud the ENB of the value of his insurance policies, and that you knew he was still alive when you first approached the bank to report his death.'

'And what makes you think that? It's not something you could possible prove.'

'I suppose that depends on your definition of proof.' Rose leaned forward to pull a loose sheet of paper from the pages of her soft leather notebook. 'I've taken a good look at your financial profile, Verity, and I think that your financial situation had become so bad that you had run out of options.' She slid the paper across the table, and watched as Verity's eyes turned reluctantly down towards the document. 'The business was going under, Leo was struggling to find a buyer, and the only way you were managing to keep your heads above water was because Toby took a risk and extended the overdraft for Pearson the Bookmaker far in excess of what the business could afford to repay. But that money wouldn't last for ever.' She folded her arms onto the table, her eyes still on Verity's face. 'I think that claiming on those insurance policies was one last ditch attempt to jettison the debts you had both run up, pursuing a lifestyle that you couldn't afford.'

'If Leo planned to defraud the bank, it was nothing to do with me.' Verity gave a furious shake of the burgundy curls. 'How do you know that Toby Dugdale didn't collude with my husband to defraud the bank? After all, he colluded with Leo to inflate the value of the business, and he knew that Leo used a false set of accounts to back up the application to extend the company's overdraft.' She placed her hands on the table. 'And the police have arrested him. You seem to have forgotten that. Toby has been arrested for Leo's murder.'

Rose gave a gentle shake of the head. 'He hasn't been arrested for murder, Verity. He's been taken in for questioning, to help the police with their enquiries. It's not the same thing.'

'Of course he murdered Leo. Who else could have possibly done it?' Verity scowled. 'He must have known that Leo was hiding out in Neil Redfern's flat, and he went there to argue with him. I told him that Leo had been using him, and he was livid. He was humiliated.' She lifted her eyes to the ceiling. 'For pity's sake, can't you see that I'm the innocent victim in all of this?'

'Victim? Possibly.' Rose turned her head away. 'But innocent? I'm afraid that's not a view I can subscribe to.' She turned back to Verity Pearson. 'You see, I don't believe that Toby murdered your husband, not just because he cared about Leo, but because he didn't have a strong enough motive. But you, I think you had a much stronger motive.'

'You think that I murdered Leo to benefit from the insurance policies?'

'No. I think that you murdered him because you'd simply had enough. It's true that Leo used Toby, but it's nothing compared to the way that he'd been using you all these years, is it?' Rose paused, and her voice softened. 'It can't have been easy for you, all this time, depending on a husband who sailed so close to the wind financially.'

Verity blinked, and her mouth contorted to stem a sob.

'He's always kept me in the dark about money.' Tears were beginning to flow. 'In the beginning, I just believed him when he told me we had plenty of money coming in. We certainly had enough to fund a move to Kirkby Park, and there was never any difficulty in obtaining credit. But over the last few years ... well, I may not know much about gambling, but I know that it's a fickle business. More and more people are gambling online, and then when the local factory closed last year the takings really began to decline.' The colour had begun to drain from her face. 'And suddenly Leo began to look worried, and talk about not being able to meet the mortgage repayments.'

'And you didn't at any point just think about selling up and buying a smaller property? Or changing your fancy cars for something a bit more affordable?'

A guilty flush suffused into Verity's cheeks. 'I suppose that's what a sensible person would have done. But sensible wasn't a word in Leo's vocabulary. He was too busy enjoying the high life, and taking me along for the ride.'

'Did you always have to go along for the ride?'

'I did think about leaving him once. But it wouldn't have worked. I was in too deep, you see? I was a director of Pearson the Bookmaker, I was drawing a salary from the business, our mortgage was written in joint names ... I was in it up to my neck, the same as Leo. Only I didn't have any means of earning an income.'

'You could have taken a job.'

'Leo didn't want me to work. He said it would humiliate him. He didn't want people to think that Leo Pearson couldn't afford to keep his wife.'

'And what about what his wife wanted?'

'I had everything that I wanted. A lovely home, a nice car, lots of holidays.'

'And freedom?'

'Freedom?' Verity flinched, stung by the question. 'I don't know. Perhaps Toby has done me a favour. Now that Leo is dead, and Toby's been arrested for his murder, perhaps I can have my freedom too.'

'I still don't believe that Toby murdered Leo, Verity.' Rose spoke quietly, her voice low and calm now.

'Of course he murdered Leo. He took bribes, you know. From Leo. Leo paid him off for arranging those extensions to the overdraft.'

'I know. He's already admitted to that. It doesn't make him a killer.'

'Toby murdered Leo. He must have done. There is no other explanation.'

'Isn't there?' Rose let the question hang in the air for a moment, and then said 'I'm afraid that I don't agree.' She sounded almost apologetic. 'Leo put you in an impossible situation, didn't he? He faked his own death, disappeared from view, and left you to deal with the fall out. I think that you were willing to collude with him at first, because you couldn't see any other options. And I suppose in your defence – if there can be a defence for taking an innocent man's life, which is what Leo did to Neil Redfern – you were probably even afraid. But you trusted Leo to sort it out. Perhaps you even deluded yourself that if Leo committed the murder, it would be nothing to do with you.' Rose drew in a breath. 'But you didn't know that you would be personally liable for Pearson the Bookmaker's debts. He didn't tell you that, did he? Or that you could be faced with a charge of false accounting if it came to light that he'd falsified the business accounts? Or that you could lose the house, and be facing bankruptcy if the insurance policies failed to pay out?' She shook her head. 'I think that when you began to realise that Leo had exposed you to so much risk, it was you who became angry. Suddenly you had a lot more to lose than your lifestyle, and all those glitzy things that made you Mrs Verity Pearson. You were facing new fears. The fear of prosecution, of exposure, of public humiliation. Tell me,' Rose stretched out a hand and placed it gently on Verity's arm, 'was your fancy lifestyle really worth Neil Redfern's life?'

'You don't know what you're talking about.' Verity swallowed back a sob, and her whispered reply crackled with a raw emotion. 'You just don't understand.'

'You're right, Verity, I don't.' Rose was speaking softly now. 'But I do have time to listen. So why don't you help me to understand? Why don't you tell me exactly how it was?'

24

Rose leaned against the wall of the ground floor corridor, and pointed to the door of a meeting room. 'She's in there. I brought her a coffee, and a bar of chocolate from the vending machine. She's very shaken, but we've had a long heart-to-heart, and I think she's resigned to what's coming next. Stacy's in there with her. We thought someone should keep her company.'

George Mulligan lifted his hand and flicked a finger towards the room, an indication for the two uniformed colleagues hovering behind him to make themselves known to Verity Pearson. 'Well, I don't know how you did it, but you've saved me a job.' He waited until the officers had closed the door gently behind them, and then pulled a crumpled packet of mints from the pocket of his jacket and offered it to Rose. 'How did you know?'

Rose hesitated. 'I hope this isn't considered some sort of police bribe.' She took a mint from the packet and popped it into her mouth. 'It began with a hunch, Mr Mulligan. Nothing more scientific than that. How did you work it out?'

'I very nearly didn't, but I was lucky enough to be handed a witness – Harry Tennant, the old boy who lives next door to Neil Redfern's flat. He told Benny that he'd heard Verity Pearson's voice coming from Neil's flat yesterday evening. Benny tipped me the wink, so I've sent Scottie over there to take a formal statement.' He took a mint from the packet for himself. 'On top of that, I told Verity Pearson yesterday morning that it wasn't her husband's body in the car. And yet Toby Dugdale claimed that when he spoke to her yesterday afternoon, she was adamant that Leo *did* die in the fire. I couldn't work out why she would do that. What could she gain by lying to Toby about it? Unless she was trying to convince Toby that she didn't know Leo was in that flat.'

'She was setting him a false trail, wasn't she? She persuaded him that Neil Redfern had somehow been complicit in Leo's death, and then told him where Neil lived, knowing full well that he would find Leo alive and kicking when he got there. Then when Leo claimed to Toby that he had acted alone, that Verity knew nothing about the insurance fraud, Toby would be more likely to believe him, and help her to claim on the policies.'

Mulligan smiled. 'Toby had continually claimed that he didn't know much about Neil Redfern, beyond knowing that Leo had used him to place those bets. And I continually missed the opportunity to ask him how he knew where Neil Redfern lived. Of course it was Verity who told him. Now what possible reason could Verity have to know where Neil Redfern lived, unless she knew that was where Leo was hiding out?' His expression became grave. 'The bit I still don't understand is why she murdered Leo. If she and Leo were acting together to defraud the bank of the insurance proceeds, why kill him? They wouldn't have got away with it, of course. We'd already worked out that it wasn't Leo in the car. But why did she have to kill him?'

Rose gave a shrug. 'Who knows? Perhaps you'd need to fathom the complexities of the female mind to work that one out.'

'If you're keeping something back that's material to the case, Rose ...'

'As if I would do that to you.' She gave his arm a familiar nudge with her elbow. 'Let's just say that I don't think it was premeditated. I think that she went along with Leo's plan to defraud the bank because she didn't feel she had a choice, but things didn't quite go to plan. And maybe when she realised just what a mess Leo had left her to deal with, she snapped. I don't think it was murder. If anything, I think it was probably manslaughter.' She tilted her head towards him. 'But that's your area of expertise, Mr Mulligan. I'm sure when you've had the chance to question her at length, you'll come to the right conclusion.'

'If I were you, Rose, I wouldn't waste any sympathy on her. She's shown no remorse for the murder of Neil Redfern. She might not have been an accessory in the strictest sense of the word, but she knew what her husband was planning to do. Neil Redfern has a sister who is grieving, a nice young woman by all accounts, and a nephew who looked up to him as a father figure.' He fixed Rose with reproachful eyes. 'If you have any sympathy to give over this case, give it to them.'

'Are you scolding me, Mr Mulligan?' Rose bit her lip to stem an unbidden smile. 'I do hope not, or I might have to ask you to leave the bank's premises, and take your entourage with you.' She nodded in the direction of the small meeting room. 'The ENB normally charges an hourly rate for the hire of office space. My fees for investigation are negotiable, of course.' The smile broke free. 'You do realise that I'm joking?'

The policeman growled under his breath. 'There's no wonder Clive Barden reaches the end of his tether with you sometimes. There's a time and a place, you know, for making fun of a situation.'

His words didn't sting, but still Rose was touched to make a defence. She lifted a hand to take hold of his arm. 'I know there is, Mr Mulligan.' She sounded grave, the flippancy gone. 'But sometimes I just can't help feeling that if I didn't find something to laugh about in all of this misery, then my only option would be to wail at the sheer bloody pointlessness of it all. And I can't believe that even a crusty old detective like you would enjoy seeing a grown woman cry.'

Ian Scott pulled the Audi to a halt outside Evie Green's neat little two-up-two-down, and turned off the engine. It was dark in the street, and a cold October mist was beginning to envelope the car, its foggy threads lit amber by the glow of a nearby streetlamp as they wafted, wraithlike, around the windows.

He pulled the key from the ignition, and then paused, daunted by the task that lay ahead. He had never been afraid to be the bearer of bad news, and tonight's duty should have been a breeze, given that the news he had to bear was hardly unexpected. Evie already knew that her brother was dead, and she already knew that the death had been a violent one. But she still deserved an explanation of the circumstances, at least the best explanation that anyone could give her.

He closed his eyes, and began to run through story again in his head, mouthing the words silently to himself, reassuring himself that nothing had been missed.

As far as we can tell ...

He winced at the words. She deserved better than that. But how much better could he do, given that all they had to work with – apart from two or three scant facts – was conjecture? Verity Pearson had known that her husband had intended to commit a murder. Leo Pearson had admitted to Toby Dugdale that the victim was Evie's brother, that he'd murdered the unsuspecting Neil Redfern on Monday night, and tried to dispose of the body at Cayton Bay.

But was that enough? He knew she would have questions, questions that he couldn't – or wouldn't – answer. Had Neil been alive when the fire was set? Had he suffered any pain? Did he really have to die? And would anyone take responsibility for his death?

He wrapped his fingers around the steering wheel, and rested his chin on the cold, hard, leather rim. How could he tell her that Neil had died so that a vain and selfish couple could settle their debts? How could he tell her that Verity would be charged in connection with her own husband's death, but that no one would stand trial for killing Neil?

He lifted his head and turned to look through the mist at the brightly-lit window of Evie's front room. The curtains were undrawn, and through the pristine white nets he could just about see her, sitting stiffly on the edge of the sofa, her face turned towards the window.

She knew he was there.

He couldn't put it off any longer. He opened the car door and launched himself out into the street, drawing in his cheeks as the cold night air invaded his lungs. As he crossed the pavement to the small wooden gate at the end of the path, he saw her rise to her feet, and cross the room to the window. She lifted her hand to him in recognition, and then slowly drew the curtains shut against the cold, dark night.

Through the gate, he hesitated at the head of the path, and slipped his hand into the pocket of his overcoat to finger three small pieces of card, tickets for the family stand at Kirkby's FC's next home game. Liam was going to need someone to replace his Uncle Neil, someone to provide some support and stability, a shoulder for himself and his mother to lean on. And even if she wasn't prepared to admit it yet, Evie was going to need someone too, not just to fill the void left by her late brother's death, but to see her through the pain of the days and weeks to come — the inquest, the trial, the publicity, the grief. DS Ian Scott had already decided that he knew the ideal candidate for both of the outstanding vacancies.

Always supposing that Evie Green was prepared to accept his application.

25

'Here's to us, then, Rose.' Benny Bradman lifted his glass in a toast. 'I think we deserve a drink tonight. These should be on George Mulligan by rights. He'd still be scratchin' his head and lookin' around for a killer if it wasn't for us.' He sipped on his pint. 'I asked him if he wanted to come to The Feathers and join us tonight, but he's bein' shy.'

'Perhaps he doesn't see it as a cause for celebration.' Rose ran a finger around the rim of her wine glass. 'After all, two people have lost their lives, and Verity Pearson is looking at a life sentence.'

Benny growled under his breath. 'I hope you ain't goin' all mardy on me again, like you did when Pandora Mitchell died. Justice is bein' done. You should be pleased.' He took a long gulp from his glass. 'I don't disagree that Neil Redfern didn't deserve to die. But Leo Pearson?' He shook his head. 'I wouldn't waste any sympathy there, not now I know what he's done. And as for Verity ... she could have blown the whistle on what her old man was plannin' to do, and she chose not to.' He rested the glass down on the table. 'Will the bank throw the book at her?'

'What, for fraud?' Rose wrinkled her nose. 'Not if I have anything to do with it. The ENB have recovered most of the money advanced to Pearson the Bookmaker, they'll get the rest of what they're owed when the house in Kirkby Park is sold. Given that Verity is going to go down for murdering her husband, it hardly matters what happens to her on a financial level. Bringing charges for attempted fraud and false accounting would just be vengeful.' She laughed under her breath. 'Clive is already celebrating because the ENB won't have to pay out on the insurance policies. I'll just point out to him that he'd be wasting the bank's money in legal costs when there's no real financial benefit to be gained.'

'And what about Toby?'

'Toby?' Rose frowned. 'Well, he's lied to the police, impeded a murder investigation, failed to report a clear case of false accounting, and assisted a third party to defraud his employer. But there is no evidence that he was complicit in either of the murders.'

'I thought his security pass was found in Neil Redfern's flat?'

'It was. But that only proves that he was there, not that he committed a murder. In any case, since Verity has confessed to killing Leo, we can only assume that Toby was telling the truth, and Leo was alive when he left him.'

'Will George Mulligan charge him with anythin'?'

'I don't know yet. He certainly has grounds to do so, but I don't think Clive is likely to bring charges for offences committed against the bank. Toby has been dismissed, and he won't get a reference. No other bank will touch him. But if he's lucky he won't walk away from this mess completely empty handed. Stacy's taking him out for a pizza this evening. She's nominated him as her new pet project.'

Benny grinned into his pint. 'I was nearly Verity Pearson's pet project.' He blanched visibly at the thought. 'You don't really feel sorry for her, do you?'

'Yes, of course I do. Perhaps you'd have to be a woman to understand that. Oh, I think she was selfish, and vain, and probably even cruel to know what Leo was planning to do to Neil Redfern, and keep it to herself. But these things are never as straightforward as they seem. All people saw when they looked at her was a trophy wife. They think that everything was laid out on a plate for her -

the house, the fancy car, the holidays - but they all came at a price. Leo Pearson might not have been openly abusive, but there is such a thing as coercion. Just imagine what her life must have been like, Benny. She must have been so lonely, not just knowing that he had a habit of being unfaithful to her, but being excluded from the financial side of their marriage, and never knowing how secure or insecure their situation was, or how dishonest Leo was being. And all the time her lifestyle, and her self-image with it, was hinging on that dishonesty, and her willingness to turn a blind eye to the truth. There was no love, no trust, no honesty – she had a luxury lifestyle, but she didn't have the peace of mind to go with it.'

'She'd been puttin' up with that for years. Somethin' must have made her snap.'

'He called her stupid.' Rose pushed her glass to one side. 'She told me that when she went round to the flat yesterday evening, they argued about the situation he'd put her in. And he called her stupid.' She held Benny's gaze. 'It's never a good idea to tell a woman that she's stupid.'

'Thanks for the warnin', Rose. I'll bear that in mind.' His voice softened. 'Is that what happened with Mike? He called you stupid?'

'If only it had been that simple.' Rose blinked back an unwelcome thought, and then her face brightened. 'I'm not going back to Hertfordshire. I've decided to sell the cottage.' She nodded to herself. 'I've come to an arrangement with Clive. He's happy to let me work out of the Kirkby office on future assignments, providing I'm happy to travel into London if he needs me.' A smile tugged at the corner of her mouth, and she pointed down to a small white shape underneath the table. 'Anyway, given what a bad influence you are on Mac, especially when it comes to his diet, I can see quite clearly that someone is going to have to step in and safeguard his interests.'

Benny tilted his head down in the dog's direction. 'I

hope you heard that, pal. Now we know she can be mean, as well as mardy. I don't know why we give her the time of day.' He leaned back in his seat. 'You're not really goin' to plead Verity Pearson's case with the bank, are you?'

'I'm seriously considering it. My heart goes out to any woman who's been treated as goods and chattels.'

Benny Bradman smiled. 'Is that another warnin' shot for my benefit, Rose?'

Rose felt a faint, warm flush make its way into her cheeks and she turned her eyes down into her almost-empty glass. 'Don't you think that's for me to know, and you to enjoy the process of finding out?'

ABOUT THE AUTHOR

Mariah Kingdom was born in Hull and grew up in the East Riding of Yorkshire. After taking a degree in History at Edinburgh University, she wandered into a career in information technology and business change, and worked for almost thirty years as a consultant in the British retail and banking sectors.

She began writing crime fiction during the banking crisis of 2008, drawing on past experience to create Rose Bennett, a private investigator engaged by a fictional British bank.

Death Benefit is the fourth Rose Bennett Mystery.

www.mariahkingdom.co.uk

Printed in Great Britain
by Amazon